Don't Lean Out
Of The Window!

Baile
Dubl

Don't Lean Out Of The Window!

the inter-rail experience

Stewart Ferris and Paul Bassett

SUMMERSDALE

First published in 1992.
Reprinted 1997.

This edition copyright © Stewart Ferris and Paul Bassett 1999

Summersdale Publishers Ltd
46 West Street
Chichester
West Sussex
PO19 1RP
UK

www.summersdale.com

ISBN 1 84024 090 3

Printed and bound by Cox & Wyman, Reading, Great Britain.

By the same authors:
Don't Mention The War

Stewart Ferris has written a number of other embarrassing books, including *How To Chat-up Women, Enormous Boobs* and several volumes of *Chat-up Lines and Put Downs*. His favourite chat-up line is 'Baaaaa', and his ambition is to compete between Pamela Anderson and Melinda Messenger in an egg and spoon race.

Paul Bassett is not really a bigoted, xenophobic, fat bastard at all. He is not totally ignorant of culture, and does not hate to travel. He is a bass player and sometimes wears a hat.

Since this book was first published, the authors have been honoured by the European Commission with a blanket ban on all rail travel within the European Union.

To our parents,
with profuse apologies.

Acknowledgements

Stephen Fry, Alastair Williams (who didn't really do any of the things we said, honest), Paul's Bird, George Stephenson, Alexei Sayle, The Person Who Invented Inter-Rail, Daniel T, Reinhard Weber, Anja Dekker, Maaike Veerman, Robert Krisch, Clare Viner, The Van Dorst Family, Lucy Rice, Arif Kus, The Oracle, Honest John, David Ryder, H. H. Matthews, Neil and Denis, Uncle Olly, E. Doyle, Shakey, Ford Prefect, A. Bezzer-Fotze, Cathy King, Covvy-Jo, Mr C, Sarah Hoity-Toity Cooke, Spam.

A special 'thank you' to those of who bought the first edition of this book, and an even bigger one to the person who actually read it.

CONTENTS

Foreword

The explanation

1 IN THE BEGINNING 16

2 CHICHESTER TO PARIS 23

3 SOUTH OF FRANCE 39

4 NOT SO NICE 57

5 CASTELLANE 66

6 BUSKING 84

7 THE FAT STRIPPER AND JOHN TRAVOLTA 93

8 WATERFALLS AND POLICE 100

9 DROWNED SORROWS AND DRUNKEN SAILORS 108

10 HITCHING 115

11 HONEY, MONEY AND FASCISTS 125

12 AMONG MOUNTAINS 140

13 THE BOOGIE AND ROCK 'N' ROLL CLUB 144

14 THROWING MORE MONEY AWAY 151

15 ZURICH AND THE PASTA QUEEN 159

16 HUMILIATING EJACULATION 167

17 THE INTER-RAIL CENTRE 173

18 OSLO 179

19 A MUG FULL OF DOLLARS 186

20 MONEY RUNS OUT 190

21 SPLIT UP 195

22 UNDER ARREST 207

23 REUNION 218

24 SEX WORLD 230

25 DUTCH CULTURE 243

26 THREE SMUGGLERS 250

INDEX OF PROFANE WORDS LIABLE TO
INDUCE CHILDISH AMUSEMENT IN
MENTALLY WEAK PERSONS 254

Foreword

Stewart

I was exhausted, dirty, smelly, hungry, and somewhere beneath all that, suntanned. It was the end of an Inter-Rail holiday. My body couldn't take any more punishment. My mind couldn't cope with any more foreign timetables and languages. My eyes were lined with echoes of the thousands of miles of tracks along which I had been hurtled. My grubby hands showed the imprints of one currency overlaid upon another as coins had passed through my possession and into various indistinguishable burger bars. 'Never again,' I said, as I stepped onto home tarmac.

I said exactly the same thing the following year. And the next. Inter-Rail is a curious addiction which even today faintly nags at me, telling me to leave the car behind this time and rough it on the train. Static beds are never the same again once you've learnt to sleep in the corridor of a train, drawn into an instant and deep slumber by the rhythmic rattle of movement. There's a strong temptation to relive those beautiful nights on dusty floors, those periods of serenity broken only by the nightly jab of a border guard's boot or the overflowing of the adjacent blocked toilet.

But it's not just the car I would have to give up — the large tent, the cooker, the bagfuls of clothes that I wouldn't wear at home let alone on holiday, the chairs and table, the notebook computer and the food. All the luxuries that train travel cannot cater for fit with only just a slight squeeze into the car boot, or preferably a large van. A rucksack implies a strictly minimalist approach to travel, and encourages incredible wastefulness that can lead to the burning of socks that have become too antisocial, and throwing books away when finished. On the other hand, this approach is entirely in the spirit of Inter-Rail, for sanity, logic and sobriety — all necessary in a car driver — can be thrown out of the window along with the discarded Jeffrey Archer and the socks that are beginning to campaign for independence and democracy. All it takes to achieve this carefree attitude is an Inter-Rail ticket in your palm.

Any system that enables unappreciative youths to trample through countries at a rate of more than one a day — for maximum disorientation — must be pretty special. We were at first naïve to the possibilities of this type of train ticket, thinking it was just a cost-effective way of getting to and from our chosen campsite in southern France. But the lure of infinite travel proved too intoxicating and our desires became insatiable (nothing new there) for there was always just one more country over the border, always that little bit further to go. And what did the extra miles cost us? Nothing. The guitars made sure of that.

Guitars provided an ongoing source of income, and hence regular food. The busking process was simple: arriving in a new city, in a new country (which was inevitable if we wanted a good night's sleep on the train) the first thing to do would be to find the nearest McDonald's to work out the exchange rate. This was calculated in terms of standard cheeseburgers, for the price of a cheeseburger provided an accurate and simple insight into the value of the currency unit.

In Austria, for instance, if a burger costs sixteen Schillings, we knew we'd need to earn about sixty or seventy Schillings each if our afternoon farting sessions were to be sufficiently fuelled. So we'd find a suitable busking pitch and play for about twenty minutes until we'd earnt enough. Then back to McDonald's, massive pig-out, long belching and swearing sessions, then back to the station and time to decipher yet another cryptic timetable. This was the key to our subsistence living, the way we managed to avoid spending too many of those precious traveller's cheques by earning what we needed, when we needed. It was a precarious living, ob, as busking often is, but there was always the opportunity of a quick getaway to another country, another McDonald's, another burger and belch session.

We were not entirely ignorant of culture: we even refrained from trying to sink Venice. But we had all seen the 'sights' of Europe anyway, all been dragged through countless churches, perpetual potteries, up and down the Eiffel Tower, and in and out of historic caves. This was a chance to escape the rigours of organised and intelligent touring, an opportunity to rebel against the normal practises of sightseeing. I took great pride in the fact that all I could be bothered to see of Stockholm was the taxi rank in front of the station, and all we noticed of Paris were a few prostitutes.

We were just there to survive, to come through the water-cannons, the muggings, the arrests, and the undesirables, and to have a bloody good time doing so. In this we were no different to most of the other travellers with whom we shared corridor floors, food and water rations, money, and music. (Whether anyone actually wanted us to sing on the trains it's hard to tell, but our voices and Paul's feet often combined with a subtle blend that could clear a compartment within seconds.)

It is easy to look at Europe and see a conquered continent, its every portion mapped, owned and developed, and its every secret long since divulged to the general knowledge of the world in books, films and conversation. But to one who came to scene long after this process had finished, there is an inevitable feeling of being left out, a sense of deprivation stronger even than that which comes of not having been born in time to enjoy the summer of '67 and other such landmarks in world history.

Walking through any capital city, it is hard to imagine that such a vast expanse of concrete and stone has not always been there, that a boundary marked by a wall between two banking headquarters may once have been a hedge dividing two fields. Europe has been designed, bodged, built, blown-up and rebuilt by our ancestors to the extent that no magic remains: no matter how remote you think you are there will always be a coke can, quietly not-decaying beneath the undergrowth.

So, faced with a continent in which past generations have beaten us to everything, what is there left to explore?

The point is, of course, that even though others may have already sunned their sensitivities on the Riviera or chilled their chipolatas in glacial snow, it doesn't negate the need for us to share the experience. It's not enough for one person to visit Belgium and tell the rest of the population how crap it is — discoveries should not be, and are rarely, hidden. Anyone who now undertakes the Grand Tour is making a voyage of re-discovery, but that should not matter. Everybody knows what is there, but it is meaningless until viewed from a personal perspective. This is what makes other people's holiday photos so boring.

The thrill of travel derives from the sudden reality of somewhere that was previously just a name or an opinion. It is as if the city in which you arrive never actually existed until the train pulls in at the station and you are able to see it with your own tired and bloodshot eyes for the first time. It is the beginning of the existence of that place, as far as the newcomer is concerned, and it will continue to exist forever afterwards.

FOREWORD

Only by actually seeing Europe, by watching the blending landscapes and sensing the change in attitudes and lifestyles, can you really have an accurate picture of the continent in your mind.

While the train trip won't allow you to discover anything new in the world sense, the triumph of exploration is a personal one. It is a triumph that helps replace introverted nationalism with a sense of the variety of social systems that can work, and of the artificial arbitrariness of national borders. Europe is a big place, but the sense of union is growing, and Inter-Rail gives young people the opportunity to recognise this . . . though it didn't work in our case.

the explanation

Paul

My parents grew up in the sixties: a decade of turmoil, rebellion, drugs and rock 'n' roll. Therefore it would be fair to assume that when I grew old enough they would see fit to tell me about some of the less virtuous things they got up to during their formative years. Everyone has their standards, ideals, and beliefs about how their kids should be brought up, so by the time I had reached the age of sixteen and they had still disclosed nothing I assumed it was just because they did not think me ready for some of the skeletons they had in their cupboards.

I waited patiently for the day of enlightenment, but no further evidence has come to light other than that my mother had the names Elvis and Tommy (Steele) embroidered on the legs of her jeans, my father once crashed a car, and one of his friends got drunk and missed an exam.

To be honest, I think there is a very real possibility that they did not do anything wild and exuberant during their teenage years. Sadder still, they are not the exception: they are the rule. Sure, some people must have spent the entire decade smoking drugs and protesting about whatever it was fashionable to protest about, otherwise film makers and television producers would have been unable to make countless documentaries and cult films about this wild era that 'everyone remembers so well'.

But by the time I was seventeen the damage was done. I had already seen *Easyrider* and *Woodstock* and I had heard Canned Heat, Janis and Jimi and I could not believe that anyone could have escaped the sixties culture altogether. I double-checked with parents of friends only to find that they had been in some kind of coma as well. I was severely disappointed. I am fairly sure that when I have kids they will ask me what I got up to during the exciting eighties and the naughty nineties and, to ensure that they suffer no similar disappointment, I have adjusted my lifestyle accordingly. At least now I will be able to say yes, I went to raves that got busted by the police, yes, I rode motorbikes, and yes, I really did hitch to Den Haag with Uncle Olly equipped only with a loaf of bread and two tins of spaghetti hoops.

I am really taking out a sort of insurance policy or disclaimer for some of my past (and future) actions, so when you read the book you will understand that I did what I did for three reasons: 1) to try to clear up the 'balance of misdemeanours' deficit that my parents left me to inherit from their adolescent years, 2) to ensure that I have a good stock of (hopefully) amusing anecdotes to tell my kids when the time comes, and 3), because some of the things I did, I did because I wanted to and there was no one there to stop me. Now you know.

in the beginning

Paul

Someone once said, 'There are no bad ideas, just ideas.' This, as we know, is bollocks. I don't know who said it but I suspect that he himself made some monumental cock-up and, as it was his idea that led to this cock-up, he felt he may be able to divert attention from his blunder by concocting this idiom. This is not going to work for Alastair however as I am certain that the germ of an idea that would lead to us being arrested, water-cannoned, accosted by a multitude of drunks, madmen and homosexuals and finally returning to England half a stone lighter and covered from head to toe in filth was most definitely his.

The idea started off in a café in Chichester. It was a Saturday and, unsurprisingly, it was pissing with rain. It was this rain that had brought our busking session to a premature end, which was a shame because on a good day we could expect to 'earn' a fair amount. By a fair amount I mean about what one of our less fortunate friends might have earned over the course of an entire Saturday, dressed in an ill-fitting polyester uniform and wearing an embarrassing 'Please ask me for assistance' badge. We, or more accurately, Stewart and Alastair, had found that busking provided a far more attractive way to get spending money than did more conventional alternatives. You could set your own hours of business, set your own breaks, you didn't have to be up at the crack of dawn to start and, most importantly, you didn't have to take any shit from a brain-dead branch manager with halitosis. I digress. One major disadvantage that I have not yet mentioned was that, occasionally, busking was not such an infallible source of income as one may have hoped. The day it all started was such a day. We had made just about enough to buy a round of drinks at Neil and Denis' café and, as we had nothing better to do with the money, this is what we did.

Pipe-dreams are fuelled by despondency. We were not short on fuel today. Alastair's idea seemed to come from nowhere. More zealous individuals might say that it was an act of God — that is, until they learned what it eventually led to; then they would say that it was an idea spawned by the Devil himself. Alastair had been to Castellane before, it transpired. Castellane was a medieval town in the more rocky end of Provence and, on that dismally damp day, it sounded like paradise. After a quarter of an hour, the idea that was recently a mere germ was now more of a 'nasty turn'. Alastair continued with his descriptive monologue — it could have been complete bullshit but we were living the part now. We could not be dissuaded. The simple fact was that we had to go to Castellane. It was around this point that Stewart tried delicately to remind us of the trifling fact that such an expedition may require a degree of financing and, skint as we were, the chances of us actually going anywhere were remote. This would not be allowed to sway us.

Financing the expedition proved to be difficult, as Stewart had predicted. For a start we needed tickets to get us to the south of France. Flying there was out: too expensive. None of us had a car at the time and so the inevitable conclusion was that we would have to take the train. Initially we were reluctant to do so as none of us had any great experience of continental rail travel and, quite forgivably I think, we all assumed that it would be as unpleasant, slow and unreliable as travelling in the UK.

We consulted a bloke who worked at the travel office at Chichester station. Never before had we met such a mine of information when it came to trains. We decided to rename this man (who was probably called Ralph or something) as 'The Oracle' as the full extent of his encyclopaedic knowledge gradually unfurled before us over the course of our many visits to consult him.

Finally, the time came to book our passage.

'Hello,' I said. 'We came in a couple of weeks back about —'

'Yes, about what was the best way to get to Castellane in Alpes de Haute Provence,' interrupted The Oracle.

'Er, yes. What we need to know now is whether there is a supplement pay—'

'Payable on the couchettes. Yes, I thought you might think about that. Let me see.' The Oracle went into deep thought for one nano-second. 'I said that if you got the 18:26 train then there would be a nominal fee.'

I consulted my notes. 'Er, yes. That's what you've written here.'

'But,' he continued, 'I also said that if you were to get to the station by 21:20 then you could probably grab a couchette on the later train without having to pay a supplement as that train only has one inspector and he only bothers to check the last six carriages as he's got gout in his legs.'

'Yes. What we wanted to know is if there is a later train that will still get us into Nice before 11:00 the next day.'

'There is the *Bizet Express* which leaves at 22:15. Hang on — I'd better check that.' He looked in his eight inch thick timetable of European trains. 'Yes. That's right. It says 22:12 here but SNCF have got that wrong because they haven't taken into account the signalling changes at Beaune. The changes only came into effect six days ago. Marvellous new computerised signalling system. Cost over eighty million francs —'

This was fascinating, but slightly irrelevant.

'Yes, but do we have to pay a supplement?' I repeated.

'Oh, yes! About twelve pounds each. But it's worth it,' concluded The Oracle.

'Thanks.'

We were torn between respecting him for his great capacity to store such volumes of information and pity that his life must have been so dull to remember even a tenth of what he did. Still, he didn't fit in with the rest of the railway staff — too helpful and professional — so he had to go. We popped down to see him some months after we returned only to find that the whole travel centre was closed and ankle deep in litter. Much like the rest of the station.

We set about the mammoth task of raising the money required for the trip with unaccustomed gusto. Our busking activity was stepped up to cover Saturday morning in its entirety and, in order to ensure that we could always busk in our preferred pitch, this would normally require an unreasonably early rise and cycle ride to the subway where we would play. On one occasion, we found that some enterprising soul had beaten us at our own game and was merrily playing away when we arrived at the subway. What the saxophonist did not realise was that a) he was on our pitch, and b) that we, or, more accurately, Alastair, was more mercenary and ruthless than he could imagine. Alastair, after a couple of minutes of indecision, walked to a nearby phone box and called the police claiming that he was a resident of a house in the adjacent 'Franklin Place' and that there was someone making a terrible noise in the underpass. We then waited for a quarter of an hour and observed (from a discreet distance) the musician being moved on. We allowed the dust to settle for a couple of minutes before seizing the now vacant pitch.

We took a job share at the café where we would wash up in a sweaty little kitchen area for a mere £1.15 per hour. We also sold anything we didn't need at the time. Saleable items included a shitty electric guitar and a shitty bicycle (though the bicycle only became shitty through the clumsy and unprofessional restoration process to which I subjected it).

Stewart

Our penultimate day in Britain saw two of us walking through the town centre on a hot Friday afternoon looking like a cross between mountaineers and Arctic explorers. Alastair carried a cheap acoustic guitar in his right hand, wrapped in a collage of gaffa tape that just passed for a guitar case. In his left hand was a small daysack, packed with rolls. On his back was a rubber duck, tied to a piece of string which was in turn attached to an enormous green rucksack that towered above his head, bursting in an effort to contain all his clothes. Tasteless Bermuda shorts, sailing plimsolls and an inappropriately smart shirt and straw boater completed the picture.

It didn't occur to me at the time that I looked equally ridiculous.

'How many cheese rolls did you make,' asked Alastair.

'Only enough for lunch tomorrow,' I replied, 'about twenty-four.' This was a slight exaggeration. There were, in fact, only twenty-three left, because I had eaten one on the way into town.

We met Paul some moments later, sitting on the cathedral green with four beautiful tanned French girls.

'Alloo,' said one of the girls. I think she said it to me, which was surprising because her gorgeous tan and long dark hair made her look like one of those cool, mysterious and sexy girls who never seemed to talk to me.

'Hello,' I said, and she ignored me.

Paul explained who they were: students from Marseille.

'Ooh la la,' I said, straining my French to its limits.

The conversation hereafter was stilted for obvious linguistic reasons, and I was concerned that it was time to get to the station. Upon leaving, we exchanged a combined total of forty-eight goodbye kisses with the girls.

'If these Continentals are always snogging hello or goodbye, how do they ever get anything done?' I asked Paul.

'They don't,' explained Paul.

Coming to the market cross we met one of Paul's friends, a newly converted hippy.

'Hey guys,' said the hippy. 'Wow,' he added shortly after, having studied us closely.

'How was 'Henge?' asked Paul.

'A bit of a downer. John got his ribs smashed by the pigs.'

'You have to be careful on farms,' I said.

'We're off to France now,' said Paul.

'Love the rubber duck,' said the hippy, pointing to Alastair's mascot.

'We've both got smaller ones,' said Paul.

'Ooh la la,' I grunted.

As we arrived at the station and forced our enormous bulks through the ticket barrier, some pangs of doubt slipped into my mind. We were only going to Alastair's house tonight, ready to leave together first thing tomorrow morning, but from now on there was no turning back — our paths were heading inexorably to mainland Europe and I had no idea what it would be like. Everything was so vague, and I felt as if I'd never been abroad before. I knew we were camping somewhere in the south of France for a week or two, and then according to how much money was left we would travel back perhaps via Switzerland and Germany. I wouldn't have believed at the time that for part of the trip we would actually tear through more than a country a day, constantly escaping from a trail of bemused girls, angry policemen, angry campsite owners, angry nutters, more bemused girls, angry restaurateurs, and other assorted angry Europeans. We each had an Inter-Rail ticket, that magic passport to unlimited rail travel in Europe for a month. But though we had no intention of staying that long, intentions rarely determine actions.

chichester to paris

Inter-Rail Rule 1: Packing. Gather together everything you want to take, then throw away anything remotely useful.

Stewart

We were in a band called Fridge at the time of the trip. Not 'Frigid', as some had predictably suggested. Alastair and I played guitar and shared the vocals; Paul wasn't musical so he 'played' bass guitar. A fortnight after our return we were booked to play our greatest gig — The Chichester Festival Theatre Studio. This was actually a large tent, but we usually forgot to mention that.

Being in a band had nothing to do with music, I discovered. Especially where Fridge was concerned. All that mattered were credibility and image. It was vital to spend at least one afternoon a week mooching around Honest John's Music Emporium pretending to be cool and hard and talking about reverb levels, PA rigs and Fuzz Boxes. Whatever they were. We told other musicians that we were going on a tour of Europe, playing loads of gigs. This sounded a lot more impressive than the truth which was that we were going camping and might play in the odd gutter for a few Francs.

The importance of credibility ensured that the first thing we checked for when we went through our rucksacks at Alastair's house were photos of Fridge, to prove to foreigners that we were rock stars. Everything else was tipped on the floor, and we argued about what to leave and what to take, and who should carry which parts of the tent. I came off well because I didn't have many clothes to start with, and as my rucksack was the smallest I was given the lightest share.

Paul

For me, the trip started the moment I hauled my rucksack and plethora of carrier bags containing clothes and useless novelty goods over Alastair's doorstep. The three of us sat around in a circle gazing in awe at the mammoth pile of junk in the centre of the lounge.

We had decided to adopt the monicker of the 'Mad Brothers' for our expedition for reasons of personal amusement. This explained why we felt the need to carry a small inflatable desert island complete with palm tree and a set of yellow, plastic bath-time ducks.

Packing turned out to be a bit of a headache when we realised that economies would have to be made. The problem was that we didn't really know what we needed, and we were all reluctant to leave anything behind. As well as full rucksacks we had the added encumbrance of one guitar and one daysack each. The daysacks were necessary to contain all the goodies donated by well-wishing friends and relatives, notably Alastair's grandmother and her Nobel Prize-winning chocolate-chip cookies. Bless her cotton socks. We had decided to take the guitars because they looked like they needed a holiday.

Thus the Mad Brothers were ready to launch their first assault on an unsuspecting Europe. Unfortunately, but not remarkably, we were not noted for our organisational skills, and for this reason we had decided all to stay at Alastair's house overnight to minimise the risk of not being able to find each other in the morning.

'Where's the camping stove, Paul?' Stewart asked me, looking worried.

'Well I only had a small space in my rucksack before I came over here, and there were two things still to pack: the gas stove, and the broken old telephone.'

'So?' asked Stewart, fearing that his tea bags would now be about as useful as his prophylactics.

'Well, the telephone was lighter, 'cos we ripped out all the insides. And I thought it would be more useful.'

The alarm clock sounded at 06:30 in Alastair's bedroom, but it needn't have bothered as we had been awake for a good hour, speculating as to what on earth we were letting ourselves in for.

After only the most cursory of breakfasts we loaded up with our bags of crap and filed out of the door and up the road to Fishbourne station.

Stewart

Paul announced his presence in the carriage with a loud, unembarrassed belch. The noble art of belching was something which he practised with the vigour of an Olympic candidate, to the extent that he was able to belch distinguishable words, although the word was usually 'crisps'. We spread ourselves across six vacant seats while the train grumbled away under our weight.

Part of the reason for travelling together was in order to keep rehearsing the Fridge songs for the gig. These were practically identical to our busking repertoire, but that was rusty too. We decided to start practising right away and took out the guitars.

When Alastair (the only one of us with a sense of pitch) had tuned them, it occurred to me to feel nervous: a sick feeling caused by a combination of the train's swaying movement and the fact that there were others in the carriage on this Saturday morning. But Paul was revelling in the atmosphere. He was in an unrestrained 'mad mood' and had to be tactfully restrained from letting fly a fart from his internal chemical weapons factory that would have destroyed the carriage. Alastair extended his natural empathy towards all those around him and thought nothing of his own safety in trying to prevent Paul's aromatic expulsion.

We filled the train with a cacophony of music and voices for a couple of verses of 'Mrs Robinson' until we realised that none of us really knew the chords yet. Or the words.

The train squealed to a painful halt at Newhaven Harbour Station and sent a rucksack crashing down from the overhead rack into Paul's lightning reflex arms. We now faced a frantic scramble to load up our things and get onto the platform.

'Which way's France?' asked Paul to a railway porter, without waiting around to hear the offensive reply.

Inside the ferry terminal the customs men let us straight through, deciding that a few sad glances would suffice to show their disgust at Britain's latest exports. Relieved at not being searched and having to explain the reason for the presence of the telephone (which was that we were mad) we wandered into the heart of the ship and claimed a row of reclining chairs for ourselves and our luggage. The ferry then performed a three-point turn and headed for Dieppe.

I tried to read, but Thomas Hardy and water didn't agree with me, and I was asleep in less than a chapter of *Far From The Madding Crowd*. We later treated ourselves to a more edifying cinema showing of *Rocky*, which was marginally more interesting than looking at the waves. Then we promenaded on the 'sun-deck', and considered complaining to the Advertising Standards Authority about it.

Inter-Rail Rule 2: Never listen to the orthodontically-challenged stranger smelling of shit who offers to get you tickets for the Paris Metro. He's a complete bastard.

The beauty of Paris in the summertime is seriously overrated. Admittedly it has many fine architectural features, sites of historic interest, and those futuristic toilets that open their doors automatically before you manage to pull your trousers up. Its cuisine is admired worldwide, as are its women, and the appeal of the Seine is unquestionable. If you're a rat. But the image of the city has for years been maintained on the relic of its sophisticated 1920's heyday, and can no longer be accurate. The city has vanished beneath a sea of tourists.

Wherever you go in the world, a crowd of tourists looks the same. What's the use of visiting Notre Dame if all you can see are people and cameras? Unless you are particularly tall in stature, all you could hope to gain from straining your neck to look above the crowd is a view up an American's flared shorts.

Paris and its suburbs now flounder like a decaying walrus upon its river. Tiny bird-like cranes peck at its superannuated flesh, destroying all of its original beauty. Its digestive system has long since spilled out and been named the Centre Pompidou, and only one graceful whisker of a tower remains. And yet, from this tower, the skin of the city still seems somehow alive. It is the mass movements of the millions of ants who have come to see what remains, but in doing so are choking its arteries.

Three particular ants were now approaching the city on the artery that led to Gare St Lazare.

'Paris looks a bit of a shit-hole,' pointed out Paul, as the train slowly ground its way through the most degenerate part of the northern suburbs.

'Where are all the tulips?' I asked, stupidly, to no one.

'Don't be a wanker,' replied Paul, inspecting an interesting bogey that he was considering sending to the Natural History Museum.

The journey from Dieppe had lasted an exhaustingly slow afternoon, leaving us plenty of time to slag off nearly every aspect of France and its inhabitants in a wholly and unreasonably bigoted manner. The compartment was shared with two other people, whom we confidently believed to be foreign. This left us entirely without inhibitions. But we were disappointed to discover that on French trains everyone sits reading in silence just like in Britain. We were buggered if we were going to stifle our voices for hours on end.

'This is a piss-boring train,' said Paul. 'I thought Froggy trains were supposed to go fast.'

'Hang on, there's the station. It looks horrible.' With that I leant out of the window to look ahead. There was a guard on another platform giving me dirty looks, so I shouted, 'Ne pas se pencher au dehors!' at him, as recited from the helpful sticker on the window.

As the brakes began to squeal and the general bustle of the station came into view, one of the two others in the compartment rose up to leave. He was a young man, carrying only the Balzac novel he had been reading. He paused before leaving.

'Your views on France have been most illuminating,' he calmly said.

I was the first to recover from the shock.

'We thought you were French, not English. That's a French book you're reading, isn't it?'

'Yeah, and I'm Australian.'

'We didn't really mean any of that, you know,' apologised Alastair.

'I 'ope not, monsieur,' said the other man, who was clearly of garlic descent. The two men left, and we felt terrible.

We enjoyed the rare luxury of being able to take our time getting off the train, as it was a terminus stop. The station was warm and busy, the noises and shouts had a distinctly continental flavour, and the odd example of graffiti was unintelligibly foreign. All except for one advert for French knickers which had been unable to escape that poetic phrase, 'Chelsea FC'.

There were hundreds of other Inter-Railers around the station, all equipped with rucksacks, beachmats, and bottles of coke. We were no longer outsiders — we were in our element.

'I think we should get to Gare de Lyon before we do anything else. The train might be delayed or something.' Alastair's statement was, of course, in no way influenced by the fact that he had just heard a couple of girls saying they were going there, and anyway the girls soon disappeared into the crowds of suspicious looking tanned men with moustaches, greasy hair, suits and training shoes: men who could barely produce one set of teeth between them.

We made our way through the smelly crowd down into the Paris underground system. 'Metro', said the sign in red lights. Paul led us through to a large underground hall with tunnels leading off to mysterious destinations. Alastair spotted a route map on the wall, and we sidled up to it. I put down my guitar so that I could press the buttons that lit up the various routes.

After several minutes of lighting up as many routes as possible, without actually bothering to work out where we were supposed to go, we were approached by a dark, greasy man with a moustache and about three teeth. He grinned. I wished he wouldn't. And then he spoke.

'*Où allez vous?*' he asked, spilling out breath that was almost solid. Paul and I both understood, but thought feigned ignorance would be a better way of getting rid of him than encouraging the communication.

'Sorry mate, we're English. Don't understand you, Monsieur le Smell,' said Paul, with a polite smile.

'Ah, English? I help you. Where you go?'

I was worried. I tried to outwit the foreigner, trying to work out why he would want to help us. The only thing I could think of was that this odd and rather repulsive gentleman was in league with someone else who was kindly relieving us of such inconveniences as cash and passports from behind our backs. With this in mind, I constantly watched the backs of the others, and kept turning round so that no one could get inside my rucksack (not that there would have been room for them anyway).

Alastair answered the man, much to my dismay. I would rather have just run off.

'Gare de Lyon,' he said, in an English accent.

'*Quoi?*'

'*Gare de Lyon,*' repeated Paul with an exaggerated Pythonesque French accent.

'Ah, is good. I show you. Come.'

We looked at each other, each suspicious and unsure. However, there was the possibility, albeit slight, that he could simply be a helpful man. So, unable to formulate a reasonable excuse in time, we agreed to follow him. He led the way into one of the tunnels like a mother duck leading her stumbling children. He walked very fast, but his scent was easy to follow. Several twists and turns and a flight of stairs finally brought us to another ticket hall. It had another map, more dodgy men, and rows of automatic ticket machines.

'I get you tickets,' he said, eagerly holding out an ape-like hand. 'For three is forty-five Francs.'

We had little change at this stage of the holiday, so Paul produced a fifty Franc note. The man took it, but put his own coins into the machine. He came back with three tickets and said with a disgusting grin,

'Is OK I keep change?' It was only five Francs. We let him have it for his trouble. Within seconds he had vanished down a distant corridor.

'We've been ripped off guys,' I realised, as we walked past the machines. 'Gare de Lyon is only supposed to be five Francs each. We paid fifteen each, plus a tip.'

'What a wanker,' said Paul, annoyed at his naïvety.

We passed through the electronic ticket barriers, then my heart sank.

'Where's my guitar?' I screamed. There was nothing in my right hand, (for a change — Paul) but I had been so worried by the toothless scarecrow that I hadn't previously noticed.

'Do you think he nicked it?' asked Alastair.

'Hang on, I put it down when we looked at the map with the stupid lights on.'

Paul sprang into action. Losing a guitar would be a serious handicap: without busking our money would run out very soon. He threw down his belongings into a corner, told Alastair to wait with them, and I stripped off likewise. Now to get out. The barriers opened one way only, and couldn't be forced.

'Give me a leg-up,' shouted Paul. I pushed him up, over the barrier, and off he ran. I felt helpless — I was the fool, but could do nothing to help. Paul might need help. He might be struggling heroically with a greasy man (nothing new there). I tried jumping over. No luck. Then I noticed at the edge of the row of barriers was an exit door. I pushed the green button, and with a hydraulic whoosh I was let through.

I charged down the stairs and through the tunnels, adrenalin pumping my legs almost convincingly enough to make me look athletic. I had to get there — I had to help Paul rescue the guitar. One more turn and I was in the large hall where it had all started. I paused to look for the map. There it was, the stupid lights flashing on and off like a pathetic disco. I weaved between the travellers in the way and caught up with it. There was Paul, standing with the guitar slung over his shoulder, getting his breath back.

We were loath to buy more tickets to get through the barriers again, so Alastair pressed the green button by the emergency exit gate for us to come in through.

'What happened then?' he asked, hoping to be told of great battles and acts of valiance.

'It was just standing where he left it,' said Paul.

'Twat', they were thinking, I expect.

Gare de Lyon turned out to be another railway station, surprisingly enough. Trains and that. But these trains were interesting, even to non-train-spotting fully-rounded human beings like ourselves, because they contained sleeping compartments, or couchettes. Now, some of you more hardened Inter-Railers reading this may think 'what a bunch of wimps — what's the point in paying for beds?', or something like that. Others may think it normal practice to rent a couchette for each overnight journey. But it is with great embarrassment that I admit to having spent a night in one of these things, purely because we didn't know there was any option. The Oracle at the railway station had booked it all for us, and we just said 'thank you very much' and paid him. But the true nature of Inter-Railing will become apparent later in our travels.

'There's the couchette train,' pointed Alastair.

We peeped in through a window. The compartment contained six bunk beds, three on either side.

'Looks pretty cosy. I hope we get three Swedish chicks on the opposite bunks,' I said.

'Naked ones,' requested Alastair.

'Knowing our luck,' said Paul, 'we'll probably get three fat Americans who spend the whole time telling us how they won the war for us. Don't worry though — I'll stink 'em out with my feet. They can sleep in the toilets where they belong.'

The train wasn't due to leave for over an hour, and I was hungry.

'Who fancies a McDonald's?' I asked.

We all did.

Passing a few prostitutes on the way to the restaurant, I worked out how many burgers I'd have to give up for half an hour with one of them and decided it wasn't worth it. My stomach was too important. The large, friendly 'M' motif soon came into view, and in we went.

Inside, the first thing we noticed was that the staff were attractive — no one had the usual 'pizza-face'. The second surprise was that they seemed intelligent. They all spoke English, and even the menu was mainly English. I decided I liked this, and that we would have to visit these cultural centres more often.

After allowing five minutes for the digestion process to get started we set off for the station again. The prostitutes were absent from our return journey, probably gone for a burger or something. Paul's purchase of a half case of Export 33 weighed him down even more, but the mild intoxicant liberalised his mind sufficiently to make him suggest it was time for us to buy our first prurient magazine, something to keep us occupied on the long journey ahead.

Of course, we had all studied examples of this particular literary genre before, sometimes studying with a rigour that would have exhausted the most ardent academic. But none of us had previously had the courage to buy one. At the large newsagent's kiosk back at the station we had to decide who would make the purchase.

'No way, I'm not going first — it wasn't my idea,' I said, defiantly. But I think the others were less inhibited by the idea — we were in a foreign country with no chance of anyone we knew seeing us. So a joint effort was decided upon: I provided the funds, then gratefully scanned the French car magazines and watched out of the corner of my eye as Paul and Alastair stared up at the top shelf.

'Look — they've got English ones in French,' said Paul in a confident voice.

'They look a bit boring. How about this one?' He took it down, and they leafed through the glossy pages of Newlook. I stuck my head deeper into the car magazine.

'OK,' said Paul, 'we'll get this one, and how about this one here — it's wrapped in cellophane, so it must be total filth. It says Chienne.'

'What does that mean?'

34

'Something for dog-lovers, I suppose.'

'We'll have to get it then. I'll buy Newlook and you get that one,' said Alastair.

'You can go first, Al.'

'Why me? You're the fattest.'

'And you've got ginger hair.'

They were watertight arguments, logical and precise. But the woman serving was not amused by all the incomprehensible banter, and was relieved to see the colour of their money. Alastair was served first, then Paul.

'Thanks a lot young wench, I'll be thinking of you tonight,' was his gentlemanly display of gratitude. I decided I ought to buy the car magazine after all.

Small groups of Inter-Railers were dotted around the floor of the main hall of the station. We made a base at the foot of a large pillar, sitting on our rucksacks and sticking our guitars and hats at the side.

I casually enquired as to the various fetishes catered for in the more explicit pages of the magazines, and was handed the copy of Newlook and told to get my laughing gear around it. It fitted neatly between the pages of the car magazine from where it could be enjoyed in greater privacy.

Alastair and Paul had wrapped their comic in a copy of Melody Maker, though this was pretty pointless since Paul's hilarious bilingual renditions of all the captions and 'stories' made clear to the entire station what they were reading.

Thus innocently occupied, we spent an enjoyable half hour with our arms over our laps. With only a few minutes left before we could board our train, Alastair suggested we have a quick go at busking. Paul said he would rather stick a broom handle up his anus, but that was his prerogative. He stayed behind to 'look after the crap'.

Alastair and I picked up our guitars and hats and jogged down the steps that led into the underground system. We pushed hurriedly past a beggar and set ourselves up opposite a fruit stall. I gave the fruit seller a tentative grin to see if he minded us playing, and, taking the blank face he gave in reply to mean indifference, we took out the guitars.

The moment Alastair put his guitar case on the floor, a Franc and some centimes chinked onto it.

'This could be a good session,' he said.

'I don't think so. I've broken a string. We'll have to leave it for now.'

'Did we bring any spares?'

'I thought you had a spare set,' I said.

'No, I gave them to Greg to put on his old guitar. You'll have to take a string off Paul's. He won't notice — he's only a bass player.'

Alastair used the Franc towards buying a peach from the fruit seller. But before he had taken a bite we received a courtesy visit from the beggar we had ignored earlier. He stood hurling abuse at us, every word of which went straight over our heads, though we assumed he was thanking our country for selling cheap lamb to them, or something.

We found Paul with a suspicious grin on his face, which I was assured had nothing to do with a broom handle.

Paul

When they went busking I settled down to read the new look *Melody Maker* amongst our bags. Imagine my annoyance to be disturbed from my intellectual reading by an intrusive drawl,

'Hi there! You must be English.'

Excellent, I thought — Americans, my absolute favourites.

'I couldn't help noticing your paper was in English.'

Rather negligent of me, I thought — Americans all over Paris and there I was reading *Melody Maker* in full view. I was in no mood for intercontinental discourse, and luckily by this time I had already made a substantial impression on the EU beer lake which meant that decorum was no longer with me.

'What's in *Melody Maker* this week?' it continued.

I wondered what made him keep talking when he get no feedback from his conversation victim.

'Where are you going? We're from Washington . . . DC . . . you know, in America. We're into rowing and mountaineering. What are you into?' I was asked.

I had to show them what I was currently into. Not content with that, I asked if it was true that the only thing smaller than an American's John Thomas is his brain, and they laughed and said how much they loved our English Monty Python humour. Then they had the cheek to ask if they could borrow *Chienne*.

Stewart

'You did what?' I asked Paul.

'They're only over there. You can see which bit they're reading from here. Don't worry, I'll disinfect it afterwards.'

At this point one of the Americans signalled that he had finished his read.

'I really hope I don't accidentally vomit on them,' whispered Paul as he went over to collect it.

'Paul doesn't have a particularly liberal attitude towards the rest of the world,' said Alastair.

'His xenophobia only applies to foreigners,' I pointed out.

Some minutes later we were on the couchette train, a huge affair with about eighteen coaches and two locomotives, searching down the narrow corridor for our cabin. We found the cabin, but there was as yet no sign of the naked Swedes.

With the other half of the cabin still empty, we spread ourselves around liberally and took out the porn for a read. Paul grabbed the top bunk, Alastair climbed into the middle one, and I, who didn't care about the implied social diminution, took the unexciting bottom bunk. There we lay for fifteen impatient minutes, pathetically willing the door to be slid open by some beautiful girls.

Sadly, this is planet Earth, and reality reared its hairy armpits once more in the form a boring French family with an irritating son. We found it hard to disguise our disappointment.

'Bloody hell,' said Paul. 'What a bunch of stiffs.'

'*Bonsoir*,' said the father. He was in his late twenties and looked incredibly dull. His greeting marked the end of our communication.

I picked the guitars off the lower bunk opposite, and wedged them underneath my bunk with the rucksacks. I was now facing the mother, who could have been attractive had it not been for the manky hanging gardens she cultivated under her armpits. The boy on the top bunk never emerged from his personal stereo, and Paul took great pleasure in reading his magazine in front of him, knowing his parents could not see. With Alastair soon asleep, the rest of us lay in an awkward silence, broken only by the occasional recommendation by Paul of a particular part of the magazine.

I lay on my front and peered out of the window from the side of the curtains. The landscape slowly changed from blends of grey and black to tones of green and brown. Properties grew further apart, and insignificant country stations flashed by at ever increasing speeds. The gradual blur and loss of light sent me into a deep sleep that was aided by the vibrations of the train, and eventually Paul must have realised he was talking to himself.

south of france

Stewart

I woke up. Where was I? I panicked. On a train. I relaxed. The train was motionless. I panicked. The bunks opposite were empty. I panicked even more and sat up. Had I overslept and been taken hundreds of miles past my destination? I looked at my watch: it was six-thirty, and we weren't due to arrive until eight. I checked for the other rucksacks under my bunk. They were still there, so I wasn't alone. I looked out of the window. Already it was daylight, and we were at a station. I could see the dull French family walking away across the platform, and wondered why they didn't get off at a later stop so that they could get more sleep.

But I could sleep no more. The amount of activity on the station at this hour was staggering. Parcels were being loaded onto the train, people were being unloaded, and tanned men in scuffed uniforms drove little trolley trains around the platform for no apparent reason.

What really grabbed my attention, however, and kept me from falling asleep again, was the transformation that had taken place to the outside world since the previous night. As we pulled away, no longer was there the abundance of green in the landscape that had existed close to Paris. Everything now was distinctly Mediterranean. Buildings were whitewashed with gently sloping roofs of knackered clay tiles. Grass, where it grew, was brown and scorched, and everywhere seemed dusty and parched. I could see farmers at work with medieval implements like scythes and handploughs, and wondered how they ever managed to produce the food mountains that people complained about on the news. The only cars to be seen were ancient Citroen DS's, rotting away in fields because general science never caught up with their futuristic innards, making them too complex for economic repair.

I lay there marvelling at these fresh new sights until Paul woke up and farted. In a panic I quickly opened the window, and the resulting rush of fresh air woke Alastair.

'I see Monsieur Marsaud and his family have buggered off,' croaked Paul.

'*Monsieur Marsaud est parti avec son famille*,' I said, mimicking the school texts that I had never understood.

'Very flash,' said Paul, 'but it's *sa famille*.' Pedantic tosser.

'I'm allowed to interpret the language in my own way. Incorrect grammar has a nicer ring to it sometimes. Anyway, I could be right and the French could be wrong. They are foreign, after all.'

'Foreign bastards,' said Alastair, in a semi-coma. 'What about them?'

But before anyone could explain things to him he had drifted back to sleep. Paul seemed to have ceased his wind-tunnel tests for the moment, and I lay back and wondered how I had ever got into this situation.

The French family now gone, and with Nice looming not too far along the coastline, Paul scrambled down and rummaged around amongst the clothes in Alastair's rucksack. After nearly burying himself in a mountain of them he managed to find the timetable of the Nice mountain railway. He stuffed as many clothes as he could back in again and climbed back onto his bunk, leaflet in hand. His suspicions were correct.

'There are no trains on a Sunday until the afternoon — hourly between twelve and six,' he told me.

'So what?'

'How do you fancy a day in Cannes? Nice is a bit shitty, apparently, so we could do our waiting in Cannes instead.'

At this point the train began to slow again, and I tried to see which station we were approaching. Paul jumped down and belched repeatedly into Alastair's ear until he woke up.

'Shit! We're there!' I shouted. Alastair hit his head on the bunk above, then fell onto his rucksack on the floor.

'Why didn't you wake me before?'

We pulled on our clothes quickly. Paul was first, and jumped out of the window onto the platform. We had no idea how long the train would wait, so we moved fast. Paul shouted to me to pass out the guitars. Alastair was still deciding what to wear. I stood at the window passing out guitars, hats and sleeping bags, with my shorts around my ankles, to the amusement of some German pile drivers on the platform. Once dressed, we threw out the rucksacks then ran into the corridor and out through the door.

The train showed no sign of going anywhere. We stood on the platform around our heap of luggage, rolling up our sleeping bags and generally trying to tidy up. Then Alastair and Paul realised two different things at the same time.

'This isn't Nice. We've got off at the wrong station, you nobs,' sighed Alastair, in despair.

'Never mind that,' said Paul, 'I've just remembered I left the porn under my pillow.'

With that he leapt back onto the train, while I briefly explained to Alastair what was happening. Seconds later Paul appeared at the window and dropped a moonie. Then the whistle blew and once more Paul threw himself out of the window.

Two English girls came across, grinning.

'Are you English?' asked one.

'*Nein. Ich bin ein Kraut,*' shouted Paul with a salute.

'*Ja,*' I said, '*Deutschland.*'

'*Volkswagen,*' said Alastair.

'Sorry, we thought you were speaking English,' explained the girl.

'English I speak a little, ja,' said Paul in his best German accent. I walked away to laugh. I don't think any of us fancied them so we were keen to maintain the charade.

'They're bloody krauts, Claire. Bloody useless,' said the first girl.

'*Wo ist mein Vater?*' murmured Alastair, as he looked in his rucksack. '*Vorsprung durch Technik.*'

This little incident heightened our determination to spread bullshit as far and wide as possible. Anything from rock stars to minor aristocracy was possible, especially to those who wouldn't understand our accents anyway. I was to convince people that my real name was Poo.

'Doesn't Poo mean *smell* in French?' I asked, both worried and excited by the prospect.

'At least it's appropriate,' observed Paul, hypocritically.

I ate one of my stale cheese rolls on the way to finding a McDonald's for breakfast, which was fortuitous because it was shut for several more hours. Alastair and I were a bit miffed by this.

'Shit,' said Paul, prefacing a monologue that would encompass advanced comparative geosocial theories on work and lifestyle patterns in European culture, concluding that foreigners were lazy bastards.

By the time he had finished, we were heading inexorably towards the beach, walking down wide streets lined with palm trees, littered only by Aston Martins and Rolls Royces. It was still dawn, and the city was quiet, though even in the absence of its population it could not hide its affluence. The streets were not covered with shit, unlike the rest of France, and the buildings weren't even made of it. Later, as people began to appear, I could see that the high living standards of the rich meant that they could also afford the expensive beauty therapy sessions that made them look healthy and attractive. Even the old women were pretty, though I was probably unwittingly basing this on Brigitte Bardot walking her cats.

The only annoying sight was of a young man driving past in a convertible Porsche full of girls. He had more luck than I ever imagined possible without actually being a member of The Beatles whose name didn't begin with 'J'.

We came to a small harbour in which were moored hugely expensive-looking yachts and motor boats. It was a millionaire's car park in the sea. We walked along the quay, drooling over the boats one by one. Most had English flags and English names like 'The Flower of London' or 'The Affluent Bastard'. In size, most were comparable to a small house or a large lorry, and all were immaculately presented.

Alastair called me over to a particular yacht he was admiring. We stood in awe before its polished mahogany deck that was kitted openly, and somewhat ostentatiously, with a drinks cabinet, a large stereo system and a television. It was also clearly marked that the gangway was alarmed. I wondered what had frightened it.

We crossed the quay and scrambled over the rocks to the beach, claiming a patch of sand with the towels. It was beginning to become warm, and joggers started to pound their way along the sand and kick through the waves. The beach slowly filled with sunseekers until we were surrounded by embarrassingly unclad women and intimidatingly muscular bronzed men. The surface of the sea became cluttered with windsurfers, waterskiers and swimmers.

Paul and Alastair walked off to explore the vicinity, leaving me in charge of base. No sooner had they left than a woman in a bikini sashayed through the sand towards me as I lay on my back gazing at a cloudless sky.

'*Monsieur?*' She spoke in tempting tones. I sat up, thinking my luck was in.

It wasn't.

'*Quel heure est-il?*' she asked.

'*C'est, er, neuf heures et demi.*'

'*Merci.*' She trudged away. Nevertheless I was ecstatic. Not only could I tell the others I had chatted someone up already, but I had also conversed with someone in French and both parties concerned had understood every word. This had never happened to me before. I lay back in the sand and felt good and confident.

'Do you fancy a Quickie?' asked a familiar voice.

'What, here on the beach?'

'No, nob,' said Paul. 'We've found a fast food place called Quick, and it's open for breakfast.'

'And Ian Botham's in it,' added Alastair.

'What?'

'Well he looks like Ian Botham, anyway. Except he hasn't got a cricket bat with him.'

'Ah, well it's probably someone else then.'

This was a boring strain of conversation, so it was promptly abandoned in favour of breakfast. At the Quickie there was no sign of Ian Botham, but already burgers were being prepared in numbers almost colossal enough to conquer Paul's appetite. We took over a corner of the restaurant with our luggage and went to order.

'*Cinq cheeseburgers, deux frites, et un grand coca,*' said Paul.

'*Deux cheeseburgers, un frite, et un coca normal,*' I said.

'*Une salade et un jus d'orange,*' said Alastair.

Paul and I forced him to buy a chocolate doughnut, which we later ate for him. When Paul was queuing up for more, Alastair and I dug out a magazine and looked at it under the table. We were still engrossed in it when Paul came back with another tray of burgers and flicked a dill pickle at me. It slid off my shoulder in its own sauce, and landed on the ample chest of a woman who was posing in a greenhouse.

Very appropriate, I thought as I wiped up the mess with Paul's napkin, then threw it back again.

'Oi, you bastard, it's your turn to buy some porn. We'll find a tabac after breakfast,' said Paul.

'I don't care,' I lied, now drinking my ice-cubes very slowly indeed, 'I'll choose another juicy one.'

'Do you want one of these burgers?'

I scoffed at him, saying I knew that even his stomach must have some physical boundaries. With that, Paul unwrapped all three of them, took out all the dills and stuck them to the underside of the table, then squashed the burgers together in a pile. Somehow, sickeningly, he managed to force them all into his mouth.

'You sick bastard!' we shouted. The sight was disgusting — more than half of the 'meal' spilled out all over the table as he tried to chew. And it was not long before his jaws gave in and spat out the rest.

'You can have it if you want, I don't mind.' He stood up and headed for the toilet to wash off the tomato sauce. I followed, feeling sick, leaving Alastair looking rather guilty as he sat surrounded by what was probably the biggest mess the restaurant had ever seen.

Paul was quite prepared for an earful of shit from the cleaner on his return, but came back to find the table completely clean, and Alastair counting some money on its shiny plastic surface.

'Where's my breakfast? I haven't finished it.'

'I know,' said Alastair. 'I shoved it in your rucksack for later.'

'You wanker!' shouted Paul, desperately searching for the sludge he feared might be staining everything he carried.

'Of course not, the cleaner mopped it up. She's taken it round the back to recycle it into lunch. I got a dirty look but no abuse.'

'Don't forget Poo's got to buy some porn,' remembered Paul.

'That's what I'm counting my cash for,' replied Alastair. 'I'll put fifteen Francs towards it.'

'Me too,' said Paul. 'We'll have the hottest one they've got.'

Outside, the streets had become hectic and hurried with tourist traffic and Sunday browsers, and most of the smaller shops were open. We found a nearby pedestrian precinct and looked around for a tabac. The precinct was narrow but at this time of day afforded little shade and seemed to stretch on indefinitely. We rested at a small, decorative, and somewhat obstructive, brick garden in the centre of the street, and Paul, being the most exhausted after his feast, sat on the brick surround.

Suddenly, the earful of abuse Paul had expected for his behaviour in the Quickie seemed to catch up with him. He found himself subjected to a torrent of incomprehensible, but presumably expletive, French words from the mouth of an old woman.

Cheeky bloody peasant, I thought, unable to understand quite how Paul had managed to upset her so much, before I realised that she couldn't be a peasant because we were in Cannes. Paul, diplomatic as ever, calmed her with the words,

'I would appreciate it if you would kindly fuck off,' and then he was able to understand her. 'She says I'm squashing the bloody flowers, I think. Stupid cow — I'm only sitting on the bloody wall.' He stood up to prove it to her, but the effort involved reminded him of the certain something on his back. 'Ah, the rucksack. Er . . .' He turned around to see a group of flowers and part of a bush completely crushed immediately behind where he had been sitting.

'Desolé, Madame,' he apologised, and we all ran off along the street out of earshot from the woman's angry rantings.

'What a stupid fuss over a load of old weeds,' I said, trying to divert their attention from the combined bookshop and newsagent's that was now in view. It was too late: they were already ushering me inside, offering to look after my guitar and bag of rolls while I surveyed the choice of literature.

The shop was not especially large, but I remember seeing an annoying preponderance of children's books, and hence many of the customers therein were annoying children, many with parents. I could tell this wasn't going to be easy. I looked for the magazine stand — it was along one side of the wall of the shop. I scanned its offerings: comics on the low shelves, thousands of almost identical women's magazines, and a few hobbyist titles. But no porn.

I felt great relief at the temporary reprieve, and happily turned round and shrugged my shoulders at the others, still waiting by the door. They were pointing at something, gesticulating high in the air and wearing victorious, dirty grins. The whole shop was watching. I followed their fingers to an archway at the side of the magazine stand. I had noticed this place before: it had dangling beads and a sign that I hadn't bothered to read, because I assumed it meant 'Staff Only'. It meant 'Adults Only'.

Shit, I thought, trying to fight my way through the beads without making any noise, which was impossible and kept me in the public eye. I found myself in a room no larger than a broom cupboard, decorated with wall-to-wall pornographic magazines. Under any other circumstances it would have been paradise.

I looked quickly for what would have been the most disgusting title, which would probably be one of those with the plainest covers, but I was under pressure and had no time to think about it. I grabbed what looked like a triple pack of porn wrapped in cellophane, and noted the figure '15' in the price. Unfortunately, my eyes were blurred by nerves, and I didn't notice when the shopkeeper rang up one hundred and fifty Francs on the till as I presented my choice. There was a mother queuing with an *Asterix* book behind me as I tried calmly to hand over a twenty Franc note for *Pertes Blanches* and held out an unsteady hand for the change.

'*Non, Monsieur, cent cinquante Francs, pas quinze Francs.*' He didn't seem angry, but he wasn't laughing either.

'Huh?' I croaked in disbelief. The porn was ten times more expensive than I had thought. I looked again at the price and could now see the zero after the fifteen. In a calm, fatherly manner the shopkeeper took me back into the booth, apologising to the mother as we passed.

This wasn't happening, I thought. It had to be a cruel dream. But I knew the others were egging me on and that I could not desert my post. The overpriced item was replaced and I was shown a shelf that contained much cheaper examples of publications that catered for my particular interest. Now the choice was doubly difficult with the shopkeeper looking over my shoulder and pointing out various titles that came within my humble price range. I gulped and picked up one with nuns and whips on the front cover. This time the sale was successful, and I ran out of the shop and down the street without waiting for the others to catch up.

It was unanimously decided that I deserved first read for what I had endured in the name of *Art*, and I sat under a shrivelled palm tree glancing at the pages and wishing that I wasn't wearing shorts. Then the beach beckoned once again, and we fancied cooling off in the water.

The sand was now hot under my toes as I danced past the topless girls into the water, wearing only my safest boxer shorts. The sea was a beautiful rich blue, darkening suddenly as the continental shelf dropped away beneath me. It was so deep, in fact, that I figured the odd turd would not do any harm, and would sink innocuously to the sea-bed without trace. I pulled off my boxer shorts and slung them on my arm while treading water, then my face reddened in the execution of this new and very strange experience. It felt so natural and clean, though it was odd to be engaging in such an activity within sight of at least a hundred people all swimming and floating around unawares.

Then I noticed something of a suspicious nature floating next to me. It looked rather like a turd, which was surprising because at the time I had not heard Mr Connolly's monologue on 'jobbies' and why they are the best thing to cling to when your ship sinks. I still believed they would sink in the sea like they do in the toilet.

Taking a wide berth around the polluted zone, I headed back towards the shore, remembering to put my boxer shorts on again before I got too close. Then the cramp struck. My right leg became twisted and useless, and soon it spread to the other leg. The shallow water was some yards away still, and I struck away with my arms. Luckily, my swimming style never much catered for any co-ordination between my arms and my legs so swimming without legs wasn't impossible, though it was difficult keeping my head above water. The thought of what the recent, enormous breakfast had done to me was frightening and I considered shouting for help. I let myself sink a little to reach for the bottom: it wasn't there. I propelled myself a little further forward and tried again. Still no luck. I thought again about help, and called to Alastair who was ahead of me, reaching the shore.

'Alastair! I've got cramp, but I'm alright.' This at least gave me some kind of security in case my arms gave out too. I pulled further, and a little further. My arms grew heavier and the shore seemed no nearer. I decided to test the depth again, and clenched my face and dropped down. This time it was not far — with my feet on the sand my face was only just below water level. I swam forward one more time and felt a huge relief at being able to stand on those twisted legs and breathe deeply until the cramp began to disappear. Finally I was able to move to the edge of the water where Alastair and Paul were waiting, somewhat nervously. They helped me over to the towels and sat me down, then Paul administered some warm water to my dry throat.

'Tastes like shit,' I moaned.

'He's OK,' concluded Paul.

not so nice

Inter-Rail Rule 3: Make sure there's actually a railway where you're going.

Stewart

The journey from Cannes to Castellane is, theoretically, quite simple: standard train to Nice, mountain railway to Annot, then bus ride through the mountains to the town of Castellane. Our chosen campsite would then be a mere short hike away. With such precision of goal, no spare time was allowed and we casually arrived back at Cannes station with only a minute to spare.

'Uh-oh, we'd better get a move on,' I said as soon as I saw several clusters of people around the few doors of the train that were still open. I ran to an uncluttered door and yanked it open, dropping my guitar in the process. Alastair and Paul continued to push their way forwards. I picked up my guitar and looked up at a sea of faces gazing down on me: the train was completely full. I half expected to see scores of Indians hanging out of the windows and clinging with accustomed dexterity to the roof. The position of each individual squashed into that end of the corridor was not exactly enviable, but as a whole they exuded a subconscious sneer which frightened me into muttering a nervous 'Pardon' in a silly accent. The door was slammed from within and I looked around for the others, who were gently easing themselves into an adjacent carriage.

The sardines burst out at Nice station into a thick, stuffy air. We were feeling hot and stressed, and were in no mood for politeness when accosted by a representative of one of those rather strange and sinister religions that flush your brain down the toilet and take all your money. Needless to say we told them in no uncertain terms where they could stick their ideas. Similar refusals were granted to offers of drugs and suspicious accommodation, though we were more than a little disappointed at the lack of offers for free sex.

We paused outside the station. I needed a *pissoir* and was relieved to see a sign for the toilets just next to the station. It was an underground inconvenience, as I discovered having descended the steps and turned a corner where an iron portcullis hung across the entrance, indicating that it was closed. I peered through it into the murky interior — there was a small transaction window inside with a tariff. It was one Franc for a piss, two for toilet paper, another one to wash your hands, and five for a shower. Disgusted, I pissed all over the portcullis and ran back up the steps to tell the others.

'Bloody hell,' said Paul, 'how much for a wank?'

We walked the filthy streets in what was, by luck, vaguely the right direction for the mountain railway. The traffic was appalling and wild, and none of the city's beggars seemed to be taking the day off. The weather may have been beautiful but the overall impression was one of greyness — of sad, rough people living in a deathly dry and dusty network of crumbling buildings. It was an unsettling contrast to the affluent perfection of Cannes, and Alastair had to reassure us that Castellane was an altogether more pleasant place.

Having officially designated Nice an even bigger shit-hole than Paris, we decided not to stop anywhere for fear of being mugged. At the station for the mountain railway we could relax, except for me, since I was volunteered to be the spokesman who would buy the tickets. Luckily, the girl at the ticket desk didn't understand a word of my mumbled French and Paul had to take over.

Many Francs the poorer we passed through the ticket hall into the station. It had been built as a grand affair, with an impressive steel and glass roof and high arched windows in one of the walls. One end was completely open, revealing the slowly inclined track that led into the hills. Some of the cracks that turned the walls into vertical crazy paving looked particularly dangerous, even by Mediterranean standards of construction.

We sat on one of the iron benches, but soon gave up trying to be comfortable. Out through the open end of the station the shimmering image of a train gradually gained in clarity as it approached. I noticed how silently it came to a halt, presuming its downward descent to be powered by gravity alone, though probably aided in its momentum by the fat peasants it was carrying.

When all the passengers — human, animal and vegetable — had spilled out of the train and it had become apparent that it was not going to be disinfected prior to our trip, we boarded an empty carriage and sat inside. With ten minutes to go there was not a soul in sight, not even a driver, and we looked forward to what had to be the most pleasant trip that day. We revelled in spreading ourselves around the shady half of the carriage: three seats for the rucksacks, three for the guitars, plus, of course, three seats for our sweaty bottoms. Then, to round things off, we thought it better to take up another three seats with our feet.

A woman and a child came through from the ticket hall and boarded the other carriage. Then came a huge, old man with a grey moustache and curiously pungent body odour who, for no reason at all, decided to move one of our guitars (in spite of the rest of the carriage being free), sit with us, and start burbling incessantly and enthusiastically about turnips or something. Paul did his best to translate, but could barely recognise a word of the ancient patois — a dialect probably unique to his isolated village in the mountains.

Still, we were due to leave in five minutes, so things couldn't get much worse. A small group of boys arrived, giggling and swearing. There were only a couple of minutes left. A woman boarded the other carriage. A minute to go. I wondered if I could hold my breath until the train started to move and fresh air would begin to flow in through the rusty vents. Three mountaineers with rucksacks and picks joined the train. Only a few seconds.

Then the floodgates opened and a horde of people scrambled aboard. There was a guard with them and he instantly grumbled at us for using what was now precious bum-space. Our rucksacks and guitars were hauled onto the doddery luggage racks above us to placate the queue of people waiting to sit down. Alastair's guitar turned out to be one too many, and we had to take turns in holding it.

As the train began to pull away the last couple of passengers squeezed through the door and joined around ten others who were standing in the aisle. The stench was horrific. Alastair tried to open the stubborn grimy window above his head, but it wouldn't budge. Paul stood up and hit it as hard as he dared with an equal lack of success. We buried our faces in our hats and learned to appreciate the smell of processed straw.

The grubbier suburbs of the ironically named city shrank below us as we crawled up the hillside. Then through a tunnel and civilisation was gone. Instead, dust and rock mingled in imaginative ways to create a semi-lunar landscape. Further on I spotted a wide but pathetically dry river trickling at the bottom of the gorge which the train was to follow for most of the remainder of the journey. There were waterfalls and the remains of rock avalanches, burnt-out cars at the bottoms of cliffs, and the occasional hillside farms struggling against the odds to rake a subsistence living.

Almost two hours later the train came to Annot, a major stop. Or so Alastair thought, but we were the only ones to get off. It was cooler now that the sun was lower in the sky, but this only served to add to the sense of isolation.

'What do we do now, then?' I asked, hunched once more under the weight of my gear.

'There's a bus that takes us all the way to Castellane.'

'All the way? How much further is it?'

'About twelve miles. The bus should be here somewhere.' Alastair was beginning to worry about the distinct lack of buses around us.

We scoured the vicinity of the station, which consisted of two huts and a hole in the ground masquerading as an outside toilet. We were all keen to investigate the potential of the latter after such a journey. There was nothing in the car park except for a Peugeot with a wheel missing.

'It'll probably be along soon,' I suggested.

'I'll wait five minutes and then ask the fascist in there,' said Paul, pointing back at the station.

After some minutes of sitting and watching our shadows grow, Paul took charge and went to seek information from the 'fascist', who doubtless thought of himself merely as a station master. Paul came out swearing.

'These useless fucking Frogs don't have a bus on a Sunday.'

'Shit. They could have told us.' Alastair checked his timetable. Under Sunday it had a picture of a bus with a line through it, though he decided it was best not to say so.

'Let me see the timetable,' demanded Paul. Alastair handed it over, innocently.

'Does it say anything?' he asked.

'Er — shit, yes. *Il n'y a pas des autobus à fucking dimanche.*'

'Twelve miles, eh?' I tried to be optimistic. 'If we walk it we'll be there by about midnight.'

'What, with all this crap on? Fuck off.'

'Let's go down to the village,' said Alastair, being annoyingly sensible. 'There might be a campsite here.'

A steep, tree-covered lane led the way down from the station into the almost deserted village. A street café was open, though apparently not popular, and a boulangerie had its door open to let in all the flies. Paul asked about campsites at the café. There wasn't one in the café, and none in the area: the nearest were at Castellane. He asked about buses: none until Monday morning. He asked which was the road to Castellane: it was back past the boulangerie.

In spite of my misgivings we opted to hitch, though only after we had stocked up with emergency supplies from the boulangerie. Being late in the day there was little left to choose from. One croissant, a pain au chocolat, and two sticks of dry bread baked in a naughty shape. We bought the lot and divided it between us, then chose a couple of drinks each. I had scoffed most of my share by the time we reached the junction with the 'main' road that led to Castellane.

It wasn't a busy road. Two cars came past in half an hour, and even though we had hidden our luggage behind a bush it seemed no one would want to stop for us. With grim, determined faces we loaded up and started to walk. I had never hitch-hiked before, and soon learnt how much a thumb can ache from this usage, and was almost pleased to hear the screech of a car skidding to a halt close behind us.

'*Où allez vous?*' called the cheerful man at the wheel.

'Castellane,' I said, in my English accent.

'*Où?*'

'*Castellane*,' corrected Paul, annoyingly.

Paul surmised roughly from what the man then said that he could take us halfway. That would do! It was a big car — a Renault 20, and it accommodated us all with ease. Paul sat in the front as the chief interpreter.

'He says he's a driving instructor,' he told me and Alastair as the car was hurled into the first bend. I heard myself say that that made it alright then, though inside I began to jellify with fear. The road followed the side of a mountain, and as its altitude increased the small descent on one side developed into a sheer drop of at least sixty feet. I gulped in disbelief: this driving instructor was squealing his tyres at every bend. Every blind bend at that. Tyres squeal when they are at the limit of their adhesion and are about to skid. I knew that. I wished I didn't.

'He says he comes this way every day and he knows every bend perfectly.'

But what if a tyre burst? Or if there were a lorry round the corner? I winced as we passed a car with only inches to spare. All I could think of were the smashed and burnt-out cars I had seen from the train on the journey up. Now I knew how they had got there — they must all have belonged to driving instructors. I tried to think that the barriers would save us: a crenelated wall of stone about half a wheel high. Stone was tough. Then we flew round a corner and found the stone missing where another driving instructor had knocked it over the side.

The road reached its highest point, passed through a short tunnel, then dropped away rather sharply. Our chauffeur decided it might be a good time to start using the middle pedal, and jabbed hard at the next bend sending the car juddering around the corner. Things were improving slightly. Below us was now a large lake, and I could see that the road forked at the bottom, close to the water.

'He says we'll have to get out at the lake. The fork bit leads all the way to Castellane.'

'*C'est lac du Castillon.*'

'Does that mean it's Castellane lake?' I asked.

'Dunno.'

'Well it can't be much further then,' I concluded, 'if it's only the other side of the lake.'

'I seem to remember it being quite big,' said Alastair.

'We'll try for another hitch. I'm not walking that far.' Paul went on in French to thank the insane driver as the car pulled up onto the gravel beside the road. I shouted '*Merci!*' and evacuated the vehicle as quickly as possible in case he should change his mind and offer to take us the rest of the way.

The wheelspin with which the Renault pulled away sprayed us with so much dust that we could barely see the sun which, from this low point, was already setting behind the mountains across the lake, spreading a large shadow which was soon to envelope us. Time was against us, and not a single car came by during the time it took to stop spluttering and swearing about the ride from which we had just escaped.

The chances of one of us getting a lift seemed pretty dire, let alone all three. Paul bravely (or lazily) volunteered a rescue plan. He exchanged some of the bulkier things he was carrying, such as the incredibly useful telephone, the tape recorder and some of his clothes, in return for the other two parts of the tent. He would walk on ahead, take the first lift and set up camp. We would wait until he was picked up, then follow on down the road and try our luck hitching as a pair. This plan suited us fine, as neither of us fancied hitching alone.

We wished Paul luck with the words,

'Hope you make it, Mr Bastard,' then sat on our rucksacks and watched him saunter down the fork that followed the edge of the lake. Above us was a roadsign, antagonisingly pointing out the eleven remaining kilometres to Castellane. It didn't sound much, but we hoped Paul would get a lift soon so that we could begin to make some progress. His bulk was becoming rather indistinguishable with the distance and the dusk when a Renault 5 came to the fork and took the Castellane road.

'Shit — she's stopping for Paul,' I observed.

'Do you reckon they'll come back for us?' He stood up to watch what was happening: Paul's gear had been put in the boot, then he was in the front seat. The car moved. 'She must be turning round,' he said, hopefully. The car carried on moving away from us steadily, round some bends, then behind a hill and it was gone.

I stared intently at the sign as I helped Alastair on with his rucksack. Eleven kilometres. Eleven thousand metres. That wasn't much. About thirty thousand paces. Er, that was quite a lot.

'Bastards,' observed Alastair.

This road was even bendier than the last one, built as a continual series of hairpin bends to follow the infinitely irregular coastline of the lake at a very slight gradient. The first hairpin took the best part of ten minutes to walk, and only brought us forward by about ten yards. This depressed us enough to stuff our mouths up with bread and water. We ate without stopping, determined to press on quickly as all hopes of obtaining a lift faded with the daylight. We couldn't, however, prevent nature from taking its course. I resisted the uncomfortable pressure within me until Alastair declared that he needed a shit and so the two of us began to look for somewhere suitable.

There was no shelter where we were: a steep grassy drop towards the lake on one side and an upward cliff face on the other. Not at all what we had in mind. I didn't know exactly what I was hoping to find on this desolate road, but I knew there had to be somewhere suitable within reach, somewhere that lessened the chances of being run over. We could even still see the fork in the road from where we had started. But the next bend was more gentle, and took us towards a tree-covered area between the road and the lake. Even from a distance it looked promising, a feeling that was reinforced by a sign depicting picnic tables.

An empty lay-by marked the length of the picnic area, and nestled in the shadows amongst the trees were two wooden picnic tables. Wow. What about some toilets? We took off our luggage and rested it on the table that had the least bird shit on it. Alastair went down through the trees to the edge of the hillside overlooking the lake. I didn't like to get so close, even if the fall was blocked by such a myriad of plant life. But even from where I was standing I could see the view that was transfixing Alastair: across the lake was a tiny waterside village, with jetties and boats, and lights that shone out a yellow warmth onto the glass surface of the water. The beauty of the scene was breathtaking and poetic.

'Shall we crap here?' I asked. But Alastair was already strolling back to fetch his tissues, and I went back to get mine. To add a little background music to the scene I stuck the tape recorder on the table and turned up the volume for Cliff Richard and the Shadows, who I'm sure would have been honoured to know that their lyrical tones were perfecting an atmosphere of such magical serenity. We each chose a secluded viewpoint and dropped our trousers to the appropriate tune of *In The Country*.

'This is a bloody nice place,' I said, and I meant it. 'I feel like writing some poetry, but it's too dark.'

'You could use the torch.'

'I don't want to waste the batteries — we might need them to keep Cliff going.'

Cliff stopped singing and the tape recorder clicked itself off in relief. Alastair was first back to the picnic table, and he turned the tape over.

'Come on pretty baby let's-a-move-it-and-a-groove-it,' sang the great-grandfather of rock. We were now fully enveloped by the night as we continued the march, but Cliff sang out ahead of us like a lucky charm, frightening small creatures and cheering us with amusingly bad songs. Music of this ilk was an acquired taste, we decided, though well worth acquiring. Probably.

We pressed on, chasing the hours into the night. Ten o' clock. Eleven o' clock. From its peak just past the picnic place the road took a barely perceptible descent. The lake shimmered in the blackness with an eerie quiet, but was nevertheless inviting. The night air was warm, and we were sweating hard to keep on plodding.

Only two cars had passed us in the last couple of hours, and one of those had been going in the wrong direction. There was no point in optimism. I was simply prepared for an all-night walk. We had long since exhausted the conversational topics of girls, college, music, girls, and what a bastard Paul was for getting a lift. The Cliff tape had been played four times over and I thought it best to switch it off for the night.

Some minutes later a set of lights appeared, seemingly stretching across part of the lake. This was puzzling. It was nearly one in the morning and we had great difficulty in interpreting the image that was vaguely appearing before us.

The road took us now in the direction of the lights, and Alastair said it was probably a bridge. It wasn't until we were a little closer that we were able to see a tall structure rising out of the rock face at the side of the road. The building was painted white and fenced off at the bottom. What he had thought was a bridge was a hydroelectric dam.

Alastair crossed to the other side of the road — the side that faced away from the lake. He was leaning over the fence looking for the water when I approached.

'What's there?' I asked.

'I can't see anything.'

I gingerly leant over the edge to look at the same nothing that Alastair was seeing. It was like a bottomless pit.

'It's like a bottomless pit,' I said, experiencing an unpleasant tingling of the plums that always accompanied a view from a great height.

We returned to the pavement and walked quickly, and slightly nervously, across the dam.

'What's that noise?' I asked, looking up to trace the engine-like sound that was reverberating through the mountains, like a bouncing ball only different.

'Must be a plane.' But there were no lights in the sky. We looked back along the road at the dam and the power station.

It was as far back as we could see. Seconds later a light ploughed down the mountainside towards the dam.

'Bloody hell. We might as well try for a lift,' I shouted, beginning to run away from the approaching car.

'What are you doing?'

'They won't be able to see us here — the next lamppost isn't far off.'

We wobbled unsteadily from our patch of darkness into the next pool of light. The car was halfway along the dam. We stood in the brightest spot, prepared our sweetest smiles, and stuck out the thumbs on the weary right arms that had been carrying the guitars.

The car seemed to be driving faster on this lit-up stretch of road. It reached the end of the dam, from where it could see us. Like something from a fantasy world it actually stopped just ahead of us.

'It's a Golf GTI,' I puffed, as I jogged towards our waiting carriage.

The driver got out, for it was only a two door model. He was a young man, dressed for the holiday season, as was his wife in the passenger seat. I told him our destination and he nodded and ushered us inside. We sat in the back with everything on our laps for the ten minute journey. To walk would have taken the rest of the night. From the lake the road went on to the town of Castellane, from where Alastair directed them to the campsite.

The car stopped beneath a large sign, 'Camp Du Verdon'. It was gone two in the morning and only the main entrance to the site was lit. The rest was shrouded in trees and shadows like a forbidding wood. I thanked the driver, Alastair thanked his wife, and together we took the gentle descent towards the main gate.

'It's deserted,' I whispered. 'How are we going to find Paul?' I could see no tents or caravans from the entrance area. There was a bureau, bar, restaurant, games room, shop and car park, but no campers.

'Most of the sites are this way,' pointed Alastair, directly ahead of us.

'Most? How many are there?'

'About six hundred. Seven. I don't know.'

My awe at the scale of the operation and the unlikelihood of finding Paul was broken by a hushed shout,

'Hey — wankers!' We turned round to see Paul sitting on a grass verge. 'You took your bloody time,' he continued. 'I've been freezing my bollocks off sitting here.'

'We've just walked about a hundred miles,' said Alastair.

'Girls! The tent's up. Follow me.' He led us over a little wooden bridge and into a Eurocamp zone. Nestled some distance behind one of these magnificent family tents was a grotty-looking brown thing in a rough patch of ground. It was sagging in the middle and was obviously not on a legitimate *emplacement*.

'What the fuck do you call that?' I asked.

'Shh! We're not supposed to be here. It's only for tonight because the bureau was shut.' Paul's voice dropped in volume, then rose, then dropped again as he remembered what he was talking about. 'If we keep quiet we won't have to pay for tonight. We can say we arrived tomorrow.'

Alastair bent down to get into the tent.

'Oh, look out for the mountaineer. He's probably asleep by now,' whispered Paul.

'Oh,' said Alastair, too tired to question matters.

'Homeless mountaineers are quite a problem in these parts,' Paul explained. 'He's alright. It's just for tonight.'

I had just thrown my sleeping bag inside and was starting to undress when a powerful beam of light picked me out. The footsteps and a clicking noise came nearer.

'*Silence!*' called the French voice behind the torch.

'*Desolé,*' replied Paul.

The light was extinguished and I could see the silhouette of a retreating man with a bicycle. I then climbed into the forlorn-looking tent, which was already reeking of Paul's uncontrollable feet.

We settled down into a cramped and uncomfortable sleep that was broken six hours later by a violent shaking of the tent.

castellane

Inter-Rail Rule 4: If you want to camp without paying, make sure you get up and leave before you go to sleep. Alternatively, why not just settle up in the morning?

Stewart

'What the bloody hell's this?' cried Paul upon waking. I sat up, then crawled over still-sleeping Alastair to un-zip the tent. The shaking stopped and a stern face peered in.

'*Qu'est-ce que vous faites ici?*' it demanded.

I jumped back and nudged Paul to take over negotiations.

'*Nous sommes arrivés très tard, monsieur.*' That was a good start — Paul had remembered to say '*monsieur*' a lot when being bollocked. '*Et le bureau était fermé. Nous voulons payer ce matin, monsieur.*'

The angry man had not been expecting such a polite and legitimate answer.

'Uh,' he grunted, and stood up. '*Dormez-pas ici ce soir, d'accord?*'

'*Oui. Desolé monsieur.*'

'What?' I asked when the man had gone.

'We can't sleep here tonight. And I said we'd pay this morning 'cos they were shut last night.'

'Oh.'

One by one we staggered out of the tent into the blinding sunshine of the morning. There was no sign of the mountaineer — he was probably half way up Mont Blanc by now. The things we had left outside the previous night were damp where they lay in the shade, but dry where the sun had begun to reach over the irregular roofline of the tent. Through the trees behind us were a line of caravans and large tents, and before lay the Eurocamp community.

'You take the tent down while I get breakfast,' ordered Paul. Alastair yawned and reminded him who was the bass player in the band.

'I put the bloody thing up!' said Paul, though this wasn't saying much.

We put in our breakfast orders and Paul went off towards the central complex of the campsite. Alastair and I began to attack the tent, and within seconds it had been fully demolished and scrambled up into a pile, though its overall appearance hadn't changed to any great extent.

Paul returned with the meal, which was ravenously devoured. Then we put on our hats, picked up our things, and walked the short path to the reception bureau to give them some hassle.

The woman attending gave her colleague a long-suffering look on seeing us, then addressed us in a strange Germanic language.

'*Je ne comprends pas*,' objected Paul.

'Sorry — you are English? No problem, I speak English too.'

Paul told her we wanted a pitch for a couple of weeks, and she sighed and told us there was only one pitch available for one night, miles from anywhere, for about a million Francs. Plus tourist tax.

'But we came here specially,' said Alastair. 'I've stayed here twice before.'

'Why didn't you say so?' She ticked a box on a registration form marked '*Client Ancien*'. 'We have a place here,' she pointed on the map, 'number four-three-five, by the river. You can stay there for two weeks.'

This wasn't exactly true, as events turned out, but we weren't to know. And so we trotted off to look for *The Gaff*, as it was to be called. The campsite was huge, interlaced by networks of sparkling streams and dusty roads. We passed a small lake before arriving at The Gaff, a corner site, directly opposite a water tap, and adjacent to a stone bridge over the stream that led from the lake into the main river. The *emplacement* was large enough for a caravan and a car, so our modest erection barely made an impression.

Paul completely emptied what was left in his rucksack, spread its contents around the inside and outside of the tent, then stacked the empty and flattened rucksack against the pole at the bell-end of the tent. We did the same until the result resembled a sort of organised chaos: clothes were piled up inside the tent, food and utensils sheltered under the wings of the flysheet while the guitars and airbeds were laid out on the grass.

Paul and Alastair then went off to the toilets, while I crawled around inside the tent to get changed. Already the heat inside was stifling, so I left the doors open. In the middle of my squirming I saw a brown-haired girl go by. She looked in and smiled as she walked past on her way to the bridge. This had to be a good sign, I thought. I quickly finished dressing: shorts and deck shoes, then sat casually on an airbed in front of the tent, strumming a guitar quietly to myself. Then I remembered my shades and rushed back into the tent to dig them out from under the pile of clothes in my corner. Now I was cool.

It wasn't long before the girl came back. I stopped strumming and asked if she was English.

'Yeah — Tracy. Where are you from?' Her tone of voice did not exactly inspire scenes of punting along the Cam on a summer's day after finals, it was more of a sunset over the gasworks. But I didn't care, being more interested in her ample body.

'Sussex. Chichester. Do you know it?'

'Blimey, yeah — I'm from Werving.'

I assumed she meant Worthing, which was only a few miles along the coast.

'What's ya name?' she asked me.

'Stewart. But call me Poo. You here with some friends?'

'Poo? That's an 'orrible name.'

'It's a long story, which I'm not going to tell you.'

'Oh, Poo. You play the guitar?' she remarked, observantly.

'Yeah, we're buskers.'

'I'm here with me parents. We're staying on the corner of the river down there.'

I hopped onto the bridge to see where she was pointing.

'The Cortina?' I asked.

'Yeah, it's the only English one around here.'

'Too many Dagos?'

'Too many Dutch, anyway.'

'Oh, is that what they are?'

Paul and Alastair then came loafing back along the gravel road towards the tent. They were too busy examining the caravans of our neighbours at first to notice my prize catch.

'Are they your mates?' she asked, with a little too much enthusiasm for my liking, and lit up a cigarette.

'That's Paul on the left, and Alastair with the hat.'

'What's all this then?' asked Paul.

'I'm Tracy.'

'Hi,' said Alastair. 'How long are you here for?'

'A couple of weeks.'

'If you need a shit we've found a terrific bog,' said Paul, helpfully.

'I had one yesterday, actually,' she replied.

'You've got her talking dirty already,' I said, impressed.

'Well you'd better make sure,' added Paul, 'that you carry on using the women's ones.'

'Paul went in the Ladies',' said Alastair.

'They're a lot cleaner.'

I needed to brush my teeth, so I asked the whereabouts of this major tourist attraction.

'It's at the end of the road,' said Alastair.

I muddled around in pre-ambulatory confusion, not knowing whether to undertake the reasonably long trek to the toilets now, which was what I had conversationally committed myself to doing, or to continue the chatting-up process in which I now faced stiff competition. I bent down inside the tent, pretending to be looking for something. She smoked. I didn't like that. She lived geographically close to home. I didn't like that either. And that voice . . . I listened to that voice responding easily and willingly to Alastair's charms. She was being unknowingly but inextricably chatted-up by him. Paul just rabbited on insanely about the toilets.

A slight sickening, pissed-off feeling was brewing in my stomach in the knowledge that my prey had been so quickly requisitioned. Not having the nerve to compete, I dug out my wash bag and announced that I was going to the bog. Perhaps Tracy would decide to go with me? But no one had taken the slightest bit of notice.

I walked off alone, staring, as the others had done, into the open doors of the neighbouring tents and caravans. Although my eyes alighted on nothing more than the inevitable family clutter, the hope was always there in the back, or rather spreading somewhat rapidly across the whole, of my mind of seeing a nubile gynaecomorphous specimen *au naturel*. It seemed highly unlikely, even though Tracy had seen me doing it. What, I wondered, was the point in shutting the door when changing? It was too safe and too dull. Leaving it open would bring excitement into people's lives, with the possibility of giving pleasure to others, namely me.

I looked up at the one cloud in despair of the cynical, unadventurous world, probably at just the moment when a naked woman walked past the open window of her adjacent caravan. The world should be more sexy, I thought, arriving at the stinking toilet block and stepping over used paper towels and nappies.

On my return to the tent I found that the mess on the pitch had been re-arranged into a different pattern.

'To catch the sun when we're on the airbeds,' explained Alastair. It was a nicer mess now: less angular, but maintaining that essential feeling of randomness and anarchy. Paul's novelty Union Jack flags had been unpacked and stuck to the tent pole with gaffa tape, making it look as if we were conquering new territory, and the telephone had been placed on a flat stone some feet in front of the tent, with the cable leading back inside to give the impression that it was connected.

'Aren't you going to show us around the campsite?' I asked, before remembering more important matters. 'Where's Tracy? Have you frightened her off?'

'Best thing for her,' said Paul, sprawled out on an airbed.

'She's gone off to look for her parents. She wanted money off them or something,' said Alastair.

'She only wanted to talk to me,' I boasted, ignoring the major inaccuracy of the statement.

'Fuck off,' advised Paul.

'Do you two want to look round then?' offered Alastair.

Paul stood up and sniffed his armpits, trying not to choke. He scrambled around the edge of the tent.

'I need a bit of de-rodent first.'

So that was what scared her off, I decided.

The body odour problem solved, we walked along the stream that backed onto the pitch until we came to the river Verdon. This river had previously got around to carving the magnificent Gorges du Verdon, but was now a lot less interested in any form of strenuous activity and was sliding along lazily on its back, sunbathing.

'Shit boys, look!' exclaimed Paul in his loudest whisper. He was indicating towards a group of people sunbathing at the water's edge, some yards in front of us. Two of the women were topless. Until that point I had thought it was only possible to see that sort of thing on a beach. I casually checked my loins for any sign of activity, but fortunately there was none.

Too embarrassed to walk past the sunbathers we turned away from the river bank and headed back into the maze of caravans and Volvos. The Dutch were very sensible people, it seemed. Their caravans were tidy and modern, and their Volvos seemed well cared-for. And, inevitably, I was beginning to notice that their daughters were all blonde. Except for the brunettes, of course. But they all possessed a beauty that seemed to transcend anything I had known before. The Beach Boys had obviously never been to Holland.

We came to the dry gravel car park that flanked the campsite's amenities area. The shop was now closed until late afternoon, but they probably deserved a rest after having worked an interminable couple of hours that morning. They wouldn't want to be saddled with counting too much money at the end of the day, after all.

'I've found 'em,' called Tracy as she walked towards us.

'I can't see how she could've missed them,' whispered Paul to us, referring with such great subtlety to the enormity of her norks that we had no idea what he was talking about until he clapped his hands onto his chest.

'Where were they?' asked Alastair.

'By the pool.'

This reminded the others that we still hadn't been to see the pool. They rather rudely pushed past her, and I reluctantly followed.

'Where are you going?' she asked.

'To the swimming pool,' I said, feeling guilty. I had expected the others to be showing more interest in her, but they were too absorbed in the staggering displays of talent they could already see coming in and out of the pool compound. 'Come on, we're just going to take a look,' I suggested, but she mumbled something about bloody perverts and lit up a cigarette in a pissed-off sort of way.

I was having doubts about my charm. Perhaps I needed more de-odourant like Paul. What did he call it? De-ratter or something. We hopped up the steps to the raised area of land behind the bureau and the restaurant to the pool. Its sides were littered with bodies: British ones in various stages of redness, and Dutch ones consistently golden brown.

'Shall we have a quick swim while we're here?' I suggested.

'What about the towels?' said Alastair.

'Now who's being a girl,' I objected. 'You don't need a towel in this weather.'

'Well you go in then,' added Paul. 'I'm wearing kacks, not boxers.'

This changed matters considerably. Even France had maximum pollution levels for swimming pools, and letting Paul's kacks loose in the water would be like tipping a dustbin load of rotting fish heads and elephant dung onto the swimmers, only not so popular.

'Well shall we get our things and make a day of it?' asked Alastair.

'It's a pity we're not hoopy froods today,' said Paul, esoterically, as we turned back down the steps.

Alastair gave me a nudge to inform me of a great discovery. Between a couple of caravans we could see two girls sitting on the grass close to the games room. They seemed to be our age, and their beauty sent Alastair into a state of semi-incoherency. One had a short bob of blonde hair and long, tanned legs, the other had honey-gold, sun-kissed hair and an even deeper tan.

'They — shall we, er, I think, the er, you know?' said Alastair. I think he wanted to get closer to find out where they were from. I looked into his glazed eyes for a moment, and this shunted him temporarily back into coherency.

'I'm in love,' he announced. 'The one on the right.'

'Not the blonde one?'

'No. The other. She's perfect.'

I had to agree that he wasn't far from the truth.

'I'm going to check out the prices at the pizzeria,' said Paul, already bored with this game and worried that if Alastair were to fall in love it would ruin our chances of getting some serious Inter-Railing done next week.

Lacking at this moment the courage to proceed any further in his new love affair, Alastair dejectedly followed Paul away from them. To be honest I was more concerned with swimming and freshening up than in continuing the pursuit any further. I knew I wouldn't stand a chance with anyone until I stopped ponging.

The pizzeria turned out to be shut until the evening, so we fetched our towels, sunglasses and a bottle of water, and were disappointed to discover on our return that the girls had moved on. Alastair was disheartened: there were thousands of people on this campsite, and they — or rather she — could be anywhere.

He climbed the stone steps ahead of us to get a first view of who was around the pool, but couldn't spot her.

'We've got to take our shoes off guys,' said Paul.

'Bastards,' I said. 'They won't know.'

Paul then pointed out the pool fascist in the corner: a sickeningly brown lifeguard sitting on a deckchair wearing reflective sunglasses and looking cooler than Antarctica.

'OK,' I conceded.

I hopped around trying to stand on one leg while undoing a shoe. Alastair hopped right around and found himself facing the grass patch where the girls had been. Or rather where they now were. They were sitting, as before, this time licking ice-creams in a manner which made Alastair want to be an ice cream. Feeling an urge to talk to her that he couldn't control, Alastair found himself pulling his shoe back on and running down the steps. I followed, for moral support, leaving Paul with the towels and instructions to stake out a nice spot for us.

'Hi,' said Alastair, nervously.

'*Hoi. Hoe heet je?*'

Trying to piece together what he could of his shattered hopes he managed to say,

'Sorry, could you repeat that?' If she spoke no English and he no Dutch they would be at a dead-end. But he hadn't bargained on the brilliance of the Dutch education system and the intelligence of its students.

'Sure. I didn't know you were English,' she said. 'It means what's your name?'

'You speak good English,' said Alastair, relieved and impressed. 'Better than my Dutch.'

'How did you know we were Dutch?' asked the other girl.

I wanted to tell the truth, which was simply that they were so beautiful they had to be Dutch, but all I could manage was,

'Most people here are Dutch.'

'Yes, that's true. It's terrible,' said the first girl, from whom Alastair had still not averted his gaze.

'I'm Alastair.'

'I'm Poo.'

'Hello Poo and Alastair,' said the first girl.

The other girl stated her name, but it was unpronounceable to us, and neither of us tried to learn or repeat it. But the first one was called Maaike.

'Mike?' asked Alastair in disbelief. 'You're called Mike? That's a boy's name.'

'No, it's Maaike. It's a little different, you know?'

'Fair enough,' I said.

'How did you get here?' asked Maaike.

'By train,' said Alastair.

The girls gave a look of slight incomprehension. I tried to remedy this by doing an impression of a train and making 'choo-choo' noises, but made such a dick of myself that everyone became embarrassed and Alastair was worried that the girls would lose interest.

'Stop it, you prat,' he said, as politely as he could manage.

'We know what a train is,' explained Maaike, 'but there is no railway here.'

'Ah,' I said, 'we walked.'

'There's a mountain railway at Annot, and we walked from there, and hitched a lift.'

Alastair gently kicked me before I could go into mime mode this time.

'Hitch-hiking. Yes, I know it,' said Maaike. She translated the phrase to her friend, which was followed by an uncomfortable silence while both parties scanned their minds for something to say.

'Are you going to the campfire tonight?' asked Maaike, to our considerable relief.

She explained that campfires took place every night in a clearing by the river. Most of the young people on the site went there after the bar had closed, and it was easier to get to know people then because during the day everyone would be indulging in daytrips and other boring activities.

'Yes, I'll be there,' said Alastair. It was almost a date. I affirmed with similar enthusiasm.

'Where is your other friend?' asked the one who wasn't called Maaike. I took this to imply that Maaike fancied Alastair and she fancied Paul.

'Up at the pool,' I said, reluctantly.

'We will be there later,' said Maaike.

'We're going now,' I said firmly, more to Alastair than to the others.

'Yeah,' he said, dreamily, and seemed to float up the steps to the pool without actually touching any of them.

'That's for girls,' said Paul, predictably, when I offered him a bottle of sun-cream. I didn't care, and spread factor five over my white body. Alastair put on his Ray-Ban style sunglasses and sat up, looking at the girls around the pool. Maaike and her friend were nowhere to be seen.

I lay on my back looking for a cloud. Occasionally a distinct shadow of a passing pair of breasts would briefly cool my face, if not the rest of me, but it was never sufficient to create the refreshing shade I sought. Already feeling drier than a Martini, I remembered the swim I so badly needed. The others agreed to join me: Alastair to fill in the time while waiting for his new love; Paul to make some big splashes that would annoy the foreign kids. I preferred Paul's motive, and we dive-bombed in Stuka fashion as close as we dared to a younger group of noisy Dutch boys. But Alastair was above such pranks and dived in so smoothly that his boxer shorts slid cleanly down his legs and were entangled around his ankles as he came up for air. I saw two girls sitting at the water's edge grin at him.

'What if Mike had seen that?' I asked.

'She's not here yet, I hope,' said Alastair, pulling up his shorts. 'And it's Maaike.'

'Yeah, something like that.'

'Nice one,' said Paul as he swam over. 'We were going to de-bag you anyway, but you saved us the trouble.'

The water was sufficiently chlorinated to wash myself in, successfully killing the ever-expanding communities of micro-organisms that had been cultivating themselves in my armpits for the previous couple of days. Then I climbed out, pulling my clinging wet boxer shorts away from my body. The others were having a vicious splashing contest in the pool, but I lay on my wet towel and closed my eyes, dreaming a myriad of images revolving around the theme of Dutch bodies.

The reverie was soon broken, however, by the falling drips from Paul's now very flat-top hair. He shook his head like a soggy dog and lay down without using his towel.

'Bastard,' I moaned.

'Bloody girl.'

Alastair then returned and did exactly the same thing to both of us, but neither of us could say anything without an implicit sex-change.

Maaike later arrived with a couple of body-builders. She made no attempt to look for Alastair, but instead settled at the opposite end of the pool and lay down between the two hunks.

Alastair rolled over onto his front, though not for the usual reason. He buried his face in his arms, and continually reminded us how devastating the situation was.

'That's a bit wanky, isn't it?' said Paul, in a consolatory manner.

We lay in the glaring heat for a couple of blistering hours. Maaike seemed quite content to stay in her place in the sun between the two body-builders, and didn't notice when we left.

'They're probably complete bastards,' I said. This made him feel worse.

'Exactly,' he said.

'Well,' tried Paul, 'she was a bit muke anyway.' But Alastair refused even to consider that she was anything less than physically perfect.

'What are we going to do boys?' he asked, at a loss.

Back at the tent we tried to formulate various plans for Alastair to follow at the campfire that night, most of which involved me and Paul chucking the other Dutch boys in the river while Alastair sneaked off with Maaike. Nothing feasible came up, and Alastair went for a wander when Paul tried to strum a guitar.

'Shall we try out that boat?' called Alastair above the din. He was on the other side of the stream behind the tent and pointing to a rowing boat that was half-hidden in the undergrowth. Without hesitating to wonder to whom it might belong we jumped in and pushed ourselves up the stream to the small lake. Once in the centre of the lake Paul stood up and rocked the boat violently, and it began to take in water.

'Don't do that!' shouted Alastair. I echoed likewise, with the odd 'bastard' thrown in for good measure. Our feet were wet, and greenish water was sloshing around the bottom disconcertingly.

'Bloody hell Paul, I wish you wouldn't . . .' I began, but saw no point in continuing as the backlash of the boat had sent Paul tumbling backwards into the murky depths.

This rendered us insensible with mirth all the way to the shower block where we endeavoured to wash off the algae-infested water. But once we were in our adjacent shower cubicles the hysterics had worn a little thin, so Paul started some serious singing.

'Bum-ba-ba-bum-ba-ba-ba-bum . . .' he began, reciting the bass line it was his job to play on one of our home-grown songs. I remembered my cue and started singing the first verse,

'Listening for the rumble and the shaking and the roar,' then Alastair joined in with the harmony,

'Standing at the wayside where we stood when we were poor . . .'

And so we sang, loudly, and attracting much attention from outside. I like to think we created melodious a cappella, but it may have been some other disease.

'Fuck me, that was good,' shouted Paul when the song was finished, somewhat altering the atmosphere created by the ballad.

When we told Tracy about this later at the tent, she suggested we call ourselves the Cubicle Choir, or the Shower Singers.

'How about the Talentless Wankers?' suggested Paul.

'Do you always swear so much?' asked Tracy, critically.

It was time to get philosophical.

'I don't really think that everything we say is some form of verbal eructation. We do say other words,' said Paul.

'Swearing can't be any more than one per cent of our vocabulary,' I added.

'Yeah, but you swear a lot as well,' she said.

'Isn't all language equally viable?' I asked.

'But that,' interrupted Paul, 'would put a Sun reporter on the same literary level as Shakey.'

'Shakin' Stevens?' asked Tracy.

'No, someone much less famous called Shakespeare. You won't have heard of him. He's a twat.'

There was no reply to this.

'What we're saying,' I explained, 'is that a 'fuck' is no more offensive than, er, well, 'flower' — if you say it often enough.'

'You what?' asked Tracy.

'Fuck fuck fuck fuck. It's just sounds. People choose to be offended if they want, others don't. Sounds aren't inherently bad, it's just their interpretation. If people choose to be offended by particular sounds then that's their problem.'

Tracy's eyes had a distant look, like a bored pupil, and Paul was sniggering at her bemusement in the face of such verbose and complex discourse.

'Fuck it,' she said, and walked back to her tent.

The path to the campfire ran through a small wood on the edge of the campsite, and at night it was pitch black among the trees making it necessary to bring torches. But the fire had been built-up before our arrival so it was bright enough there to see. We sat on wooden picnic tables and studied the various faces in the flickering yellow light.

'Any sign of Mike?' I asked Alastair.

'Maaike. No, don't think so.'

She couldn't have been far behind us, though, because she soon arrived with her blonde friend and no hint of any bodyguards. It was time for Alastair to get to work.

Paul and I left him to it and went over to introduce ourselves to a mixed group of Dutchies that were gathered around a howling ghetto blaster.

'That's 'The Fall' isn't it?' asked Paul to the boy who seemed to be in charge of the music station.

'Yeah, it's their latest album,' said the boy.

'I thought so,' said Paul. 'We play in a band too. The Fall supported us on tour last year.'

I had never even heard of The Fall, but I presumed from the look of sheer amazement and respect on the face of the Dutch boy that they were well known among trendier circles.

'Wow,' he said, 'is that true?'

'Yeah,' lied Paul, 'we're on a tour of Europe at the moment, just taking a break for a few days. I'm the bassist, Poo here's the lead-singer.'

Attention turned suddenly to me. In the space of ten seconds I had been verbally transformed by Paul from a non-entity in the shadows to a superstar commanding envy and respect from all assembled foreign teenagers. Paul had given away the secret of his lowly status as a bassist, and was now, quite rightly, ignored.

'What is your band called?' asked a voice in the darkness. The voice froze my attention instantly towards it, and not simply because I was afraid to admit to being in a band that no one had ever heard of. It was the quality of the voice: deep and husky, its accent so tempting that I wanted to touch it. It was sexless and at the same time the sexiest thing I had ever heard. My lips were burning to touch the unseen mouth from which the words had come, to embrace the concept of absolute beauty that existed in those five words like a Platonic Form.

My mumbled mention of a certain kitchen appliance in response was lost among a further round of Dutch and English questions, presumably on the subject of bands — a subject which was now far from my mind as I tried to peer over the dark shoulders to see the darker shape of pure gorgiosity behind them that had spoken to me. I squeezed my way through to her. This was the girl I had been looking for for so long, the personification of all my hydrous reveries. Our conversation was neither long nor profound, since I was soon dragged back into the bullshit game to defend Paul's impressive claims, but I was determined to seek her out the next day, if only to see her face.

Paul ran back to the tent to fetch a tape and a pen, with which he crossed out the words 'Van Halen' and wrote instead, 'Fridge'. This was then played on the Dutch machine to general exclamations of approval and assent. Even though I had given away our secret to the already sceptical girl with the magical voice, Paul was eventually able to return to the tent feeling good; Alastair and I were walking some way above the trees. Tomorrow I would find out what she looked like.

busking

Paul

I woke up feeling like a joint of meat slow-roasting in my mother's oven. The others were still asleep and this annoyed me.

'Oi! Wake up, scumbags!' I shouted, shaking first Stewart then Alastair by the shoulder so that they would have to share in this unreasonable level of heat with me. Alastair was first to wake.

'What do you want?' he mumbled in his normal quasi-hibernatory drone.

'I want you to be awake so I've got someone to talk to.'

'Shit. What time is it?'

'Daytime. About nine-thirty and I need some breakfast.'

'But we haven't got any food,' pointed out Alastair.

'*Exactement, monsieur.* That's why we need to go shopping. Are there any supermarkets around here then?' I asked.

Alastair said that there was a place called Genty which stocked a product range sufficient in variety to satisfy our discerning palates. He then went on to wake Stewart in an unashamedly violent manner which terminated with Alastair shoving his bum in Stewart's face and farting energetically thereon.

'Shall we do some busking today, guys?' asked Poo, after recovering from his forced inhalation of noxious gasses.

'It's OK with me. Where shall we do it then?' I replied.

'In the town there's a lot of little squares,' Alastair informed us. 'We should have some luck if we try one of them. There's always loads of people walking about.'

Unanimous approval was given to this idea and having gathered our guitars and Alastair's rucksack for the food we set off across the campsite.

The road into Castellane passed a few other campsites and a nightclub called the Moulin de la Salaou. I could see the heat-haze coming off the road and was glad that we had chosen such a well shaded site. One site to the right had no trees, no pool, no shop, no toilets and no tents. In fact, it was a field, not really a campsite at all.

'This'll do nicely,' said Stewart as we arrived at a small square in the town. In the middle of the square was a rusty, ornate fountain and the buildings surrounding it were mainly medieval town-houses with the exceptions of an ironmonger's and a bar called Jo-Jo's.

Stewart and Alastair withdrew their guitars from their cases and began to tune up. I would have to sit on the proverbial touch-line for this one as Stewart had taken the G-string from my guitar to replace his broken one, incorrectly assuming that I would not notice because I was 'only a bass player'. Bastard. After only a few minutes of playing they had already attracted a fairly substantial audience. This was to set a precedent for our subsequent busking sorties in Europe.

I noticed that Alastair and Stewart were also attracting some admiring and possibly even amorous glances from the female contingent of the crowd and I began to resent the fact that due to the lack of a suitable instrument I could not be in there, showing off as well. I cheered up a bit when I remembered that I would get a third of the money for doing nothing at all. The boys came to the end of another song amid rapturous applause.

'Could you do some bottling, Paul?' asked Alastair, reluctant to miss out on any potential revenue.

I was none too keen on the idea and decided that if I were to ignore him he would have to start another song and therefore be unable to ask me again for another couple of minutes by which time, hopefully, he would have forgotten. The plan fell through as Alastair repeated his request.

For those of you who have not encountered the term 'bottling' before, it is the practise of actively extricating money from people by rattling a hat, half-full of money, under their noses. Normally it would have been a humiliating task but, having reminded myself of how much my parents would disapprove of such behaviour, my mission became a lot easier.

The patrons of the café were very generous but I was distracted from my bottling duties by the sound of coins hitting the pavement. It took a couple of seconds to work out what was going on: several residents of the surrounding town-houses were leaning out of their windows waving money at me. Now, I was the centre of attention for once and I wasn't going to let the situation slip away.

I ran to the area of pavement directly below one of the windows in question. The toothless woman on the fourth floor dropped another coin and I dodged about on the pavement below, lining the hat up with the path of the falling money. Given the fact that, when in P.E. lessons at school, people would select blind, paraplegic, clinically obese, or even dead people to be on their team in preference to me on account of my appalling hand-to-eye co-ordination, the chances of success now were very remote. Amazingly, the money fell squarely into the hat with a reassuring chink.

The novelty of The Amazing Coin-Catching Man was enough to make other residents reach for their purses and throw more money down to me. It proved to be a very worthwhile move financially, for when we counted the cash at the end of the session we found we had enough to cover the predicted expense of our impending shopping trip, about two hundred Francs.

The old woman in the flat above the square proved to be such an infallible source of income on all subsequent busking sessions that we took her a bunch of flowers in gratitude. The insanitary stench kept us from entering her apartment fully, but while she thanked us excessively at the doorway we could see inside that nothing had changed since the war, and she was probably still waiting to be liberated.

Another ten minutes of walking saw us at the edge of the car-park of Genty. The store had a petrol station for which there was a huge queue, and a few independent traders were selling candles, herbs and honey outside the main building.

On entering, I realised what a long time it had been since I had had the pleasure of visiting a French supermarket. Alastair insisted on buying some wine because he was more sophisticated than us, and I could not resist such reasonably priced Export 33 and Camembert. Stewart on the other hand restricted his purchases to chocolate milk, brioches, tissues and processed cheese.

I was glad to leave the supermarket some forty minutes later. There wasn't anything wrong with the place as such but somehow the smell of the shop was so different from supermarkets at home that I felt a bit uneasy about buying something as fundamentally important as food there.

As we started walking, Alastair's rucksack, brimming with goodies, began to dig into my shoulders.

'Fuck this. Your turn, Al,' I decided after about ten minutes.

'I reckon we should try hitching back,' he replied, trying to dodge his duty.

'Yeah, why not? After all, you and Poo are so good at it.'

We stood at the beginning of the road back to the site, thumbs outstretched, trying to look as cute and harmless as possible. After ten minutes of no offers Poo decided to treat himself to a chocolate milk to pass the time. No sooner had he opened the carton than a silver Volvo estate with Belgian plates slewed to a halt amid a cloud of dust.

'Luck's in, boys!' I shouted back to the others as the benevolent driver agreed to take us the pathetic mile and a half back to the site. Alastair climbed in and I handed him the rucksack to put on his lap. Then Stewart passed his chocolate milk to Alastair for him to hold as he got in: unfortunately, Alastair was stuck under a ton of rucksack. The chocolate milk globbed steadily from its container onto the deep carpet of the floor and all hell broke loose, much to the confusion of the driver. Stewart ripped open the packet of tissues and set them to work on the brown puddle, expecting at any moment to be thrown out of the car.

Being Belgian, the driver did not possess the normal set of reactions that you would expect from an archetypal Volvo driver. Instead, he took the permanent discolouration of his floor very well, and took us to the campsite without complaint. Then with a cheerful wave drove off towards Moustiers. Weird or what?

Back at The Gaff we considered the problem of refrigeration, and concluded that a submerged storage area would be best. On the other side of the bridge adjacent to our pitch was a trickle of water flowing from the boating lake to the main course of the Verdon. If we were to arrange a few stones in such a way as to prevent the food being washed away we could half-immerse our foodstuffs therein, thus refrigerating them. Before we got round to building the fridge however, such was the extent of our hunger that we ate most of what we had bought.

Later in the day Stewart and Alastair went to the table-tennis room, undoubtedly to see if they could score with some women. I would have liked to have gone and joined in but I accepted the fact that I didn't have that certain je-ne-sais-quoi necessary for communicating effectively with girlies and with this in mind I decided to spend the rest of the day taking aesthetically pleasing photographs of the surrounding countryside and generally feeling sorry for myself.

Stewart

There was an image of the girl from the campfire implanted firmly in my brain, leaving little room for anything else such as co-ordination of hand and chocolate milk cartons. I found her by the poolside, and after several minutes of encouragement from Alastair I heeded the advice of the acknowledged expert in these matters and went over to her.

'Hello,' I said. Shit, I thought, what a crap start. Where do I go from here?

'Hello,' she said.

'I was at the campfire last night.'

'Yeah, I thought so,' she said, adjusting her inadequate wet bikini and sitting up. She remembered me! Paul's bullshit session must have made an impression on her. I looked at her closely. It was the first time I had been able to see her face properly, the first time I had seen true beauty. Her eyes were sparkling emeralds, her skin a deep gold, and her voice had the same alluring, seductive accent that made me go weak at the knees. (Pass me a bucket — Paul.)

'Do you want to play table tennis?' I asked, pinning my entire future happiness on her answer.

'Yeah, why not?'

Why not! She put a large T-shirt on over her bikini, but certain wet patches immediately began to show through, which was most distracting during the game and probably explained why she beat me. But I had won on a much higher level — I had won her friendship, and that was worth more than any plastic ball that went ping-pong.

She was called Anja. It was a name I hadn't heard before, but it was a beautiful name, pronounced 'Anya'. Her presence intoxicated me that afternoon as it had done the previous night, and having established that she was there for a couple more days I felt it was safe to take things slowly. She would have to be treated with respect and tact, for her sense of humour was biting and subtle, even when she was creating puns in a foreign language. With this in mind I opted to play it cool until the next day.

Paul

We met up again at The Gaff for dinner. Today's highly original culinary offering was tinned ravioli. Had I brought the camping stove with me instead of the telephone the making of a wood fire and the consequent problems of balancing a billy-can on top of the conflagration would not have presented themselves, but we didn't let this trifling matter bother us. After all, a broken telephone was bound to be invaluable on mainland Europe.

When the sun had gone down we made our way to the campfire. The orange glow being reflected on the rising smoke of the fire was enough for us to find our way to the social event of the evening without getting lost. When we arrived I was pleased to note that there seemed to be a marked absence of anyone official-looking and I took that to be a carte blanche for my behaviour over the course of the evening. Thoughtfully, we had also brought a case of beer with us to help the evening pass.

We were feeling generous on this particular evening, probably because of our unexpected success at busking, so we felt that we could afford to dish out some beers on the house. The scene was fairly idyllic and we were unhappy when one Dutch kid decided to spoil our evening by trying to pick a fight. The kid in question was called Igor and for this reason started at a disadvantage as far as I was concerned. The strangest thing was that he had a chip upon his shoulder about what the English had been up to during the Second World War. I could have sworn that we were on the same side.

'Eh! What did you English do during the war?' he taunted. 'I'll tell you. You sat at home in your allotments and read newspapers and grew vegetables. You scum.'

'I think not,' remarked Alastair. 'What's your problem anyway?'

'The English are like toilet paper,' he explained.

'Stupid roast beef,' braved a French voice in support.

'I hate you all. You are cheeseheads,' concluded Igor.

The kid was obviously drunk and unfortunately for him so was I. Alastair's diplomatic attempts at pacifying him were to no avail and I could see that Igor wanted to get physical. At this point I thought that it would be a good idea to use my superior height and bulk to resolve the matter. I grabbed him in a bear-hug, thus immobilising his arms, and waddled over to the now waning camp fire. With a heave that required all my available strength I dropped him feet-first into the fire amid a shower of sparks. That'll learn 'im, I thought. To this day the 'Igor incident' remains my most gratuitously violent act.

When he had swiftly removed himself from the flames and he and his friends had withdrawn, presumably to find re-enforcements, we decided that it would be prudent to call time and retire to the tent.

On a lighter note, Alastair asked us if he could have some money to take Maaike out to dinner. I told him to stick that idea up his Gary Glitter. I was only jealous of his sexual magnetism.

the fat stripper and john travolta

Paul

I was the last to wake up this morning, thankfully from natural causes. The others were outside the tent discussing women for a change. I stuck my head out of the relative shelter of the tent into the scorching early morning sunlight.

'What on earth is that unholy smell?' I moaned.

'Probably your feet, matey,' taunted Alastair. I could not believe that such a foul stench could have gone unnoticed by anyone with a nose. Seeing that the others had no intention of seeking out the source of the aroma I ventured outside to conduct my own investigation into the air pollution. Following the instructions issued by my nose I was led around the tent and eventually under the fly-sheet. I tentatively picked up a warm, opened milk carton and shook it about. The fluid sensation I was expecting to experience through the cardboard walls of the carton did not happen. With increased caution I dared myself to look inside. As anticipated, I found a nodular, gelatinous, coagulated mess, teeming with macroscopic pond life. I made public my findings in a manner that would probably have been hard to miss.

'Oh, that was probably me,' replied Alastair, devoid of shame or regret. I tried to throw the repulsive contents over the offending bastard but he deftly dodged the oncoming organic napalm, letting it splatter onto the path where it would attract even more bacteria and flies. 'I'm in love,' he explained when I told him it was all his fault.

There was a market in the main square at Castellane this morning. It was a particularly provincial one, which meant all

DON'T LEAN OUT OF THE WINDOW!

it sold was honey and herbs. This was fine if you were into that sort of thing, but I wasn't and found it boring.

There was a strange, balding man wearing a dinner suit and rubber sandals jigging about a bit behind us. Some people were watching him and listening to his strange, tuneless voice singing odd, wordless songs. And he had a barrel organ that he turned with varying degrees of steadiness, as if inventing a new time signature for every bar.

Poo and I watched him for a few painful moments, didn't put any money in his hat, and went off to find Alastair who was having a fascinating time examining the honey and herb stalls and buying bagfuls of useful condiments.

'Do you actually have any use whatsoever for those things?' enquired Poo, referring of course to the half dozen or so bags of herbes de Provence which Alastair was triumphantly displaying to us like a junior angler with his first minnow.

'Of course I have,' he said, indignantly, 'I'm going to give them to my Mum.'

'Waste of money,' I said, 'you can get them in Sainsbury's for less than a quid.'

Alastair became very defensive, stating that the herbes de Provence that you got in England were not from France at all, but, despite the blatantly shite nature of what he was saying, I couldn't be bothered to argue with him.

For want of anything better to do we decided to make a move home to The Gaff. I could feel the sun burning my calves so I tethered them to a shady tree. My legs were getting red as well, and this only served to remind me how anaemic I must have looked to the natives.

We slumped around the tent, too exhausted even to swear at each other. Feeling charitable, I wandered over to our makeshift fridge and collected a bottle of beer each for Alastair and myself and a bottle of Orangina for Stewart. I noticed that the entire affair was completely waterlogged due to an unforeseen increase in the volume of water leaving the boating lake, but I couldn't be bothered to tell the boys and risk having to rectify the situation. Calmly returning to the tent was a far better course of action, I thought.

We spent the remainder of the afternoon at the boating lake, floating on the disintegrating airbeds which my parents had kindly loaned us on the understanding that we took good care of them. All afternoon Stewart and I had to endure Alastair's incessant ravings on the subject of his impending date with Maaike. During my lie-in that morning, Alastair had approached Stewart on the subject of taking her out for dinner and as, unlike me, Stewart's genetic make-up prohibits any unpleasantness, he had agreed to grant Alastair the necessary funds for his venture.

From that point on, consulting me was deemed to be unnecessary as I was 'only a bass-player'. Thus, the plan of action for the evening was that Alastair should take Maaike out to a restaurant (and in so doing spend the remainder of the money that we had set aside for the rest of the holiday) while Poo and I remained at The Gaff eating crappy tinned food.

Stewart

Alastair disappeared into the toilet block after lunch to get ready for the date, emerging about six hours later looking exactly the same as before.

Paul and I enjoyed our 'crappy tinned food' that evening, burnt ravioli being a particular favourite of mine. I decided that Alastair could do the washing-up the next day as I had helped to finance his five star candle-lit meal, and left the smeared billy-cans on the grass as close as possible to the centre of an ant-infested zone. Our own evening preparations in the toilets took less than ten minutes but were sufficient to remove at least fifty per cent of all objectionables from our bodies.

At the campfire that evening there were some suspicious-looking types seated on logs at the far side of the fire, by the river. They were wrapped in untouristy woollens and ragged cloaks, and carried certain facial and odoriferous deformities that would not have gained them legitimate access to the campsite. However, no one was talking to the gypsies and they were silent amongst each other, so we paid little attention to the matter, preferring instead to concentrate our interests on more exquisite creations.

There was no sign of Anja tonight, much to my disappointment, so I made do with a small bottle of warm beer and the remains of a bar of Milka. I spoke to a few Dutchies, as usual, but there were no riveting conversations to be had. My legs just went slightly wobbly as the beer intake slowly increased and the fire burned down.

At about ten o' clock Alastair came back, inextricably intertwined with Maaike and so in love he nearly sat on the smouldering embers instead of the picnic tables. I didn't stay to listen to the verbally copulating couple, and went instead to talk to Paul and Tracy. When I looked back Alastair and Maaike were gone.

Some of the older kids from around the fire were leaving to go to the nearby nightclub, but Paul and I didn't fancy the idea and returned, tired, to the tent.

Paul

As we rounded the final corner and crossed the little bridge to The Gaff we could both detect that something was not quite right. The tent was there, but in our minor alcoholic haze it appeared to be moving. We could hear Alastair's dulcet, mellifluous tones wafting out of the tent doorway as Stewart and I stood face to face wondering what to do about it. Stewart took the incentive and approached the quivering erection.

'Alastair,' he whispered, trying to keep things as subtle as possible, 'can we come in?'

'Bugger off and come back in a few hours,' came his equally hushed reply.

We gave him another thirty minutes, which was for us a rather shivery half hour at the now almost deserted campfire, before returning to see if they had finished.

They hadn't.

'It looks like we're going to have to go to the Salaou after all,' Stewart informed me.

'Bollocks,' I replied in disgust, reluctantly following him up the path that led to the nightclub.

Stewart

The Moulin was not a windmill but a watermill, served by a waterfall that crashed out of the rockface behind the building. It had been tastefully restored in the original Louis XIV style with wooden beams and shitty walls, embellished by disco lights and suspended speakers.

Avoiding the bar we fought our way through the throng of teenagers and off-duty staff from all the town's cafés and bars and into the main dance room. There we sat adventurously on a wooden bench designed for those who didn't wish to make prats of themselves on the dance floor, which was us.

I noticed a gap gradually forming among the dancers, revealing a lone dancer strutting his funky stuff. I recognised him as the assistant in the campsite shop who transformed into a professional show-off at the pool every afternoon and held a monopoly on all women who liked that sort of thing (ie rippling muscles, sickening tan, and a bustling trouser department). Fortunately that didn't include most of the Dutch girls, who were mercifully blessed with a rather more sophisticated taste, although we had our doubts about Maaike.

We decided the dancer was doing his best to imitate John Travolta. His legs were a blur of movement, his arms shot this way and that in sharp thrusts, and his head jerked back and forth like a chicken. The gap around him was now large enough for his ego to perform uninhibited, and he had the full attention of the audience.

'What a dickhead!' shouted Paul in my ear. I was inclined to agree, though I was pretty amazed that Mr Travolta's legs didn't fly off at a tangent to his torso and pierce a few breasts in the crowd.

After some moments of this unique entertainment a new attraction appeared in the corner. Clearly jealous of the attention Travolta was getting, the new dancer took his place in the centre and started to wobble his body a bit. John Travolta became pissed off by this intrusion and stood aside to let the fat old bastard take over.

He was a sweaty, balding old man wearing a large suit over his corpulent form. He tottered around drunkenly enjoying his new-found stardom, and, encouraged by the sarcastic wolf-whistles from parts of the audience, decided to liven up the show. First his jacket was slung across the room, soon followed by his tie and then his stained shirt. Large rolls of hairy flab now glistened in the intense light of the stroboscopes giving the impression of a lardy dumpling dancing in stop/motion photography. Inevitably, his chubby hands found their way down to his belt-buckle amid gasps of horror and sexual anticipation from the crowd.

At this point the disc-jockey decided that he couldn't handle any more teasing from this sex monster and stopped him from revealing anything that might have resulted in copious quantities of vomit covering the floor.

Paul

I had had enough of the club and Stewart needed little persuasion in following me back to The Gaff. When we returned, still sniggering about the portly spectacle, we found the tent still shaking with the amorous activities of Alastair and Maaike. I was shagged-out and really couldn't be bothered to wait any longer. I approached the jiggling tent intent on ejecting the two lovebirds.

'We're home now,' I observed, to no effect. 'Do you think we could have the tent back?' There was still no reply and so, reluctantly, Poo and I retired to the campfire to wait a little longer.

The campfire was little more than a pile of glowing embers and the surrounding area was totally devoid of human life, or gypsies. A quarter of an hour in the cold was all that we could endure: when this period had elapsed we returned to the tent, adamant that we would not be fobbed-off with any more excuses.

We found the tent to be totally motionless and an internal inspection revealed Alastair fast asleep. What a bastard, I thought — we'll have words with him in the morning.

waterfalls and police

Stewart

I could have sworn our tent had poles when I went to bed the previous night, but when I woke up breathing directly through the cotton lining on my face and unable to see a thing I thought someone must have put me to bed in a large postal sack. Clearly the slight earth movements the previous night had taken their toll and the fragile structure of our cheap tent was not up to it.

My unsubtle coughing woke the others.

'What the bloody hell's this?' moaned Paul, echoing exactly what he always said when he was woken in any way other than by a surplus of sleep. Alastair awoke amid a flurry of similar complaints that the tent had collapsed, possibly having forgotten that it was his fault in the first place. One thing was agreed upon, however, and that was to get out of the tent and re-set it immediately. Several minutes of bitter complaining later the task was complete, but by this time we had exerted ourselves to such an extent that it would have been impossible to get back to sleep.

Paul

Reluctantly, we re-entered the tent and emerged a few minutes later fully dressed and ready for breakfast, after which it was necessary to visit the latrines. Due to Sod's Law, after the obligatory singing in the shower session, my bowels expressed a wish to empty themselves. The others waved goodbye and I went off in search of a hygienically acceptable toilet in which to defecate.

From my throne I could hear an English camper doing his washing-up and talking to his son.

'Have you washed your face?' he asked.

'Yes, Dad.'

'Have you brushed your teeth?'

'Yes, Dad.'

'Have you washed your hands? Have you made your bed?' he continued. I felt a strong feeling of empathy with the poor kid.

'Have you changed your pants today?' he went on.

I felt the need to be crude as I had only sworn once or twice since I had got up.

'Have you licked your bollocks clean?' I shouted over the top of the cubicle door. I was glad that I was sitting on the bog at the time for the ensuing laughter that I suffered was acute enough to have caused the soiling of my undergarments had they not been around my ankles at the time.

When my mirth had subsided and I felt composed enough to stand, I completed the job in hand and then left the cubicle to wash them. When I opened the door, I was confronted by a small man wearing a Durham University T-shirt, standing with his hands on his hips and wearing a pathetic excuse for a scowl on his middle-aged face.

'What in heaven's name do you think you're playing at?' he attempted to bellow at me. 'That boy is only six years old and he doesn't need to hear words like that.'

'Well,' I replied, 'as he's almost certainly got a set of bollocks himself, he'll probably need to know what they're called at some point so why don't you explain things to him?'

The man did not see the funny side.

'I demand an apology,' he insisted.

'What do you want to apologise for?' I asked him, as I began to run back to The Gaff, laughing my head off.

Stewart

Paul told us his fascinating tale as we followed Alastair on his mystery tour to somewhere called The Waterfalls. We had been instructed to wear amphibious clothes and shoes and to smear some high factor smeg cream on our exposed parts.

We walked through the site of the campfire, then bounded over the boulders at the side of the river.

'I'm not going in there!' I moaned. The water was freezing, and in the middle it was waist deep.

'It's undoubtedly a lot cleaner than anything in England,' said Paul. 'When Blake wrote 'This green and pleasant land' he was referring to the rivers, not the fields. Make the most of it.'

This didn't make it any warmer, and my extremities shrunk into a painful non-existence as we traversed the deeper points.

On the far bank was a small stream, unnoticeable from the campsite. The stream flowed unevenly through the wooded flatlands at the base of the mountains that overlooked Castellane. Other than the odd bubbles over a stone there were not any waterfalls to speak of, and we thought that maybe Alastair had lost his marbles in a freak wind. However, things soon changed as the sound of tumbling cascades reached our gunky ears. Round a corner was a series of mini waterfalls, each about a foot high, and each presenting as much of a challenge as climbing something a foot high. Still not very impressive, we thought.

'It gets better,' said Alastair, unconvincingly.

We trudged on up about fifty of these miniature waterfalls, swatting flies and tripping up in the slimy mud that had gathered in the pools.

Paul

The first major waterfall we came to looked very daunting. The lip of the fall was some twelve or so feet above ground level and the noise created by the sheer volume of water was deafening. Fortunately for us, we were in previously-charted territory and one former pioneer had thoughtfully erected a kind of gang-plank up to the top of the fall. The makeshift walkway had been constructed from two telegraph poles lashed together, the end of which was balanced precariously on some big oil drums.

The water at the bottom was murky and waist deep, though the focal point of the entire scene was the upturned carcass of a rotting sheep. Thankfully, as the water had a cooling effect on the remains of the dead animal, the thoroughly unpleasant smell which one associates with corpses was whisked away before it could get too out of hand. Nevertheless, none of us was particularly keen to loiter in the freezing cold mutton gravy for any longer than was absolutely necessary.

As we climbed over the parapet we entered another world, an ethereal one that had existed in our minds right at the beginning when we had drawn up our plans in the café on that rainy Saturday. The water was crystal clear as it ran through a series of small, almost artificially perfect pools. The bottoms of the pools were completely smooth, and because the sun was beating down with such ferocity the water seemed to lose some of its bite which gave them the feel of being Mother Nature's own bath tubs.

The steep, narrow valley through which we were walking was dotted with caves far above us. Caves are very few and far between on the South Downs and these huge gaping cavities in the rock face, although inaccessible by a matter of a good one hundred feet, held us genuinely captivated as we imagined the stone-age men who may have lived there in times when our parents were young and sprightly.

As we continued our voyage of discovery, a familiar smell found its unwelcome way up our nostrils, growing in intensity until the source of the odour became visible when we rounded another outcrop. There, in the water, upside down, was another dead sheep, this time exposed to the catalytic rays of the sun.

'Oh shit!' I cried in disgust, realising that the water we had enjoyed bathing in up to this point had all passed over the rotting entrails of the sheep. We were not going to go back however: we could not accept defeat and so decided to circumnavigate the stiff. Alastair went first, cautiously picking his way across the scree that surrounded the body.

Then it was my turn. Although Capricorns like myself are supposed to be sure-footed (if you believe all that astrology bullshit), on this particular occasion my celestial, sentinel-goat was doing a poor job of protecting me. Just at the crucial moment the loose stones under my feet subsided, allowing my right foot to slip off the rock and straight into the decomposing mass right up to the ankle. I started screaming and hopping about, kicking my leg around frantically in an attempt to throw off any offal which may have adhered itself to my shoe. I spent the next five minutes or so washing my foot in the water upstream of the sheep to the accompanying jeers of the others. Thankfully, I did not contract any diseases from this incident but I never really felt the same about my feet for the rest of the holiday. (Neither did we — Stewart.)

The whole trek took about two hours to complete. During our return journey, some interesting plant life caught my eye by the side of the road. Upon closer examination I concluded that it was the very same plant that we had seen in our drug awareness lectures at school and decided to take it back to the tent and maybe smoke it later on. I couldn't help thinking how ironic it was that if I had been naughty and not been to the lecture to start with, then I would never have noticed the plant at all. Another interesting find on the side of the road was a sheep's skull which we ghoulishly decided to take with us as we thought that we could probably find a use for it later.

Alastair and I decided that the best thing that we could do to the skull would be to make a sort of trophy of it and, with this purpose in mind, we constructed a mini-Stonehenge on our pitch, in honour of 'John who got his ribs smashed by the pigs'. Rather than going all the way to Wales for the stone we opted to use local stuff, using the skull as a centrepiece. Meanwhile, Stewart was occupied in the preparation of some tinned ravioli for dinner as he couldn't see the point in doing something as puerile as recreating national tourist attractions of England in a foreign country.

That evening we attended the campfire once more in the hope that Stewart would meet Anja and Alastair would meet up with Maaike. I could entertain myself as I was 'only a bass player'. Sure enough, the two loverboys met up with their Dutch girlies and spent a considerable portion of the evening with them. I, on the other hand, had the misfortune to be landed with Tracy again. Her incessant verbal torrents on the subject of Worthing were beginning to irritate me almost to the point of violence and I resolved that the only realistic course of action would be to get drunk which, as we had again brought an ample supply of beer with us, was not difficult.

For some unknown reason, the fire was burning its fuel far too quickly tonight and as no one could be bothered to fetch more wood — not even the gypsies, and I thought they were good at all that outdoor stuff — the only option left open was to throw the camp tables on the fire. Although I wholeheartedly approved of this idea, I was not going to be seen to be involved in it so I stayed well out of the way as Igor and some of his mates heaved the huge pieces of garden furniture onto the blaze. No sooner had this been done than a group of three or four policemen arrived on the scene demanding to see everyone's passports. We began to crap ourselves thinking that someone had implicated us in the table burning incident.

The coppers made us return to our tent to fetch the relevant documents and when we arrived there, we found Poo reclining on his li-lo and rather defiantly refusing to go and surrender his passport to the waiting policemen. Alastair and I were feeling uncharacteristically co-operative for some reason and duly went back to exhibit the passports. We need not have bothered. The only reason that the policemen had been there was to find out who was a gypsy and who was not and then to round up those who were and arrest them accordingly. Needless to say, we were relieved by this revelation and decided to stay for another beer to celebrate the fact that we were not the victims of the latest infraction of human rights. Then again, we were in France — in Italy things would be different.

My cold shoulder approach with Tracy was not working as well as I would have liked. She was still latched on to me and I could not shake her. To be honest, I suppose I was too Brahms and Lizst to care what happened so when she grabbed me and stuck her tongue down my throat, I thought 'Oh good! I've scored'.

Providence was once again with me on this particular evening and, with no warning, my bladder decided that it was full and that the rest of my body would have to take it to somewhere private where it could empty itself. I made my polite excuses and sauntered round to the back of a bush that stood on the bank of the river.

Suddenly, reality caught up with me. What was I doing with this moose? I racked my brain for a pretext for leaving Tracy and returning to the tent. My brain had, for the most part, shut down as a result of the alcohol I had consumed and the small portion that was still functioning was only running a skeleton service. I almost allowed panic to set in but my survival instincts came to the rescue: I would have to make my escape down the river.

I arrived back at the tent saturated from the waist down, but that didn't matter. At least I had escaped what would undoubtedly have been a topic that would have attracted much derision for the rest of my life. Alastair returned alone about half an hour later looking a bit anxious: Tracy had told him that I had gone to the river for a piss and maybe I had been washed away and drowned. We had a good laugh about it, but I lost a lot of sleep wondering how I could avoid her for the rest of the holiday.

drowned sorrows and drunken sailors

Stewart

An early rise this morning was necessitated by the lamentable departures of Anja and Maaike. Alastair and I languished beneath a dark cloud that cast its shadow over us alone, blinding us to the beauty of the trees and the river, and emphasising the turds and the Ladas. We made ourselves as presentable as was possible before nine in the morning and set off in search of our respective departees.

I met Anja half-way to her tent. She was heading towards the shop to stock up on a few essentials for the journey back to Holland. Unfortunately, I wasn't one of them. I bought her a Bounty Bar as a romantic going-away present, then walked back part of the way to the tent with her, stopping short of being within visual range of her family in order to increase my chances of indulging in labial union. This opportunity was obtained with the limp excuse of,

'Oh, I'd better get back to the others.' It was probably this line that in fact ensured that I didn't get a kiss, for she must have thought I was keen to be rid of her. All that happened was an exchange of addresses, courtesy of the pen and note-book that I just happened to be carrying. I promised to visit her in Holland but could not find the courage to embrace her before she left.

Alastair was sullen and quiet, sitting on an airbed back at the tent. I felt empty inside, but that was because I had visited the latrines on the way back.

'Perk up you miserable buggers,' said Paul, sympathetically. 'We've got some shopping to do.'

'You get it,' said Alastair, 'I'm too busy being unhappy.'

'I'll come,' I offered, knowing that a six-pack of chocolate milks would cheer me up no end.

We hitched a lift into town in the back of a bread van that was stacked high with empty bread crates, against which we lolled and tottered unsteadily. Clearly French standards of hygiene made allowances for dirty hitch-hikers in food transportation.

From Castellane centre it was another ten minute hike to the supermarket where we were pleased to discover that the place was actually open for a full five minutes before adjourning for its three hour lunch break. We didn't buy much this time, perhaps in premonition of our sooner than expected departure from Castellane, though probably because we had to tackle the aisles at a run.

I stopped to gather my breath near the drinks section close to the door by the rear warehouse. While I was making a comparative study of lemon syrup prices a large man came out of the staff door and started ordering various assistants about. He was wearing familiar clothes, and yet there was something odd about them: they were on him, not flying across the disco floor like on the previous occasion when our paths had crossed.

I double-checked the man's identity with Paul, who confirmed that our supermarket manager was indeed the stripper, which probably explained the bareness of many of his shelves.

Paul's expertise in the art of hitching evinced itself on the return trip in the form of a BMW convertible, the rear seat of which was infinitely more comfortable than the bread van. The driver and his partner were German, so Paul took charge of the verbal exchanges on the short journey. The driver was keen to know if Paul was impressed by his scarlet 325i, which he was, and his partner asked if Paul had been to Germany, which he had. They dropped us just inside the campsite entrance road with a polite tug of the peaks of their leather caps. A charming couple, I thought, except their moustaches were just a little too bushy.

We had been a little hesitant about travelling topless in one respect, however. There were some rather large and heavy-looking black clouds beginning to be sucked in by Alastair's depression and it looked as if at any moment the rain would turn the BMW into something that might resemble a scuttled boat.

As we headed back to the tent I heard a spit, spit, splatter. I told Paul not to be so unhygienic; he told me to hurry up because it was starting to rain. We weren't sure whether Alastair was fully back in the real world enough to put everything in the tent, so our presence was essential.

We found him sitting in a puddle, spreading factor five on his arms and morosely whistling a Christmas carol.

'Feeling better?' I asked.

'No,' he replied.

'Well hurry up then,' said Paul, throwing clothes and guitars into the tent. Alastair followed him in and I was close behind with the shopping. The rain was falling hard on the tent fly-sheet and the river seemed to be making more noise than usual.

Paul peered up at the sky through the door, reeling inwards with a drenched face and cursing a lot.

'It's solid black up there,' he informed us. 'This could go on all day.'

'Are you sure everything's inside?' I asked.

'Well, 'Henge is still out there, the phone, and so's the airbed — it was wet anyway,' said Paul.

I shifted my bum and it felt as if I was sitting on a waterbed. I was. The ground beneath the tent was sodden and leaks were beginning to trickle through the groundsheet. Paul bravely took another look out, the sound of the zip being drowned by the echoing rumble of thunder.

'Shit — the water's flowing under the tent! The river's nearly over its banks!'

'We've got to dig some channels,' ordered Alastair, returning to planet Earth in the nick of time. For some reason he and Paul stripped to their boxer shorts, as If indulging in some rain worshipping ritual, and ran dancing and singing into the storm. They cannibalised some of the sharper elements of Stonehenge for the purpose of digging drainage channels around the tent. These diverted the new streams that were running down the campsite into the Verdon and prevented them from carrying our tent with them. Then they put rocks on the airbed as ballast and came back inside, rather wet.

'What's that over there?' I asked, pointing outside at a small blue packet of something.

'It's just the Entrotabs,' said Alastair, dismissively.

'But they'll get soggy. What if we get the thr'penny bits?' I asked.

Paul once more leapt into action like Superman.

'Save the Entrotabs!' he said in a corny black and white film sort of way, and dived out into the sodden mire to rescue the neglected medicine.

With everything now inside, and channels dug around the pitch leading into the Verdon, the only worry was the height of the river itself which seemed to be increasing by the minute. The river was fed from the lake around which we had walked, and the dam had obviously been opened to stop the lake getting too wet. We could see parts of the river bank slowly crumbling into the water, reducing the size of the campsite probably by a few yards. No doubt we would get the blame for it.

But the longed-for flood didn't occur. The storm abated, the river level reached its peak and started to ebb, and hundreds of damp campers crawled out of their shelters to start clearing up the mess. Paul was particularly upset to find that his botanical specimens gathered the day before had been spirited away by the wind and were now probably enjoying a new existence some miles away. We told him not to be so sentimental: we had to get on with cleaning ourselves up, for tonight was Junior Disco Night at the Club House.

Our enjoyment of the disco that evening was negated somewhat by our embarrassment at being on average twice the height of everyone else, so we quickly left and prepared the beer and guitars for a fun session at the campfire. This Friday night must have been the last night for a large number of Dutchies judging by the level of attendance at the fire. Now that we had been there a week we were recognised both as buskers and as being the only young people on the campsite without our parents. The cumulative result of this was that we were continually asked to play various songs we didn't know at all, which we replaced with our usual songs that we knew a little.

It was annoying not having picnic tables to sit on, but our performances were in such demand that there was no time for sitting anyway. Alastair and I forgot about our departed loves and sang loudly and uninhibitedly into the still night air.

'Play Drunken Sailor,' shouted a drunken Dutch boy.

'Yeah, play it,' shouted another.

It was almost midnight and our voices were tired.

'No, we'll stop now. People will be trying to sleep,' I said.

'No, you must play. It is alright. It is Friday night.'

'No, our voices are sore,' objected Alastair.

'We will sing,' said one of the voices.

'This is the last one, then,' I said.

And so, in the middle of the night, we found ourselves leading a multi-lingual rendition of *What Shall We Do With The Drunken Sailor?* with about twenty Dutch youngsters all clapping their hands and stomping their feet in the gravel.

After several repeats of the chorus we finally declared enough was enough and started walking away from them in defiance of their screams and shouts for more. Alastair and I held back a little, revelling in the adulation, and almost tempted to continue, but Paul was adamant that it was too late and marched a few feet ahead of us up the shingle.

Suddenly, over the mound that separated the campsite from the campfire, came two figures sinisterly silhouetted against the stars like vampires about sweep on any virgin flesh. We were, quite rightly, crapping ourselves. But Paul, carrying Alastair's guitar, was the first to come within their range and they set upon him violently.

'*Vous avez reveillé l'entier camping!*' shouted M Fasciste in Paul's face as he shook him by the shoulders in a rather unfriendly manner. His wife stood by him, looking equally angry.

'*Desolé Monsieur,*' said Paul, dropping his fudge, but still, to our amazement, managing to function in French. Myself, Alastair and a large Dutch contingent stood bravely silent while Paul took the blame for the disturbance on all our behalves. The fingers of the fascist pointed at me too, my guitar making another obvious target, though thankfully I wasn't required to grovel in a language of which I had little mastery — something which Paul was now doing very well indeed.

When Paul was set free and the evil apparitions drifted away to haunt someone else, he translated what they had said.

'That's it. We've been thrown off. We've got to go in the morning.'

I thought his voice was remarkably steady considering what he had endured in his martyrdom.

'Tomorrow? Do we have to pay?' I asked.

'Yeah,' said Alastair, 'they've got my passport details.'

'Shit,' I said.

'So what?' said Paul. 'The only bus leaves at about seven in the morning and if they can't be bothered to give us sufficient notice to be able to pay when the bureau is open then they can fuck off.'

'Hang on a minute,' said Alastair, 'I'm not having Interpol waiting for me when I get home.'

'Girl,' we said.

'But I suppose all they would do is write to me first of all telling me to pay up.'

'Yeah,' said Paul, 'and then you can write back and tell them to fuck off.'

'Or pay,' I added, tactfully.

When we had convinced Alastair that being thrown off meant that you weren't supposed to pay at all, we found the idea of leaving Castellane quite alluring. We had been thrown off the campsite! Now we could set upon the rest of Europe.

hitching

Inter-Rail Rule 5: Always ensure a member of your party has sufficiently whiffy feet to stink out a compartment if you want it to yourselves. This is usually no problem.

Paul

Stewart had borrowed an alarm clock from a Dutch girl called Inge, assuring us that it would wake us before dawn. At the pre-ordained time of five thirty the alarm was strangely silent, but so intent were we on an early departure that we were awake anyway. It was six in the morning by the time we had dressed, and the air had an unpleasant chill to it. Alastair and I hastily dismantled the tent while Stewart jogged off to return the faulty time-piece, returning with a jar of traditional Dutch camping-honey that Inge's father thought we could use on our travels. We were keen to avoid a confrontation with M and Mme Fasciste again and we tried to make as little noise as possible.

One thing we were unsure what to do about was the useful telephone that was sitting on the grass, looking rather sorry for itself. There was a lot of travelling to be done, and the only thing to do was to leave it behind. But where? The bonnet of an English car was decided upon, and I left it there with relish and a little salad cream, having first scribbled the phone number of someone I didn't particularly like on the paper disc in the centre of the dial.

Stewart returned a few minutes later holding a jar of honey and accompanied by a lad who towered even above Stewart's six foot frame.

'This is Justin von Leeurtens,' announced Poo. 'He was singing with us last night at the campfire.'

'Hello,' said the giant, 'I am sorry you have to leave. That was bad luck last night and I liked your singing.' He went on to give us his address in Nijmegen in case we were ever passing through. We gave him ours too because he was a true Fridge fan and there weren't many of those about. He stayed with us and helped us finish packing up our crap before escorting us to the camp entrance and acting out an emotional farewell.

The road to Castellane was not deserted at six-thirty, but no one was stopping in response to our upturned thumbs. By the time we arrived in town, we had missed the only bus of the day that provided a connecting service with Annot and the mountain railway. This provoked a lot of swearing within the Mad Brothers' camp on the reasoning behind running one bus service per day at seven minutes to seven, and plenty of abuse was directed at me for incorrectly believing that the bus left after seven. All the imprecations and speculation did not alter the fact that we were still fifty miles from where we wanted to go and we had no way of getting there.

To cut a long and somewhat boring story short, we spent about eight hours on the side of the road trying to hitch to Cannes, at the end of which time no lifts had been offered in spite of the fifty Franc notes waved at the drivers, and we reluctantly trudged back into the town to decide what to do. An hour of investigation and exhaustive walking around the town later, we found ourselves at Bar L'Etape buying coach tickets costing all but twenty pounds of our remaining holiday money.

When the coach finally arrived, we were not in the least surprised to see that it was about thirty years old and only fit to transport livestock, though we were too relieved to be moving again to care.

Since this total failure to procure a lift, I have become reasonably proficient at hitch-hiking and have therefore been able to draw up a short list of hitching tips for those of you who are contemplating the joys of the upturned thumb (ooer!).

Fundamental Rules Of Hitch-Hiking
(as compiled by Paul and Uncle Olly)

1. Stand, don't sit, facing the traffic
2. Try smiling — it may not feel natural but it will help
3. Hold a board stating your destination
4. Don't bother trying if there are more than two of you
5. Go by train
6. Buy a car
7. Stay at home

The interior of the coach to Cannes was more pleasant than the outside had suggested. We were also fortunate enough to have the entire back seat to ourselves. We spread out our crap to make sure it stayed that way and went to sleep.

We stepped out into the noise and dust of the dirty end of Cannes (ie where the bus station is) and hauled our crap over to a nearby concrete flowerpot, this time ensuring that we did not crush any flora or fauna. We had unanimously decided that we should try to visit at least one other country before we made a run for home: we still had twenty pounds or so and it would be a waste of an Inter-Rail ticket otherwise. In the event of the money running out prematurely we could always try busking, although we didn't really know what to expect. Having made sure that all our rucksacks were as secure and comfortable as possible, we set off in search of the train station.

'Why do we have to go to Venice? I bet it's crap,' I said, displaying an incredible level of bigotry.

'Because it's about time you took in some culture, you complete pig,' replied Alastair.

'It's OK, I've been there with my parents,' said Stew. 'Bit expensive though.'

'Oh look, the train's only going to be three quarters of an hour. That's a bit of good luck,' said Alastair. I grunted my disapproval. 'Mellow out, Paul. You never know, you might even like it,' he added in a way that sounded so much like one of my parents that I felt like hitting him.

We drifted over to the required platform and plonked our crap down on a spare bit of filthy concrete. Stew and Al sat me down on my rucksack and began to extol the fine architectural virtues of Venice. I must admit that after ten minutes I was quite looking forward to our visit, but I was yet to be convinced of the logic behind building a city in the sea when there was nothing wrong with the surrounding land mass. Could the medieval Italian Tourist Board really have thought that far ahead, I wondered?

By now we were beginning to get rather concerned at the increasing number of babbling tourists who were arriving in droves on the platform. We hoped they weren't all going to board the Venice train, but, of course, they were. About five minutes before the train was due we elbowed our way to the front of the platform in order to be able to procure for ourselves a vacant compartment. We could see the distant train approaching, finally decelerating as it drew into the station. I imagined the locomotive must have felt like an asthmatic boy after a sadistic PE tutor had just made him run the fifteen hundred metres and then told him that it wasn't good enough and that he would have to do it again.

By this time the locomotive had passed and the empty carriages were flitting before us. Alastair turned to us and said,

'Take my guitar and follow me.' It was obvious that he'd had another of his great ideas. He started to run along the platform parallel to the train like a Londoner chasing a bus. When their speeds were equal he jumped up onto the footplate and grasped the handrails on either side of the door, clinging on as if his life depended on it, which it did.

Stew and I realised the logic of this manoeuvre was to make absolutely sure that Alastair would be the first at the entrance to the carriage and thus be able to secure some seating for us in the face of overwhelming competition, and we were mildly impressed by this unusual display of forward thinking. What impressed us even more, however, were the unanticipated side-effects. With Alastair clinging to the side of the train like a limpet and with his rucksack adhered to his back in a similar manner, the new width of the train on the platform side was sufficient to catch other passengers completely off-guard. The human appendage was swept through the crowds knocking many of them over and causing others to drop their luggage in order to remove themselves from his path.

We sauntered up the platform after him, looking around furtively in case any victims of the human cannonball saw us and associated us with the reason that they were currently dusting themselves down and picking up their bags. No one did, fortunately, since most were Inter-Railers too and looked just as scummy as us.

Alastair's face appeared in the window.

'Over here boys!' he called in a gruff voice designed to attract the least attention. We passed the three guitars and the two remaining rucksacks through the open window and then climbed through ourselves. Alastair sat in a corner and pulled his boater down to cover his eyes, hoping he would now be sufficiently disguised to escape a vicious lynching from the casualties outside.

The compartment was designed for six, which perfectly suited the three of us and all of our crap. But we knew it would be unlikely that the space would remain our own for the whole night when there were such crowds still trying to get on. With this in mind, Stew shouted,

'Quick Paul — get your shoes off!' Ooer, I thought. The curtains were drawn, the door was shut, and I knew one whiff of my feet would be enough to anaesthetise any head that poked its unwelcome way through the door. 'Come on Paul,' he continued, 'we're used to it.'

But I had hardly made an impression on the complexities of the Hi-Tec laces when the door slid open and two girls squeezed in. They looked a couple of years older than us, and viewed us suspiciously. They turned out to be Danish and were unfortunately going all the way to Venice, hence there was no chance of finding ourselves with more space again later in the evening.

Twenty minutes of sitting and making polite conversation to the Danish girls passed before I decided to wander about a bit and explore my new environment. I wasn't far from our compartment when I saw two lads standing in the corridor, smoking a suspicious-looking cigarette which I correctly identified as a reefer. Sadly I could not work out the language they were speaking, but they quickly spotted that I was English.

'Eh man,' said one, sounding like a cross between Bob Marley and Marlon Brando, 'you smoke hashish.' This sounded more like a ultimatum than a question, but at the time I didn't even smoke cigarettes. The word 'no' was just on the verge of being blurted out of my mouth when I remembered my code for precarious living. What would my parents do? To start with they would have taken a plane instead of a train, but that wasn't the point. Undoubtedly they would politely refuse and then quickly move on to stay out of trouble. That settled it.

'Yeah, man! Nice one,' I replied, taking the joint from the outstretched hand, wishing I was black and had some dreadlocks so that I would look a bit more credible. I knew I wouldn't be able to inhale much, being a non-smoker, and therefore took the precaution of handing it back after a couple of drags, saying thank you, and theatrically staggering back down the corridor in order to avoid making an idiot of myself by choking. Obviously I wasn't stoned, but I didn't want to let my two hippy friends know I'd been wasting their ganja. The most important thing, however, was that I had flouted the law and done something of which my parents would definitely have not approved.

'Hey guys,' I said, hanging through the doorway of our compartment, 'I've just had a joint with two hippies.' Stewart looked at me as if I'd said that I had just pushed a nun out of the moving train, but that was because he'd seen too many government drug-awareness adverts on TV.

'Are you floating then?' asked Alastair.

'No, not really.'

'Bit of a waste of time, then, was it?'

'No, not really,' I replied, realising that it must have affected me somehow to make me give the same answer to two different questions.

The train started to decelerate again. We huddled together by the window, gazing out into the twilight to ascertain our location.

'Hey, it's Monte bloody Carlo,' exclaimed Stewart.

'Best we visit it quickly then,' I suggested. The three of us oozed out of the compartment and stood by the door. When the train halted we jumped out. I rotated through 360 degrees on the platform, looking at all the lights on the hillside, and inhaled deeply. 'I bet we're the only people in Monte Carlo not to have to pay to breathe the air,' I commented, pointlessly.

'Prob,' said Stewart.

'Let's get back in before we get charged for standing on their platform,' said Alastair. So we did.

Shortly after we had returned to our compartment, the door slid open once more and two young men stuck their heads in and looked around. It was obvious to me that they were English for several reasons. Firstly, they were both wearing jeans in mid-summer, secondly, one was wearing a grey, crew-neck jumper, and thirdly, the other was wearing a 'Girton College' T-shirt.

'Ullo John,' said Poo, greeting them in the traditional Alexei Sayle fashion. From this point on they became known as the two Johns, though one was definitely called Christopher.

We made room for the two Johns in the compartment as they seemed to be OK kind of guys. It transpired that they were from Exeter university, which made me think 'if they're so clever, why are they sharing a compartment with us?'

After a long half hour (about forty minutes long) exchanging exaggerated anecdotes we decided it was bed time. The two Johns were experienced Inter-Railers, and they knew some tricks that we didn't. They told us that the six seats could be transformed into three small beds by a cunning system of rails and little wheels. With this feat of engineering accomplished everyone dived onto the padded vinyl platform that passed as a bed in order to obtain sleeping space for the night.

I, however, was too slow. With the other six already in, the only available space was the gap under the beds. It was five feet long, three feet wide and less than a foot high. I squeezed myself into the gap and found that my head protruded into the corridor, which meant keeping the door open all night, and my hips were too wide to allow me to turn over onto my side. It was the most uncomfortable night of my life.

I hadn't been asleep long when someone ran along the corridor and booted me in the side of the head.

'Oi, fuck off!' I shouted before I realised it was an armed, uniformed man wearing a peaked cap. Whistles were being blown boisterously everywhere and dogs were yapping wildly. I correctly deduced that we were at the Italian border. Everyone else then woke up in a decidedly irritable mood. A food vendor pushed his trolley laden with overpriced cans of coke and hot dogs along the platform and stopped outside the window. He shouted something in Italian at the top of his voice to proclaim his presence.

'Bugger off!' shouted Alastair in return. 'We don't want your sausages interfering with our sleep.' The two Johns seemed quite entertained by this little outburst, but the two Danes didn't share their sense of humour. I think they might have been educated at a convent or had a grounding in morality or something. The train stood at the station for forty-five minutes in a typical display of Latin inefficiency before we were allowed to proceed.

I didn't sleep much more that night. I spent most of my time with my head out of the window: Genova, Milano, Padova — the names meant little. In the end I gave up and fell asleep. I woke up half an hour later in Venice to the sound of Stewart repeating the words, 'Yuk, it's really sticky' over and over, but knowing him as I do I thought it best not to actually look up to see what he was talking about.

honey, money and fascists

Inter-Rail Rule 6: Don't sit down in Venice.

Stewart

The trek across Italy from Ventimiglia to Venice was insufficient
to allow a full night's sleep, but with the two Danish girls lying
beside me in the compartment I didn't mind. At least Alastair's
warnings of thieves climbing in through the windows while
the train stopped briefly during the night proved unfounded.
But during the last few miles sleep managed to win me over
and with Venice only minutes away I slipped into a semi-
conscious state.

The sun shone in weakly across our sleeping bags, but
something was making me warmer than the yellow rays would
suggest. Something felt very warm. I tried to pull the curtain
further across to introduce some shade, but the curtain was
warm too. And rather sticky. Strange sexy thoughts flew
around my unawakened mind until I forced my reluctant eyes
to open a little more. I could now see that the curtains were
streaked with an unpleasant something, and I found myself
quietly cursing dirty, uncouth foreigners. Not finding a clean
patch of cloth to wipe my hand with I looked up to the luggage
rack for some sort of rag, only to find that the unpleasant
something was dripping from my daysack onto my seat, via
the curtain. Inge's father must have given me the honey as a
joke, I bitterly thought. The glass jar had been very thin — I
knew that because I could see bits of it floating along the
cascade of honey.

My predicament forced a premature goodbye to the Danish
girls and the two Johns on the platform because there was no
way I could tackle any of Venice until I had beaten the honey

monster. The station washing facilities were fortunately and unusually excellent: my honey-soaked wallet and traveller's cheques were finally separated in a delicate operation. The hot-air blower soon dried them, albeit to a crispness not normally found in paper forms of currency. The jumper, 'borrowed' from my father, was harder to restore. It proved to be so full of sticky glass fragments that wouldn't wash out that I decided to bin it. The same judgement was reluctantly passed on the small daysack.

Finally out of the station, we saw our first canal. It looked like a brown, stagnant pond, but I could tell it was moving because some of the boats were being overtaken by the drifting bottles and cans. There were brown tide stains on the stone sides of the buildings opposite, but pigeons were doing their level best to paint the place white. It was a beautiful sight.

'Mmm,' I exclaimed, breathing in deeply, 'this fragrance must be Canal Number Five.'

I had been to Venice before, so I pretended I knew where to go.

'This way,' I said, unconvincingly, leading us towards an aquatic dead end. The other direction took us to the Scalzi Bridge, over the Grand Canal and into the labyrinth of ponts and passages that was to provide us with such a lucrative day's busking.

The density of the Americans was staggering — the flows of tourists were thicker than the water, and it was hard to find an Italian anywhere. We set up first on a small bridge linking nowhere in particular with somewhere nondescript, and began playing to the constant stream of people keen to view the two places. For the first time in our playing experience, paper money began to flutter into the hat, and was instantly weighed down by handfuls of coins. We couldn't contain our excitement for longer than a ten minute session: the hat was nearly full and we were dying to count it. However, there were only supposed to be a few days of our holiday left, so there was no time. We packed up, moved to another bridge and another unsuspecting set of tourists, and started again, with exactly the same result.

Moving on to a further pitch, we passed a poster proclaiming that 'Venice is sinking'. Oh good, we thought, dismissing the rest of the message which was a plea for cash. It was tempting to aid the sinking process by jumping up and down a lot, but we didn't have the energy. Still, if the appeal really raised enough Italian cash to save Venice, the weight of the coins would probably have the same effect as a lead lifebelt around the city.

Cashing up in one of the few banks that were open on a Sunday was a major task. We only bothered to change a few hundred of the larger coins into notes that could be taken out of the country, leaving the rest in large bags and filling our many combined pockets. We had little idea what the total amount earned that morning came to, though it was later worked out to have been in the region of a hundred pounds. Sifting through the coins I found some Swedish Ore. I had never been to Sweden, and thought I probably never would, and that it would require a substantial twist of fate if that coin were ever to be of use to me. Foolishly, I dropped it into the nearest drain.

We paused for a break and sat on the smooth stone steps of a church that was set in a small square and had become mercilessly surrounded by take-away pizza shops in its later years. Paul was wondering what to do with the US Dollars we had been given among the other coins and notes in the hat, being loath to hang on to them. He walked into the centre of the square, which was bisected from every angle by passing tourists, where he seemed to be listening to any voices that were in earshot. Finally a woman with a baseball cap and tartan shorts wobbled by.

'You look suspiciously American,' we heard him say. 'Take these.' He produced the small wad of Dollars, stuck them in her hand, and returned to us engulfed in paroxysms of laughter.

I tried my hand at the same thing later on in the day, and I must say it was a good feeling. I don't think the Americans minded too much, either.

The next busking session took place in the grand setting of the Rialto Bridge. It turned out that one of the shopkeepers on the bridge had had the decency to die, leaving his well-situated shop closed for us to busk in front of. We dumped our shit along the metal grille that covered the window and set up facing the centre of the top of the bridge. It was the most famous and popular bridge around, and the money filled Alastair's straw boater faster than we could say something that took quite a long time to say.

When the novelty of earning money again wore off a little, we packed up and prepared to walk down the other side of the bridge.

'Hang on a minute,' said Alastair, as I handed him the heavily weighed hat to carry. 'I'm not bloody carrying it.'

Neither were Paul and I. I helped myself to the notes, but stated quite categorically that it was Alastair's duty as the only non tone deaf member of the busking group to carry the loot.

'Bugger this,' he declared, and went to the side of the bridge, took a handful of coins from the hat, and tossed them into the canal.

'I want a go!' I said, and took the next handful, savouring the feel of the disappearing coins.

We were in a band called Fridge at the time of the trip. Alastair and I played guitar and shared the vocals; Paul wasn't musical so he 'played' bass guitar.

Left to right:
Stewart, Alastair, Paul

Paul experiments with a bottle of pop in Cannes while Stewart counts his guitar strings, deciding that five is plenty.

The largest fountain in Cannes failed to remove any trace of Paul's stubborn Inter-Rail stains.

Today was Paul's turn to tidy the Gaff. It was a nicer mess now: less angular, but maintaining that essential feeling of randomness and anarchy.

Stewart and Alastair attempting a musical redistribution of wealth (in their direction) within the Castellane economy.

Paul demonstrates the note of 'C'. He has subsequently mastered most of the chord of 'E minor'.

Impersonating the Beatles worked better here than when we sang.

A corner of a foreign field that will remain forever England . . . until they clear it up.

'We constructed a mini-Stonehenge on our pitch. Rather than going all the way to Wales for the stone we opted to use local stuff, using the skull as a centrepiece. Meanwhile, Stewart was occupied in the preparation of some tinned ravioli for dinner as he couldn't see the point in doing something as puerile as recreating national tourist attractions of England in a foreign country.'

Above: We spent about eight hours trying to hitch to Cannes, at the end of which time no lifts had been offered in spite of the fifty Franc notes waved at the drivers: reluctantly we bought coach tickets costing all but twenty pounds of our remaining holiday money. When the coach finally arrived, we were not in the least surprised to see that it was only fit to transport livestock.

Left: Paul asleep next to the train toilet, covered in piss.

Below: The two Danes, the two Johns, and the two authors prior to committing numerous offences in Venice.

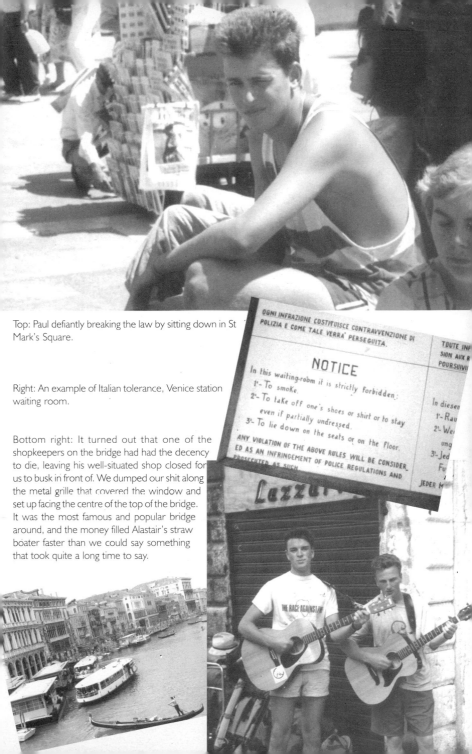

Top: Paul defiantly breaking the law by sitting down in St Mark's Square.

Right: An example of Italian tolerance, Venice station waiting room.

Bottom right: It turned out that one of the shopkeepers on the bridge had had the decency to die, leaving his well-situated shop closed for us to busk in front of. We dumped our shit along the metal grille that covered the window and set up facing the centre of the top of the bridge. It was the most famous and popular bridge around, and the money filled Alastair's straw boater faster than we could say something that took quite a long time to say.

OGNI INFRAZIONE COSTITUISCE CONTRAVVENZIONE DI POLIZIA E COME TALE VERRA' PERSEGUITA.

NOTICE

In this waiting-room it is strictly forbidden:
1ª- To smoke.
2ª- To take off one's shoes or shirt or to stay even if partially undressed.
3ª- To lie down on the seats or on the floor.

ANY VIOLATION OF THE ABOVE RULES WILL BE CONSIDERED AS AN INFRINGEMENT OF POLICE REGULATIONS AND PROSECUTED AS SUCH.

Top left: Waluliso, an Austrian nutter.

Top right: Paul Simon, disguised as Daniel the groovy Austrian busker and philanthropist.

Left: Alastair and Paul, fresh and alert after 24 hours of non-stop luxury European train travel.

Below: Stewart asleep on a bench covered in spiders.

'There is only so much natural beauty and poetry a mind can take, and so it became necessary to free ourselves from paradise and to slum it once more on dirty pavements. These offered no aesthetic appeal but were less taxing on the mind. In the cities you didn't need to keep saying to yourself 'fuck me what a lovely fjord/glacier/penguin'.'

'We were stranded near the North Pole at the remotest possible point from a McDonald's, and no pizza delivery service on Earth was going to send out a moped. The mist was heavy on the hillsides, but you couldn't eat it. The grass was lush and green around the tent, but you couldn't eat it. Even the hairy bar of soap in the shower block took on the appearance of a piece of cake, but we had to resist.'

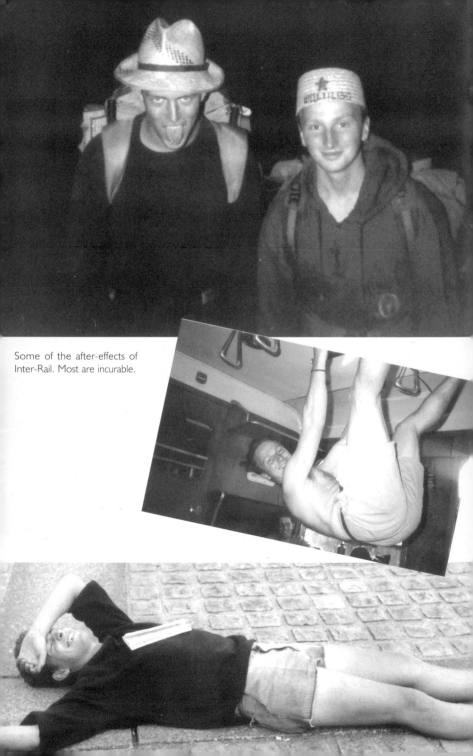

Some of the after-effects of
Inter-Rail. Most are incurable.

'Oi, my turn!' shouted Paul. He grabbed the hat, which was still more than half-full, and tipped its entire contents into the feculent depths.

St Mark's Square was bustling with pigeons recycling the peanuts given to them by the tourists by crapping them straight back on the ground. I found a patch of ground that wasn't quite so sticky and started to get out my guitar.

'Busking again, are we?' asked Alastair.

'Yeah, there's thousands of people here. We'll make a fortune,' I said.

'Not another one,' moaned Paul.

Before we could begin to play, however, a friendly policeman came over and glared at us. I asked him if it was alright for us to play, and he shook his head. Back went the guitars, and we sat on the steps of the statue behind us.

'No, no,' called an Italian voice, excitedly. It was the same policeman, desperate to inform us that it was illegal to be seated in a public place. He sternly handed us a leaflet, in four languages, which explained the courtesy and respect expected of tourists in Venice. This included such reasonable laws as the prohibition of displaying one's sleeping bag — the penalty for which was the confiscation of the bag — and the banning of beach wear. Keeping your shirt on at all times was obligatory, and the violation of which we were guilty was 'No sitting or lying down in a public place'.

'What about all those wankers at the cafés?' asked Paul.

The policeman indicated that sitting at a café was allowed. A very generous concession on the part of Venetian lawmakers, I thought.

Paul

By this time we were hungry to the point of implosion and made the finding of a burger bar the primary objective until the caverns of our bellies were totally filled.

'I know where there's a burger place,' said Poo. 'My parents took me there when we were here last. Let's go.'

We should have known that Stewart would be without a clue when it came to directions, but the scorching Mediterranean sun had done strange things to our minds and we foolishly believed him. We spent at least an hour looking for the place before concluding that the best way of locating it would be to follow the Americans. I didn't like the idea much but really there was no plausible alternative. The plan worked and fifteen minutes of being forced to listen to nauseating drivel was rewarded by a medium-sized burger restaurant.

The tills in the restaurant were some of the largest I had seen in a burger joint, but the denominations we finally used to pay for our tuck, having counted out piles of it on the tables, filled most of the small change compartments. The woman serving, who was probably a topless model on her days off, did not complain and kindly filled our water bottles for us, for which we were eternally grateful.

Arriving back at the station we exuded an unmistakable air of self-congratulation. We had managed to net in one morning the same amount as we would expect to earn back home for three Saturday sessions and, even better, we had done it illegally. This gave the money swishing about our many pockets a pleasant black-market feel. We noted with interest that whilst we had been away capitalising on the fact that Italy produces absolutely no popular musicians whatsoever (Pavarotti doesn't count), the station had turned itself into a Mecca for disgusting-looking Inter-Railers and hitch-hikers who adorned every available piece of masonry outside the building.

One particularly fetid example approached us saying that he was totally skint and hadn't eaten for over a week. Could we spare him some money? I noticed he was barefooted and that his feet and shins were so dirty it seemed that he had painted them grey himself. I asked him why his legs were so badly discoloured.

'Well, some bastards robbed me in Verona and they took my shoes too. Then I walked here.'

'What? Barefoot?,' I asked in disbelief.

'Yeah, no shit.'

This I considered unlikely. I rummaged around in my pockets and pulled out two fistfuls of change. I'm not sure how much it was exactly — probably a mere ten thousand Lire.

'Sorry I can't help more,' I said, now realising why Alastair had insisted that he should retain all the paper money for safe keeping. I dismissed the notion that Mr Barefoot could possibly be interested in a pair of my shoes: after all, his feet were merely dirty — mine were positively diseased. The unfortunate fellow thanked me repeatedly and limped off, presumably to buy himself some food.

We made our way inside the station and set up base in the front right-hand corner, marking our territory with our crap. We unanimously agreed that it was about time we had a money count. Grand total: 208,000 Lire. I suggested that we might have some fun and games with some of the cash which, in effect, had as much significance to us as Monopoly money. Alastair selected a 1000 Lire note and then affixed it to a thread of cotton. Having made sure that the cotton was secure, I ran out into the middle of the concourse as surreptitiously as possible, deposited the note on the floor and then scurried back to the relative safety of our base.

Predictably enough, after a few seconds, a man saw the note and stooped to pick it up. As he did so we began to reel in the cotton making the note dance tantalisingly away from him. He took another step. We repeated the procedure. He took another step. We were astounded by his stupidity. Alastair yanked the note out of reach once more. This time, however, the man realised that it was not the wind blowing it. Slowly he raised his head, his eyes following the course of the thread until we were staring each other in the face. He wasn't amused and for a moment we thought he might come over and give us a severe beating. He didn't. We mused for a few seconds about the wisdom of repeating the prank and decided that it would be well worth the risk of being severely twatted to watch someone make an idiot of themselves for our amusement.

After we had embarrassed a few more people with the bank notes we moved on to coins. We found that by making a small loop of gaffa tape we could adhere coins to the floor in a way that would require a Herculean effort to free them again. Additionally, the chances of removing the coin and retaining all of one's fingernails were very slim. After watching three or four people remove their fingernails, one 'lucky' individual succeeded in removing the worthless coin from the floor. He could keep it: we didn't mind. I think we all felt that the entertainment we had enjoyed for the previous twenty-five minutes was well worth the few thousand Lire that it had cost us.

We progressed, on Stewart's recommendation, to trying to write a song. We knew that playing a guitar in an area like the station where there was a proliferation of officials would be dodgy so we thought it would be best to keep the noise down. Had we been sensible, we would have waited until we were in a more tolerant country to do our songwriting. But we weren't sensible: we were the Mad Brothers.

Alastair extracted his guitar and quietly began to improvise some chord sequences. No sooner had we started than two Italian girls saw us and asked in broken English if they could stay and listen to us play. We agreed, providing they did not attract any unwanted attention and, I imagine, Stewart probably had some ideas involving them for later on.

Shortly, a group of uniformed train drivers entered the station talking loudly among themselves. At the time we did not recognise them as train drivers and mistook them to be a group of typically volatile Italian policemen. Alastair hurriedly tried to put his guitar away. Had he simply stopped playing we would probably have passed unnoticed, but Alastair's frantic rummagings alerted the drivers to a potential source of amusement lurking in the corner. The drivers made their way over to us and started talking frenetically at us in Italian: a language that none of us understood, though it became obvious from their gesticulations that they wanted us to play to them. Stewart tried some French on them believing the two languages to be almost identical.

'*Nous ne pouvons pas jouer ici . . . je regrette. Desolé, messieurs!*'

The train drivers, however, would not accept this as a satisfactory answer — probably because they didn't speak French, or perhaps because they were using Stewart's favourite trick of feigning ignorance to attain a desired end. The drivers continued their request for some live music in a way that was so forceful that we decided that the best way to get rid of them would be to play along. Alastair withdrew his guitar once more and we struck up a hushed verse of *The Boxer*. The drivers were typically excessive in their enthusiastic response to this popular classic, clapping and cheering wildly and digging deeply into their pockets for some loose change.

The men left us with another 2000 Lire that we didn't really want but we were thankful that they had gone. Before Alastair could even start to put his guitar away again, however, a set of doors flew open and two furious-looking policemen burst out screaming at the tops of their voices. They stood in front of us, the more excitable of the two standing, hands on hips, with his chest puffed-out for maximum intimidation. Then he began shouting at us in an incomprehensible babble. As they say, actions speak louder than words, and we were in no doubt that he was not at all impressed that we had profaned his holy station by indulging in the satanic practise of playing music: shame on us. Most of his fury was directed at Alastair but the two girls who had decided to sit with us were equally unimpressed by his behaviour. They began swearing back at the policemen in Italian.

'Sorry, mate,' said Alastair, dropping his guitar and holding up his hands in an attempt to give the impression of passive surrender. The girls continued screaming their dissent until the calmer of the two policemen grabbed them both roughly by the hair and dragged them off to some far-flung corner of the station (the dungeon maybe?) like some kind of wild animal with its prey.

'Fucking hell,' I croaked, unable to comprehend completely what had just happened.

'Silenzio!' screamed the policeman, agitated by the fact that he could not speak English and probably thinking that I was being flippant. Stewart and I watched in horror as he unfastened the press-stud on his holster and withdrew his pistol.

'We're too young to die!' I protested, to no avail. The policeman immediately trained his Beretta automatic on me for having the audacity even to speak in his presence. He held me in his sights for a couple of seconds, then retrained the weapon on the source of his anger: Alastair. It was very obvious to us that he believed Alastair had committed a serious transgression, though on the other hand I'm sure that Alastair was very sorry too.

He stood there pointing his gun and psyching us out for a full minute, which in the face of impending death seemed much, much longer. I think that after a minute he must have realised by the smell emanating from our shorts and the look of terror on our faces that he had succeeded in scaring us out of our wits and that we would be unlikely to start playing music again when he left. He had to be sure, however, and pushed us outside, pointed to an area of concrete, making it obvious that he wanted us to stay there.

Thus we set up a new base on the top of the steps and tried to slip into anonymity among the other travellers who had congregated there.

'What a fascist bastard,' I said, checking that he was out of earshot, ob.

'I've got to check my boxers,' said Stewart, standing up and tentatively tapping his backside to check for any residue that he may have involuntarily secreted. 'Shall we try to do that songwriting now then?' he proposed, having reassured himself of the cleanliness of his underwear.

'Yeah, I reckon we'll be OK out here,' said Alastair. 'After all, we're not busking or anything so they can't touch us . . . I hope those girls are alright.'

Before we could even begin to get our guitars out of their cases the policeman with whom we had just had our *tête-à-tête* came out of the station and incredibly managed to single us out from the rest of the crowd for a bit more harassment. The fascist again vented his aggression on the (relatively) innocent Alastair. His boisterous rantings attracted the attention of a number of other travellers who made it evident by their insulting gesticulations behind his back that they liked this copper as much as we did. After another session of unintelligible shouting, Venice's paradigm of law enforcement trotted down the steps towards the city centre. A group of Danish Inter-Railers sitting on the steps nearest us suddenly burst into song. The little ditty which they had decided to perform was an English one, apparently popular at soccer matches in the seventies,

'Who's the bastard, who's the bastard, who's the bastard in the blue?' they chanted over and over again. Some other groups decided to join in with the singalong until there were at least twenty people roaring their disapproval of the Italian police force from their seats on the station steps. The song gave me a pleasant feeling of solidarity and camaraderie with the other travellers, but, needless to say, the excessively excitable policeman did not appreciate the spirit of the moment. Spinning round to identify the reason for the commotion he saw that he was drastically outnumbered and stalked off again toward the city. He couldn't have shot us all anyway, I thought: those pistols only hold thirteen rounds and to kill us all he would have needed to persuade us to stand behind each other in a line so he could, to coin a phrase, kill two birds with one stone.

Bearing this confrontation in mind we agreed that it would be prudent not to air our guitars again until we were out of the country and so sat on the steps relaxing and drinking warm, quasi-stagnant water from our bottles. We tried to put the unpleasant incident to the back of our minds and began actually to enjoy our view of the wide station frontage that led down to the canal. This state of relative Nirvana did not last long, though.

'Hey! Look over there,' shouted Alastair, worriedly.

We craned our necks to see what he was so excited about. Right on the other side of the steps were two policemen with a large box on wheels. Attached to the box was a hose which they were using to blast the travellers in an attempt to make them leave and therefore restore Venice to the appearance given by all the tourist guides. Some moved away immediately, others stayed to have a free shower but probably regretted it later when they discovered that the water was being pumped straight out of the canal. We didn't seriously think at first that they would do that to the whole stretch of steps, but as our neighbours began to comment sarcastically 'Welcome to Venice' it appeared that the police welcome was extended even to us lowly buskers. We bravely opted for the 'get out of the way approach' and walked down to the side of the canal to sit on the bank and watch the sun go down over a backdrop of civil disturbance and angry shouts.

Our enjoyment of this was spoiled by the millions of hungry mosquitoes which were patrolling the area. This time we reluctantly moved to the official station waiting-room.

On the wall in the waiting-room was a public notice of typically Italian tolerance. It read in four languages:

In this waiting room it is strictly forbidden:

1)   *To smoke,*

2)   *To take off one's shoes or shirt or to stay even if partially undressed,*

3)   *To rest or to lie down on the seats or the floor.*

Any violation of the above rules will considered as an infringement of police regulations and will be prosecuted as such.

'That's nice,' said Poo.

'If we're not allowed to rest does that mean that we have to run about?' asked Alastair, rhetorically.

'Yeah, and if we get sweaty doing it we've still got to keep our shirts on. Clever eh?'

'Can we go to Austria?' I asked, trying to change the topic of conversation. 'I've always wanted to go there.'

'No we can't,' retorted Alastair, looking for an argument and then realising that there wasn't one to be had. In any case none of us was particularly keen on arguing after such an exhausting day. 'OK, why not?' he conceded.

'I thought we were going back home now,' said Poo.

'What's the point when we can travel anywhere in Europe for free?' I asked.

'Yeah,' agreed Alastair. 'What is there to go back for anyway? It's the middle of summer. Let's see how many places we can visit.'

This discussion marked the beginning of our transformation from mere travellers with Inter-Rail cards to genuine Inter-Railers — an entirely different species.

Having studied the timetable we decided to go to Innsbruck via Verona. The train wasn't due for another two and a half hours so we agreed to get some rest, taking it in turns to keep watch for any fascists that might pop in to the waiting room on the off-chance of being able to shoot a rail passenger.

By the time the train left we were almost refreshed and full of great expectations of Austria. As the train pulled out of the station and I knew that it would be unlikely that any policemen would be aboard the train, I could not prevent myself from opening the window and shouting, 'Venice sucks'. Well, it did.

among mountains

Inter-Rail Rule 7: Think about going by car instead.

Stewart

A border guard's boot prodded me during the night as I lay sleeping on the corridor floor of the Innsbruck train. Without bothering to open both my eyes I held up my passport and squinted at him. He didn't bother looking inside it as it was a British one. Then with a few more kicks, a few more cries of 'Ouch, what the hell's that for?' and further shouts of '*Ausweis!*' the door at the end of the corridor was slid shut and the carriage was once again quiet.

I woke up properly at about six, as the train was making its final approach through the mountains towards Innsbruck. Without getting out of my sleeping bag I sat myself up and looked out of the window. The track seemed to be about half way up the hillside in a valley of lush green. Below us was an empty road, clean black with shining white lines, neatly bordered by trimmed grass. The dust and unpleasantness of Italy seemed a world away from this squeaky-clean toytown land of colourful chalets, snow-capped mountains and Hitler.

We rolled up and stuffed away our sleeping bags just as Innsbruck station started to envelop the view.

'It's too early to play,' said Paul, 'so we'll have to see what time the McDonald's is open.'

We piled our bags into some station lockers and went exploring. First impressions of the town were disappointing. All the buildings were of sixties and seventies construction and were hence extremely ugly, and the road pattern was slightly less imaginative than that of New York. But our sixth sense led us directly through the grid to the McDonald's, where we sat on the steps and waited for its eight o'clock opening.

'What's the exchange rate here?' asked Alastair, looking at the menu.

'Well,' I said, 'cheeseburgers are eighteen Schillings here. They're a bit less than a pound at home, so there's probably about twenty Schillings to the pound. Just think of the cheeseburgers as being the international currency unit — it's worth the same wherever you go.'

According to the menu we had enough Austrian cash from the pool of assorted foreign coinage that we had earned in Venice along with the Lire to pay for a modest breakfast, after which we would have to earn some more for elevenses and lunch. This plan, however, started to go wrong immediately following the breakfast part. Nobody told us we were setting up our guitars outside the entrance to the police station. No doubt some passers-by afforded us a nervous glance or a puzzled look, but no one bothered mentioning our potentially dire predicament.

We were in the old part of the town, which we found by accident while wandering the gridwork of roads at random. There was an ancient archway, behind which the real Innsbruck had remained almost unchanged since one Thursday in the Middle Ages when a duck was burned alive for having allegedly been turned into a horse and then back into a duck again by the Devil. Or some such load of bollocks, anyway. The streets were cobbled, many of the houses had large wooden beams exposed among the brickwork, and the doors were set under dark overhangs of arched stone, making the north-facing ones melt into the shadows. This was why we could not at first see the small brass plaque on the door behind us that informed more observant individuals of the presence of a police station.

Alastair was tuning the guitars as usual when the door of a craft shop, on the other side of the small cobbled square in which we were setting up, flew open with a bang. A frightened-looking man dressed as scruffily as ourselves was being ushered outside by two policemen. One of them pressed him against the wall while the other frisked his quivering body.

'Shit guys,' I said, edging back into the shadow behind us, 'he must have been busking round the corner.'

No one found this remotely amusing, however, because the two policemen and their handcuffed prisoner were now marching directly towards us.

'Looks like we're next for the hospitality treatment,' whispered Paul as he joined me under the doorway.

Still they came closer. Never had our instruments been put away and replaced with innocent expressions so quickly as on this occasion. Then Paul nearly vomited with shock,

'This is a bloody pig station! We were going to play outside the bloody pig station!'

I looked for the first time at the plaque that said 'POLIZEI' and broke into a run. There was a narrow street leading away from the square and away from the arresting officers and their sty, and I was down it and round the corner in an instant. When the others caught up with me I was pleased to note that they were not handcuffed. But then it probably wasn't illegal to tune a guitar outside a police station: this was Innsbruck after all, not Venice.

When we had calmed down a little we reasoned that if the policemen had wanted to reprimand us they would have shouted something. So we defiantly found another square, read all the inscriptions on the nearby doors, and started bringing in some cash in return for giving the locals a little culture. It was not as lucrative as Venice but it kept us in burgers and milkshakes for the rest of the afternoon.

Finally it was time to move on. The circle of mountains that overlooked Innsbruck was inviting, and I knew that Inter-Rail legends tell of many of our predecessors sleeping rough in the fields on the lower slopes, but we were geared up for train travel and Paul wanted to go to Vienna.

'But Vienna's in the middle of nowhere,' I protested, looking at the map.

'It's in the middle of Austria,' he corrected, wrongly, 'and what do you call being surrounded by mountains anyway?'

'Rather cold,' I said. 'I mean it's not on the way to anywhere.'

'That depends where you're going,' said Paul.

At the station there followed a five-minute altercation between Paul and Alastair over who actually had the key to the locker, at the end of which I remembered that it was me. I didn't own up: I just unlocked it, gave them their rucksacks, and told them to shut up, which they didn't. Then we sat on the floor inside the station waiting for the arrival of the night train to Vienna, passing the time with the aid of chocolate and mutual lessons in swearing in various languages.

the boogie and rock 'n' roll club

Stewart

We piled out of Vienna Westbahnhof desperate for a tray of burgers. Among the various offers we received on the station forecourt a pile of junkfood was not one of them, so we commenced a search of the city, hoping to find a McDonald's in time for the eight o'clock opening that our Innsbruck experience had taught us to expect as the norm.

Dodging the early morning trams we crossed the main road outside the station and headed down some of the busier roads until we came to a long, wide pedestrianized street. We strolled along it until at ten past eight Paul spotted the oasis, its yellow and red sign nestling down a side street, and we ran towards it.

'Half past ten? What are the bastards playing at?' he wondered. Again we were forced to start the day moping around, doing nothing until after nine when we could sing a few songs and get Vienna bopping to work.

The takings were less than they had been the day before, so after breakfast Alastair suggested we play some more. This was a difficult thing for me to do on a full stomach, and I met the idea with about as much enthusiasm as if he had asked me to carry his rucksack for the next fortnight. But money had to be made, and we compromised by walking a little further through Vienna and finding a different pitch.

A few hundred yards yielded the discovery of a cathedral, set back in Stefansplatz. It had a colourful roof made of zig-zag patterns, and one or two beggars decorated the main entrance. In the square itself was a man dressed in white robes like a Roman, with a laurel crown on his head and a big apple in his hand. The other hand held a long white staff which he used to tap the ground in rhythm to the tape recorder strapped under his gown to gain attention to his unusual predicament.

Another bloody nutter, I thought, dismissively. But Paul could understand what he was saying, and was listening attentively.

'He calls himself Wa-lu-li-so,' he translated. 'It means water, air, light and apples. No, not apples; sun. He's talking about the failure of the summits at Geneva and Reykjavik, and saying all you need in life are the elements in his name.'

'He's off his trolley,' I observed.

'No, he's cool,' decided Paul, and went over to talk to him, much to my embarrassment. Waluliso had finished a brief monologue and his small crowd was dispersing. Alastair and I departed likewise rather than risk getting entwined in a conversation with Paul and his weirdo friend.

We decided to busk a little way around the corner, where Paul could easily find us if he felt like it. He eventually waddled along during the fifth song and pretended not to know us. That's it, I thought, he's been brainwashed and sent along to collect his white robes and his apple. Then he noticed how much money we had earned.

'Bloody hell boys, that's not bad for Austria, is it?' He dropped his things and sat on a doorstep behind us, waiting to be given his third share for his hard work.

Then someone else approached us just as the session was drawing to a close. He was a young man, and was the spitting image of Paul Simon, even down to the guitar case.

'Hi guys, how's it going?'

We gave no response.

'I'm a busker too. I live here. If you want to stay in Vienna you can stay at my girlfriend's flat.'

This was the last thing I intended doing.

'My name's Daniel. I will be busking here between six and eight tonight. Meet me here and we can go for a drink.'

Daniel gave us a wave and went off on his philanthropic way.

'Let's get out of here,' I said.

'What's the problem?' asked Alastair.

'We don't want to stay in Vienna tonight, do we?' I asked.

'Why not?' said Paul.

And so the discussion progressed, resulting in the tentative decision that if we did stay we would first lock all our valuables in the station lockers overnight, but the final decision would be delayed until we had got to know Daniel a bit better that evening. I hoped he would turn out to be sufficiently dodgy to make us move on to another country that night. Now that we had started travelling I didn't want to stop, but my opinion was in the minority and therefore worthless. I felt like a bass player.

McDonald's received another, more lengthy visit from us that lunchtime, after which it was back to Karntnerstrasse for more music.

Paul

Our performance had attracted a sizable crowd of onlookers, which had to be good for business. The spectators had arranged themselves in a semi-circle around us and were watching us intently. I was watching certain members of the audience with considerable interest too; in particular the two strikingly attractive girls standing to my right in the front row. When we came to the end of a verse and we had a few bars reprieve before we had to start singing again, I leaned over to Alastair to inform him of the presence of these two objects of desire.

'Check it out. Two o'clock,' I whispered.

'Yeah, I know. I've seen them already.' I should have known no women worth looking at would have escaped Alastair's unerring eye. Shortly afterwards, a policeman came and moved us on for busking outside permitted hours. These were between six and eight in the evening, when the streets of the city would fill with musicians and people like us, which makes competition very fierce. As we were packing up our stuff and mentally preparing ourselves for another foray into McDonald-land, the two girls approached us and introduced themselves as Liesbeth and Ans from Schinveld in southern Holland. They were accompanied by a young man who introduced himself as Robert Krisch, an Austrian.

Stewart took an immediate disinterest in the women from a sexual standpoint as he was still besotted with Anja and neither of them was well enough upholstered for his discerning groin. I, on the other hand, was definitely interested, and had no objection to being friendly with them. They invited us to go for a drink and, from that point on, my holiday romance started up.

The girls appeared to be a bit too cultured for us and were none too impressed that we did most of our eating either in the street or in McDonald's. However, they attempted to endow us with some of their spare charm and finesse by taking us on a guided tour of Vienna.

First port of call was a rather upmarket café with tables and chairs in the street. When the bill arrived I was very relieved to see the girls grab it before I had to. Not very gentlemanly, I know. After that we visited the Schonbrunn, a kind of palace painted a pale shade of yellow. As architecture was the last thing on my mind at the time I'm not sure who used to live there, but the beautiful gardens provided a perfect backdrop for a romantic perambulation on a midsummer's afternoon. I don't recall if there was an entrance charge for the place but if there was, we certainly didn't cough up for it; our continental hosts were taking care of that side of things.

The rest of the afternoon was spent relating our life stories to each other whilst reclining on a picturesque lawn in the centre of the city. I liked this place, I decided, and I would have to return one day. Robert worked for AEG and was on holiday. For this reason he had truckloads of money which he felt he had to spend on us. We made it as clear as possible that we didn't really have anything to offer in return for his kindness but he carried on spending regardless. Liesbeth and Ans were still students but almost certainly from wealthy backgrounds, and as for us; we were smelly scumbags with guitars. Life is sometimes too good.

Later on that day we met up with Daniel again as he had suggested. Getting to his place required a long trek across town which we decided to make by tube as we were too lazy/tired to walk. Public transport in Vienna is a great thing: it is free to students during the holidays (at least I think that was what the signs affixed to the windows on all the trams and trains said).

Daniel's flat was an incredible affair. It was just one room but as it had such a high ceiling he had made a mezzanine floor out of scaffolding upon which lay his bed and other bits and bobs. Underneath was his sofa and living area. After we had dumped the small amount of crap which we had brought with us on his floor he ushered us out again and told us we were going to a club that he visited frequently and might be of some educational value to us. The journey required the use of the city's underground system again but we weren't going to lose too much hair over it; Daniel seemed pretty clued up about these things and it would not have been cool to express any doubts or anxieties about the legality of what we were doing.

The club was situated on the second floor of a dingy-looking, concrete structure. No amount of sixties documentaries could have prepared us for the sight with which we were met as we walked through the door into the club. For a start, there was no furniture to speak of, just boxes and podia covered with oriental-looking rugs. On the walls all around the room was painted a surreal mural, and the contents of the atmosphere would have supplied a narcotics factory with raw materials for a month.

Daniel asked us what we wanted to drink and duly went off to fetch it. When he returned he explained a little about the club. Most of the details elude me now but one impressive feature that has lodged itself in my memory is the way in which the club was funded. There was no charge at the bar when you collected your drinks; people who used the club were trusted to make contributions to it when they got their pay-packets to the amount that they had drunk since their last donation. The business-minded people who are reading this will be by no means surprised to learn that since our visit (but not as a result of it) the club has closed down. Nonetheless, the idealistic concept appealed to me.

The exceptionally subdued reddish glow that passed for lighting in the club came from a selection of candles and tiny lamps. This flickering light did strange things to the mural so I got up to examine it a bit more closely, but could make neither head nor tail of it. I concluded that the picture had almost certainly been painted by someone on acid or something similar and that to understand it one would have to be in the same condition. Even Stewart the Sanctimonious One agreed with me about this. After I had put a few beers away I went back to the wall to see if it made any more sense. It didn't, which proves the difference between beer and drugs.

Daniel would not accept any cash from us in return for the drinks on the following principle: when he travelled the world with no money he met people who did have money, food and accommodation. These people helped him out. He would like to repay the favour to the people to whom he is morally indebted. Obviously, however, they have no need of his money and so on. Therefore, he helps other people who were in the same situation as he was on the understanding that they do the same when they are able to in order to continue the train of goodwill, co-operation and generosity. I thought that this was an excellent principle by which to live and I would encourage all other Inter-Railers to do the same, as it is ultimately to everyone's benefit.

throwing more money away

Paul

After the customary farting and cursing ritual of getting up the next morning, we thanked Daniel for his hospitality and the use of the only shower we expected to see for the remainder of the trip, and felt guilty for having initially doubted the integrity of so magnanimous a man. We coaxed him into a quick photo of him with us, before he had to turf us out onto the streets as he had some business to attend to.

This was not a problem, however, as Alastair and I had already arranged to meet Liesbeth and Ans at midday in Stefansplatz. After a little discussion, Poo, in a commendable display of altruism, agreed to look after the crap in Westbahnhof on his own for the entire day while Alastair and I enjoyed ourselves. We asked him if he had enough food and money, though forgot to wait for the reply before skipping off to town in search of our icons of female perfection.

We found them where we had agreed to meet them, dressed in even more expensive-looking clothes than they were wearing the day before. I felt like a football thug at the opera. I was not aware of the concept of 'a bit of rough' at the time, so I could not comprehend why they were with us. But I wasn't complaining.

On the cultural amelioration programme for today was a visit to an art gallery, a visit to a museum, and a stroll around the Jewish Quarter. Some of the girls' finesse must have rubbed off on me as, for the first time — and the only time, come to think of it — I actually appreciated some of those pretentious sculptures of nothingness which are so prevalent in the art galleries of the world's major cities. My mother would have been proud of me, but she wasn't there.

I found the suppression of expressing a wish to eat at McDonald's extremely difficult, but I couldn't blow everything for the sake of a couple of cheeseburgers.

Later on in the day we bumped into Robert Krisch, who immediately insisted on taking us to a café. Robert took us around a few more sites of architectural and cultural beauty that afternoon but I wasn't paying much attention as I already had one on my arm.

At the conclusion of our tour, Robert announced that he would like us to meet a friend of his who was working in a nearby shop. We waited patiently outside the shop while Robert went inside to fetch his mystery celebrity. When Robert finally did emerge from the bowels of the shop he was accompanied by a big chap with a smiling face. His name was Reinhard and he greeted us as if we were his long-lost children.

'Would you like a drink?' he asked in English of a quality not normally found in English shop assistants. What could one say? We followed him to yet another café, this time near Stefansplatz where we had met the girls that morning.

There we spent a very agreeable hour or so, telling him of our European misdeeds, before we remembered Poo, sitting alone on the cold marble concourse of Westbahnhof. He would probably have developed piles by now, I thought. We told our host of Poo's dilemma and that we really should be getting back to him. Reinhard didn't mind; he simply paid the bill, rallied the others and followed us to the station.

Stewart

To some, looking after the rucksacks all day would have been restrictive, but I revelled in the thought of the unrivalled freedom to be found within a six feet radius of the baggage.

Specific parameters such as those turn decision making into an easy process, simply by cutting out ninety-nine per cent of options. This is very relaxing for the mind.

I was left at mid-morning at Vienna Westbahnhof, having sculpted a little corner of floorspace out for myself with the shit. I was quite happy on the floor — it was marble, and polished daily by a runaway vacuum cleaner with wheels and a cowboy rider. On either side of me against the wall were various vending machines, to the far left were stairs to a bureau de change and other shops, and in front of me on the other side of the marble concourse were escalators leading to ticket booths and trains.

Few people hung around near me. They either walked straight over to the escalators or disappeared down one side or the other. But the general density of people was sufficient for me to go largely unnoticed.

Sitting on the fleshier part of my rucksack (the bit with the dirty clothes sealed in an almost radiation-proof bag), I started fidgeting with the various pockets. One had 'useful' stuff like matches and string, another had a toothbrush and toothpaste squashed in with Thomas Hardy, and another had energy sweets and a first-aid kit. But the last pocket, jutting out from the rucksack, hung down limp and heavy. I thought I was groping a feminist. I picked the pocket up and it flopped back with a deep chink.

This was where I had put all those worthless Italian coins. I pulled the zip open slowly, allowing myself to fall into a brief fantasy of discovered treasure, long buried since the day before. I took out a handful of cool coins: in Italy they were probably enough to buy a gobstopper at a vending machine, provided it had a cash box the size of St Mark's Square and was emptied after each sale. The biggest coin was one hundred Lire, and it looked as if it would roll well.

It's quite amazing the level of enjoyment to be gained from throwing money away. The experience on the Rialto Bridge had loosened my desire to hang on to all the coins, and wastefulness was to be my chief occupation for the day.

I looked around: still no one was watching. I rolled the coin firmly towards the centre of the concourse, in front of the escalators. It came to rest in full view of myself and of everyone walking past. And there it sat, a large, bright silver coin, for a full two seconds before a middle-aged man in a coat bravely stooped to pick it up. I pitied the look of disappointment on his face when he realised it was Italian, and, according to the only available subsequent logical option, worthless.

The next coin was smaller but prettier and more valuable (relatively speaking). The five hundred Lire coin had a gold coloured insert, and looked more striking as it lay on the marble floor. I sat still as an old woman picked it up and looked around. Seeing only me paying attention she walked over and asked if it was mine. I lied, red in the face.

I soon rolled another, and another, until the floor became quite littered with money. Some of the coins were a mere five Lire, and I found it hard to believe that such a coin, whose value was practically negative, could still be in use. It wasn't even much good for rolling, being so light the slightest breeze blew it over and wafted it up into the atmosphere. Well, nearly. The number of coins on the floor was now almost sufficient to make it look like a pattern in the marble. For some moments there was no change (excuse the pun): the runaway vacuum cleaner was going round and round in circles out of control some yards away from the money, doggedly trying to pick up a stubborn cigarette stub (no doubt glued to the floor by another forward thinking Inter-Railer); and no one seemed to be paying any attention to the cash. My supply of coins was exhausted and I sat waiting for more action.

Nothing seemed to happen for some moments until there was a tinkle as someone accidentally kicked one of the coins and sent it flying across the station. People began to look down, and the next thing I knew there were bent bodies everywhere, stooping to pick up what was to me no more than litter. What clean people these Austrians are, I thought. The mood of excitement could not last — one look at the coins in their hands was enough to tell them they had wasted their time. Some shoved them into their pockets despondently, others dropped them back to the ground with a surreptitious glance at the ceiling. Only the children kept their smiles.

The only thing to do now was to feed myself with some unhealthy junk from the nearby dispensers. A couple of foraging trips, a bloated stomach and a full bladder later, I realised the inherent flaw in the plan of me guarding the baggage all day. I no longer had enough Austrian cash to pay for lockers for the gear which meant I wasn't free to visit the toilets. Suddenly my freedom was gone and I wished someone I knew would walk past.

This, surprisingly enough, did not happen. I checked the locker prices and found that I had enough Schillings left to pay for one locker only, and it would be a matter of squeezing as much into it as possible and carrying the rest with me. Fortunately it was like a TARDIS on the inside, and I managed to fit in two rucksacks on top of each other. Then off I trotted into the toilet carrying a rucksack and three guitars, feeling very proud of myself.

Paul

We found Stewart exactly where we had left him, but something was not right. Alastair was quicker than I.

'Where are the other two rucksacks?' he demanded.

Poo told us that he had put them in a locker or something and not to worry. Then we decided that maybe we ought to introduce him to Reinhard. Reinhard greeted Stewart in the same way that he had initially embraced Alastair and me.

We remained in the station restaurant until eight that evening, the money for the constant stream of drinks coming from Reinhard's seemingly bottomless pockets. I couldn't work out why the Austrians were so friendly — we weren't even on their side in the war — but this *entente cordiale* and the Dutch lovelies created spectacles with the rosiest tint through which it had ever been my pleasure to look at the world.

It was an emotional farewell when we finally parted, with every party promising to write to one another.

'Where are we going, Poo?' I asked once the train was rolling.

'Zurich,' he replied.

'Oh,' I murmured and slumped against the train window in my own little dream world.

My dreams were broken about five hours later by the familiar sound of guitars being tuned.

'We're having a jam,' announced Poo. 'Come on. Get the tape deck out; we'll record it.'

'Rolling Stones mobile studio, somewhere in . . . is it Switzerland? It's dark, anyway.'

I paused the tape recorder and tried to think of something else to say.

'We're ready now,' said Alastair.

'Take one,' I said.

Stewart's guitar thumped out the chords E, A and B for a few bars until Alastair came in with an ad-lib solo, making the rendition of *Wild Thing* no longer recognisable. But we hadn't managed to record very much when the inevitable fascist threw open the door and asked for our tickets.

'Fahrkarten!'

The Rolling Stones never had this trouble, I thought. We scrambled around in the messy recording studio searching for our tickets, then resumed our historic session when he was gone.

'Yo,' said a face, some minutes later, sliding open the door again and peering into our compartment.

'Yo?' we said.

'You guys play the guitar I see,' he observed, innacurately.

'We might do. What's it to you?' asked Alastair.

'We're having a jam,' he said. 'Wanna join us?'

We didn't particularly want to, but being musicians it was important to indulge in certain social activities with strangers, and jamming was one of them.

We followed the Inter-Railer to his own compartment which was crammed with hippies of various stages of degradation, from us at the bottom to the fiddler at the top. In between was a tambourine person, two guitarists (including him), a harmonica player and a flautist. They took up all the room in the compartment, so we huddled outside with our guitars around our necks, trying to keep up with the twelve bar blues. One by one we stopped at the end of the song, as each of us reached the magic twelve at different moments.

It was an evening of great camaraderie, in the true Inter-Rail tradition — all differences in musical taste (their's was better) and ability (they had some) were forgotten as we played to the rhythm of the tracks into the night and onto the next disastrous destination.

zurich and the pasta queen

Paul

It was about nine in the morning when we arrived at Zurich, but being comfortably settled lazy bastards we decided this was too early to think about getting up and opted to stay on the train to Basel, which would give us another hour and a quarter 'in bed'.

Having enjoyed our deferment of consciousness for the full amount of time, it was time to seek out breakfast in Basel. There was a McDonald's close to hand, of course, and we sampled its fare with willing palates, especially as it served beer in a handy-bendy plastic cup with a straw.

We took our drinks out of the restaurant and into a square with a big concrete pond in the middle. In the pond were six or so mechanical wrought iron things going 'umph-umph' and moving their stupid arms and heads about in a pointless, but no doubt artistic, manner. Pathetic water jets accompanied this un-inspiring spectacle, and we sat, unintrigued, for a good few seconds before deciding it was crap.

We were nevertheless in no particular hurry to get to Zurich, and spent the day loafing around Basel and swearing every now and then. But Zurich had to be visited some time because, er, something to do with the letter 'Z' I think, but we had to go anyway.

It must have been about 1800 hours when we arrived at Zurich station. I was immediately impressed by the overall cleanliness of the place and the way that almost everybody seemed to have something to do, and even those who were doing nothing were managing to sprawl or meander in an aesthetically pleasing way. In fact, Zurich was probably the most pleasant station we visited over the whole trip, but at the time my mind was set firmly on Vienna and as far as I was concerned the Austrians could do no wrong — not even the railway staff.

The station interior was orderly in design and well signposted, but we inevitably stumbled out of the train, falling over other people's baggage in a vain attempt to find a sign that might give us an idea of where we ought to be heading. The horribly sad truth was that as per usual we had no idea of where we wanted to go or what we wanted to do or even why we were there. We eventually realised this and found a vacant piece of concrete upon which we could re-group and assess the situation.

Stewart, ever the bread-head, suggested that we play a few songs. Alastair, on the other hand, was equally determined to do a bit of sharking (nothing new there) with two girls he had seen a bit further up the platform who were having trouble with their leaking water bottle. I was not consulted on the evening's agenda, but then I was 'only a bass player'. The others let me drift off into my own little world of Viennese cafés and Dutch tourists while they argued the toss with one another.

'Oi! Oi! Wanker!' I suddenly rejoined the real world as Alastair let me know, in his own special way, that he and Stew had reached a decision and that we were about to go. The plan turned out to be a compromise: sharking, then busking.

Sad to relate, the sharking was not exactly a complete success. The girls were English, loosely speaking, but the look of total resentment that hit their faces when they heard our south coast accents suggested that we were not worth the steam off their piss. After a few moments of pained expressions from both parties Stewart asked if they would like us to fix their water bottle. We were bombarded by another salvo of

Mancunian bad-language and disbelief in our ability to effect such a repair successfully.

It was obvious to the Mad Brothers at this point that these girls were a sad bunch, but we all knew that a bit of gaffa tape could drastically alter the quality of their lives — for better or for worse, depending where it was placed. By now all of us, even the excessively effervescent Alastair, realised that we were going to get no further with these women. So with a quick flick, tear and stick from our precious roll we left them to it and strolled off up the platform, leaving them awestruck behind us with their newly waterproofed bottle as we went in search of some lovely, lustrous Swiss Francs.

On a sort of sub-ground floor level we found a little shopping complex housing the Swiss equivalent of Sock Shop, Our Price and Casey Jones. This, we decided, would do as a busking pitch.

The Swiss obsession with cleanliness and order manifested itself within ten minutes of us starting our set in the form of a security guard who had been instructed by persons unknown to rid the station of itinerant English 'musicians'. My normal reaction would have been to kick up a stink and crassly remind him of who won the war, but I had my rose-tinted spectacles on that day and neither Stewart nor, strangely, Alastair, had the wish to cause any trouble. We gracefully accepted his authority and agreed to move on.

Buskers must be something of a novelty in this part of Switzerland because despite having been silent for about three minutes we still had a substantial audience. We counted the session's takings and were astonished to discover that we had collected the equivalent of about £17. Now for a feast, we thought. Even after our counting session three people still watched us with considerable interest. These people, I thought, must be the Zurich Bahnhof hardcore nutters.

It turned out I was right. As we tried to leave, one of the three, an elderly woman, held up her hand to stop us. She started talking to us in German and consequently Stew and Alastair's faces adopted a confused and anxious look. I translated as she started her speech.

'You play beautiful music.'

'Nice one, cheers,' replied Alastair, nodding his head in acknowledgement.

'I never give money to musicians. They are beggars but you . . . but you, your harmonies are lovely.' Having understood this I realised that she could not possibly be talking to me and that I was merely an interpreter.

'I am a poor, poor woman, but your music is so good I give you this.' She threw two Francs to the ground where the hat had been about ten minutes earlier. I think she may have done this just to make sure that we knew she was mad, but we had met enough insane Europeans by this time to know one when we saw one. She continued, 'This money is for my son's dinner but I know he won't mind when I tell him about your music.' Praise indeed! Ethically speaking we really should have refused her offer, but we wanted to get moving and we knew that the hysterical woman would only delay us further if we insulted her generosity.

'*Vielen dank*,' was all I could manage, feeling sorry for her hungry son.

'Yeah, well cheerio, missus,' said Stew as she ambled off to wherever nutters hang out in Zurich — another part of the station perhaps?

Our ordeal was not over. The next of our disciples approached and introduced himself to us (thankfully) in English as Massimo. Luckily for us all he wanted to do was say thanks for the show, but disastrously I let slip that we had been in Venice a few days earlier. Venice was his home city and, needless to say, he started citing street names, restaurants and clubs we had never heard of and asking us if we had been there. Then came the fatal question,

'Don't you think the people are friendly?' This was too much for Alastair, as he was still traumatised by having a gun pointed at him by the Venetian policeman —

'No way, mate! All the Italians we met were wankers. I thought fascism died out in 1945 but I was bloody wrong!'

Massimo did not find this quite as funny as Stewart and I, and we unsuccessfully tried to suppress a smirk. He got very passionate and Latin about the whole thing, swearing, gesticulating and spitting before turning on his heels and storming off, still cursing wildly. As soon as he was out of earshot we all fell about laughing like twelve year olds on cider.

We were surprised to note that our third spectator was still there and was showing no sign of leaving. He, predictably enough, only spoke German, and so it was time for me to put my translator's hat on again and get weaving.

'What are you going to do with that money?' he asked. It seemed a forgone conclusion to me that we would be going to McDonald's, but I checked with the boys just in case.

'We are going to McDonald's to pig-out.'

'With thirty-eight Francs? You can't eat for that much and anyway there aren't any McDonald's in Zurich.'

The others looked amazed at first, but then remembered that no place in the world had been denied the unquestionable, multifarious benefits of a McDonald's restaurant.

'Tell him he's full of shit,' suggested Stewart. Although I had to agree, I wasn't going to tell him just in case I got punched.

'Well, what do you suggest then?' I asked him, diplomatically.

'Do you like pasta?'

The boys affirmed that they did, and I conveyed this to the man, thinking that he may be about to recommend a cheap pasta restaurant. No such luck.

'Well why don't you come back to my place, meet my mates, then we can have a shower and see the town?'

Panic! My brain went into meltdown. For a few moments I could not bring myself to tell the boys what had just been said. The man adjusted his pose to one that was even more camp, just to remove any shadow of doubt that may have been lurking in our minds as to his sexual preferences. We had a quick team-talk and reached the conclusion that an evening spent with him and his mates would have spelled a definite end to our collective anal virginities.

'Ah, sorry . . . Alastair doesn't like pasta. He's just remembered.' It was a feeble and thoroughly pathetic excuse, but the quality of our bullshit was the last thing on our minds.

We left the station as quickly as possible whilst making sure we didn't appear to be too unsettled by the whole affair. In the event there turned out to be a number of McDonald's in Zurich, so finding one was not a problem. A couple of hours later, thoroughly gorged by a massive pig-out burger and belch session and thinking that we had probably seen enough of the city for one evening, we returned to the station.

Guess what? He was still there, probably on the look-out for some other pretty boys to 'entertain' for the evening.

'Hello again. Hungry, I guess?' he quipped.

Even the normally calm and reasonable Stewart had lost his patience,

'Tell him to piss off, Paul. I know you can say that.'

Alastair didn't have to say a word: his face said it all.

'Er, hi. No, we have already eaten so we're about to leave the country. Very nice country but we have to go now,' I replied, again opting for the non-confrontational, tactful approach.

'You can't leave by train. No trains out of Zurich after 21:15. Let's see the city!'

'There must be a train somewhere,' said Stewart, somewhat confused.

'I will find out,' he offered, and slipped into the adjacent information office to fabricate evidence that could trap us for the night.

A couple of girls caught Alastair's infallible eye and in a split second he had formulated a plan and put it into action. He ran up to them.

'Are you English?' he asked.

'American.'

Talk about out of the frying pan . . .

'Listen, you probably won't believe this but there's a bloke in there trying to pick us up. Will you be our girlfriends for ten minutes or so?'

'You're right, I don't believe you — we won't, so get lost.'

There was something in the tone of her voice that told me the plan wasn't going to work. Maybe someone had tried the same approach before with less honourable motives — who knows? But despair would not be allowed to set in — the Mad Brothers were made of sterner stuff.

Alastair and I found ourselves facing each other: we turned to Stewart and a kind of telepathy took over, catalysed by the 'tour guide' who had been watching through the glass wall of the office. He had caught sight of us again and began to home in like a torpedo.

'It's *au revoir* time,' said Stewart.

Stew and Al moved off at a brisk pace, looking as if they knew where they were going, and I followed. We gave our over-hospitable friend the run-about for a few minutes until we lost him, finally pausing for breath by a timetable.

'Time, Paul?' asked Stewart.

'21:26.'

'Right! Platform eighteen; 21:35; Brussels. Let's go!'

He had taken charge of the situation so Alastair and I followed him dumbly. We didn't even pause to consider the wisdom of visiting Belgium; we were just happy to have found an escape route.

21:35 saw us leaving Zurich behind us and heading north. Stewart and Alastair were joking loudly about our escape from the cocoa-shunter but I was in my own little world again, saying a silent thank you to Mr Matthews, my German teacher back at high school. Perhaps, if he hadn't been such a good teacher, we may all have been changed men that evening. Nice one, Mr M, I thought.

humiliating ejaculation

Inter-Rail Rule 8: Skip Belgium.

Stewart

My first impressions of Belgium were of blissful blue skies, portrait quality landscapes and an overall feeling of well-being. And then I woke up.

What we saw was not necessarily worse than views from a train in any other country, but the aesthetic appeal of waking up in a Brussels suburb can only be compared with waking up in another Brussels suburb, which was not the best incentive to remain in the city. Concrete, dirt, dust and decay are my memories of that morning, and that's leaving out the bad ones.

But being liberal minded chaps we were prepared to give the city a chance. The first Brussels station was too shitty for words and didn't deserve a chance. So was the second, but we got off there anyway. From the platform I could see a street leading away from the station. It had run-down shops with broken neon lights, thick, impatient streams of traffic, and more dirt and dust. An American serviceman overheard our exclamations of general disapproval and volunteered to voice his own opinion of the place.

'I've been here a goddamn year,' he said, 'and it fucking sucks.'

Gosh, we thought, we'd better get out of here quick if there were Americans too. Having already fled Switzerland the night before we were now forced by events beyond our control, namely the uniform shittiness of the station, its surroundings and its passengers, to flee Belgium as well. As we had arrived in Belgium last night via France (and Luxembourg, which I missed entirely having bent down to tie my shoelaces as we passed through), it was now time to go to Germany.

The fortunate beneficiary of our initial foray into the land of sausage was to be Aachen, a place I remembered from the war films in which it was bombed a lot, for one reason or another. Then we took a smart train to Dusseldorf.

Shouting *'Nicht hinauslehnen!'* and doing Nazi salutes out of the train window at the guards is not the most sensible or indeed tactful thing to do in Germany, and I'm surprised that our immature antics didn't get us into any trouble, like starting another war. But our cowardice meant that we were always careful to pick a guard who was on a different platform when our train was about to leave.

Another pastime developed on the dull run from Aachen to Dusseldorf required access to the very back of the train, which in this case was just a widened space at the end of the corridor with a windowed door facing the retreating track. As the train pulled away from the smaller stations Paul and I would take turns in revealing certain unpleasantries at the bemused travellers on the platforms behind us. But it was not for this reason that we were thrown off the train.

German train timetables, we later found out, are covered with small symbols which we totally ignored. One of these referred to supplements payable on certain faster trains, and, of course, we were on one of those. When the fascist inspected our tickets he demanded a supplement of twenty Marks each. We pooled our foreign coin collections. All the Marks in the pile had been earned busking in places other than Germany, but even in their Fatherland they were useless for they came to fifty-seven, which wasn't enough. The only option we were given was to get off at the next stop. It was a civilised ejaculation, but nevertheless humiliating.

I looked up at the grand station, arched overhead with massive nineteenth century iron girders and panelled with dirty glass and felt glad I wasn't a German window cleaner. The sign said Koln, or Cologne, home of the famous odour.

Paul had a few old shilling coins, which are the same size as the German Mark. We found it difficult, however, to con any machine into accepting them. With increasing annoyance, Paul systematically tried each of the many vending machines on the platform, only achieving success with a locker. As a token of his disgust at the inadequacy of the situation (our next train was due in five minutes so we had no need of a locker) he took the locker key and put it in his pocket. In a few minutes it would be well on its way to somewhere where it would be of no use whatsoever. That would show them.

Five minutes later there was an *Untermensch* class train going in the same direction as the one from which we had been thrown, this one being better suited to our position of relative impoverishment.

Dusseldorf, when we finally arrived there on the slow train, afforded little inspiration. We looked dejectedly at the destinations board, not knowing where in Europe we wanted to go next. Head back home? Hit the East? Or back down south for a bit more sunburn. Sod it, we thought, let's defer decision until the next station.

We reboarded the same train that we had arrived on and jumped off again at Bremen. It was late afternoon and I still hadn't had lunch.

'Let's eat before we decide where to go,' I said.

'I've already decided,' decided Paul. 'We're going to find somewhere to eat.'

In the centre of Bremen was an old cobbled square, furnished with a variety of restaurants and cafés which we were too stingy to visit. Paul and I put our bottoms on a bench while Alastair ran over to a nearby bakery and bought some heavy, black German attempts at croissants, which we reluctantly ate in silence.

'My feet bloody ache,' moaned Paul, some time later, his fingers hovering tentatively over the stained laces, poised to unleash a Pandora's Box of unimaginable horrors upon us.

'What do you think you're doing?' cried Alastair.

'I'm going to take off my shoes.'

'What about the four minute warning?' I asked.

'You can't do it,' said Alastair. 'They've been on your feet since Vienna.'

'That's why I've got to take them off.'

He took them off, slowly, lingeringly. For a moment nothing happened, and then it hit us: a wall of nauseating odour slammed into our noses and clogged our nostrils, almost knocking us back off the seat with its power. This was what Inter-Rail was all about. This was what it smelt like. In the same way that those who never fought in the trenches can never know what it is to face living, breathing and eating mud as a prelude to getting shot, those who have never been Inter-Railing can never know what it is to live, breath and eat the odour of Inter-Rail feet. When it is difficult to find somewhere to wash there is little incentive to do so. When periods of sleep between trains can be as little as a couple of hours at a time, it is easier to stay fully dressed than to be caught wandering bleary-eyed around a platform in your underwear. The net result of these aspects of Inter-Railing — aspects which few potential adventurers anticipate — was that Paul had kept his shoes on for several days on the trot, and now the innocent town of Bremen was being made to pay for it.

Alastair and I made a break for it, charging across to the other side of the square where stood a twenty feet high statue of a chap called Roland, who was currently wrinkling his nose in disgust, his huge bronze shield affording no protection against ordnance such as this. Our luggage was left to its contaminated fate at the epicentre. Occasionally the odd whiff of what we had escaped from would grate by on the breeze, but from that distance it was diluted enough to be survivable. There was now no one in the square within a thirty feet radius of Paul and his little problem.

Paul scrambled around in his rucksack, dragged out and pulled on his other pair of Hi-Tecs, and hermetically sealed them around his feet. Then he seemed to be looking for something else, but paused to throw the old shoes some feet away from him. Then his hand plunged back into the rucksack and emerged with something shaped like a hand grenade. Good, I thought, he's going to blow them up. But all he did was to spray the offending items with his 'Lynx' de-rodent, then circled the air around him with the life-saving jet.

We courageously returned to the scene of the incident. Where the odours of Good and Evil met there was a thick, rotting stench in the air as if the battle for supremacy was still raging, and the de-rodent certainly did not have the upper hand.

Paul picked up the damp, glowing shoes by the extremities of the laces, vowing that his replacement shoes would not come off until we were on home soil. Then he told us to follow him back to the station.

'No way,' I said. 'You go behind us.'

'Well hurry up. Let's get out of Germany before they trace me.'

'It won't be hard while you're carrying those things,' Alastair observed.

We had never considered going to Scandinavia, but seeing Copenhagen on the list of destinations we thought it would be a safe haven from polluted Bremen. Paul tied his shoelaces to the window handles on the train, and dangled the shoes outside. Safe at last, I thought. But suddenly there was a whoosh of stench as the shoes flew back in again. Some considerate soul had noticed them from the platform and decided we ought to have them in the compartment with us. After much choking the shoes were shoved out again, and this time the window was secured firmly to prevent a repeat performance. Thus we were safe for the duration of the journey.

To our amazement, when it came to a necessary bit of island hopping from Puttgarden in Germany to Rodby Havn in Denmark the train was actually rolled onto the deck of the ferry, and there was no supplement to be paid. My first instinct was to shit in the train toilet, which would fall straight onto the deck. But we were up at the back end of the train from where the guard sensibly began systematically locking each toilet door. Besides which, I could not be that malicious against a nation that was cool enough to have once hosted a Sex Festival. However, someone at the front of the train succeeded in flushing their faeces onto the deck before the guard had reached his cubicle, and a little man had to sweep it up with a dustpan and brush.

We saved our substantial deposits until arrival at Copenhagen, where we were astonished to discover a purpose-built Inter-Rail Centre at the station, designed to keep scum like ourselves off the platform and away from offendable passengers.

the inter-rail centre

Stewart

No one had told us of the existence of the Inter-Rail Centre, and we hadn't bothered reading or carrying an Inter-Rail guide book, so it was a welcome surprise. We descended the steps in the middle of the station concourse, between the post office unit and a drinks stall, and down to the reception desk. Here we were asked to show our Inter-Rail tickets, offered a condom each, and pointed down another flight of stairs.

We found a room that resembled a school dinner hall, crammed with tables and chairs made of a wood that succumbed easily to the graffiti knife. There were about twenty Inter-Railers sitting around: some were cooking, some were eating, and some had finished eating and were inscribing their feelings about it in the wood.

Paul was not given a choice about taking a shower there, as we were not going to get on another train with him if he didn't freshen up. While Paul was washing a third of his body weight into the drains beneath Copenhagen I was reading the message board. There were scribbled notes in all languages, though a large proportion were in English.

Girls wanted — meet us in Athens station on the 4th, 1.00 for serious sunbathing and optional sex. Adrian of the Adriatic and Clive.

Sarah Jenkins — sorry we missed you. Catch you up in Madrid.

Warning — there's a bloody thief here. I just left my bag for two minutes while I went to the loo and some bastard nicked my wallet. So be careful — I'm bloody pissed off about it.

I left a message saying 'I love you' to a girl I had met briefly at a party earlier that summer who told me she would be going Inter-Railing at the same time as me.

'What's the point of that?' asked Alastair.

'This is Denmark. If she sees her name on a wall in a country she's never been to before, she'll be suitably shocked. And it's not signed.'

With Paul restored to as near humanity as was possible under the circumstances we turned left out of the station, crossed a large roundabout with some fancy statue thing in the middle and surrounded by important-looking buildings, and hit the high street.

Busking today was successful for twenty minutes, in a pedestrianized street in front of a clothes shop, until a lorry pulled up in front of us, almost flattening Alastair's hat. But the driver didn't mack us for making him walk a couple of extra feet between the lorry and the shop like an English driver would have done. He jumped down from his cab with a smile and started talking in English about guitars. He played in a band, he explained, and would we play a couple more songs for him? He was fascinated by the way in which we managed to simplify all the songs we played. I didn't realise we did simplify them so much, I explained, but he was convinced that most Beatles songs had not been written in the key of 'C'.

I was a little put-out by this revelation, and declared that enough was enough and that it was burger time. I faked an amiable farewell to the lorry driver and we buggered off to Burger King.

Paul

I decided that I liked Copenhagen. Its picturesque gardens and canals inspired me to take some arty photographs, ie photographs which did not feature one of us in the foreground, in blatant contravention of Alastair's golden rule of holiday snap taking.

The boys were busy busking but, due to the unwashable odours still emitted by my feet, they had decided that it would be better for business if I were not there to deter potential punters from parting with their cash. Also, we were feeling a bit guilty at the lack of real sight-seeing and culture consumption that we had undergone up to that point. Thus I was on a mission to take some photos which would give the impression that we had done something normal on at least one day of the trip. Our parents would be pleased by this, and would doubtless want to know what we thought of the Sistine Chapel and all that when we returned. I managed to find a nice statue of some geezer on a horse and a quaint bridge, both of which I took pictures, but the little mermaid must have popped off for a swim because I couldn't find her.

I returned to find the others packing up and declaring what a crap session it had been; only enough for another short visit to Burger King.

The merits of Burger King had failed to keep us in Copenhagen for any longer than it took us to eat ten cheeseburgers, for we set off once more for the station from which we would venture even deeper into the hitherto unexplored wilderness that was Scandinavia.

'Stockholm OK for you then?' Poo asked us both as we left the restaurant.

'No worries,' I replied.

We marched onwards to cross the road. Having performed our Green Cross Code to a satisfactory standard, we endeavoured to cross the not-very-busy-at-all road that was the last obstacle between us and the station. We had just made it to the other side when a violent hissing of air-brakes made us look round to see who or what had caused such a hasty halt. There was nothing to be seen — no bodies and no broken glass. Then there followed another hiss and a bus door opened and the driver came running out towards us. This made no immediate sense to any of us. The driver started ranting at us in what I assume was Danish. When he had ascertained that none of us had understood a single word he changed tack and continued ranting in English.

'You are foolish boys,' he scolded. 'You are breaking the law doing this.'

'What? Crossing the road?' I asked, incredulously.

'Crossing the road not on a pedestrian crossing,' he corrected. 'You must use them at all times. There is the nearest one,' he added, pointing at some very distant road markings.

'Oh, yeah,' retorted Alastair, sarcastically. 'Dream on, mate.'

The driver continued for long enough for us to learn that jaywalking is considered a serious offence in Denmark, but as we would soon be leaving and the realisation of our departure would not be dependent on crossing any more roads, we didn't worry too much about it. I would just like to know what his passengers thought about sitting, unattended, in their bus for five minutes while their driver went on a wild one with three foreign tourists.

On the platform I could tell we weren't the only ones planning to get to Stockholm. There was a dense crowd waiting for the train, and new tactics had to be developed to ensure that one of us was first aboard. The train carriages each had two doors, about thirty feet apart, and Sod's Law was likely to dictate that we three would be caught equidistant between the two doors, making us last on and least likely to find a seat. Stewart's solution has since been developed into,

Inter-Rail Rule 9: Spread members of your group along the platform as the train arrives to maximise the chances of one of you being closest to a door, and thus first aboard. This person can then reserve the required number of seats or a whole compartment, depending on their level of odour. Potential Inter-Railers may wish to note that Paul is available for hire.

The approach worked: one of the doors stopped just in front of me, and I only had to barge past a couple of other passengers to get into the carriage ahead of everyone and reserve a group of seats. The others took their seats with me five minutes later, while the standing passengers looked down at us malevolently.

The train to Stockholm was just too boring. At one point the boredom reached such a monumental level that we were forced to break out the emergency rations of tuna and salad cream. They coalesced in my enamel mug to form an amalgam that looked almost as bad as it tasted. Another high point of the journey was having a chat with a Swedish man who worked for Saab. I was quick to disengage my brain from this conversation but whatever was said must have had a significant effect on Alastair as he later bought three of them. This was all, still, far too boring. Sleep was definitely more fun, and I only awoke when Alastair poured the contents of his water bottle over me to inform me that once more a European capital city was about to be bestowed with the dubious honour of a visit from the Mad Brothers.

As we left the station, I was relieved to see that exploring Stockholm city centre held as much fascination for Stewart as exploring the interior of my Hi-Tecs would have done for anyone of sound mind and in possession of an operational sense of smell. Much to Alastair's contempt, we opted to sit on a bench on the banks of the Riddarfjarden, opposite the Stadshuset, tunelessly grinding out old ABBA songs with no musical accompaniment until we could sing no more. Alastair, who must have ingested too much tartrazine that day, seemingly with boundless reserves of energy ran off into the city to take some more arty photos to show our parents. None of them came out properly when they were finally developed so Poo and I had the last laugh.

Other than that, Stockholm had nothing more to offer us that night — or at least, we couldn't be bothered to get off our weary arses and look around Volvo-land for ourselves. Oslo, then, would be the next port of call.

Thus, it came to pass that the Mad Brothers would enter their third country in twenty four hours in their never-ending quest for something or other that they would find cool enough to write home about. At least the train that would take us to our next exciting destination was clean and actually had enough seating available for everyone.

Oslo

Stewart

Norwegians, we discovered, were hairy brutes with horns, rough skin and fish breath. The men were pretty rough-looking, too. We more or less stumbled from the station straight upon Karl Johans Gate which took us into the city. As Paul and I had not bothered to drag ourselves around Stockholm this was our first true taste of Scandinavia since Copenhagen the day before, and it felt good to be finally out in the open air.

We wanted to do some busking so that we would have some Norwegian currency, and soon found a pedestrianized part of the centre. There were no fountains or closed shops or backdrops of any kind to play in front of, so for the first time we set up in the middle of the street with people passing us on either side. We were pleasantly surprised to find that English buskers were something of a novelty in this part of Oslo, and there was soon a large crowd around us despite a mediocre and tired early-morning performance.

It wasn't easy to sing in the centre of the street because the sound dissipated quickly into the open space, and the circling crowd made us feel self-conscious. I remember my 'oohs' in *She Loves You* were a little wobblier than usual, but no one seemed to notice. Things appeared to be going well, it looked as if we were getting away with a lousy performance on grounds of pure novelty, and the money in the hat would at least pay for breakfast. But it was a while since we had been accosted by anyone mad, and a visit was due.

'Aaaaargh!' she said, by way of introduction.

We looked at her somewhat nervously, trying not to be angry that she had frightened away our audience. She was in her mid-thirties, reasonably well-dressed, and had long, fine brown hair that seemed well groomed. She stared at us for a few seconds before adding,

'Aaaaargh!' She seemed unhappy about something, but it was hard to tell exactly what. Maybe there was a knife in her back, or she hated Beatles songs? Whatever the reason we couldn't play while she stood shouting at us, so we fetched back the hat and began to pack up.

'Aaaaargh! Aaaaargh!'

'I quite agree,' said Paul, putting away his guitar. 'But I think full European integration is inevitable really once we sort out these little communication problems, don't you think?'

'Aaaaargh!'

'Yes, you've got a point. Do you do Esperanto as well?'

'I see the joke,' she added.

'Sorry?'

'I see the joke.'

'And which joke would that be?' I enquired.

'Maybe she doesn't like the song. I think we should change it,' Paul naively suggested. We could think of nothing better to do at the time and so adopted this as our only course of action.

'Something more appropriate maybe,' said Alastair. 'After three . . .'

'I . . . once had a girl . . . or should I say . . . she once had me?' we sang, hoping that this would appease the woman. It didn't.

'Aaaaargh! Aaaaargh!' She walked away, screaming at pigeons and lampposts and anything else that disagreed with her, and we walked in the opposite direction.

Further along the road was a smaller crowd, just three or four people looking at a painter's easel. He was sketching one of the older buildings in front of him, but it was a rather weird interpretation for someone of his advanced years. But then he was wearing a hat.

'Shit, what's that supposed to be?' I asked rhetorically, leaning over his shoulder.

'That,' he announced, 'is what the building used to look like. It was rebuilt in a different style.' His accent was perfect Oxford English, the revelation of which sent me cowering behind the others in shame.

'Are you English?' asked Alastair.

'I've been in Oslo for seventeen years now,' he told us, without a hint of the bloody-English-you-can't-escape-them-anywhere mentality in his voice. He was a real ex-patriate, and we were suitably impressed. 'Are you on your way to the palace?' he asked.

'What palace?' asked Alastair.

'It's just up the road. The Norwegian Royal Family.'

'I didn't know they had one,' I mumbled.

We bought a bag of food and took a picnic to Slotts Parken that overlooked the road down to the palace and the gardens. It was an unusually pleasant cultural experience for us, especially at that time of the morning, and our interest lasted a full five minutes before we itched to get travelling again. It was time to see some more of the country, especially the fjords.

I told the others about the fjords I had seen on the way into Oslo.

'Bollocks,' said Paul.

'There was a fjord Taunus, and a fjord Escort.'

'Ha bloody ha,' he chortled, greatly amused.

'Let's get out of here before he tells any more crappy jokes,' decided Alastair, obviously afraid for his ribs in the face of so much laughter. I couldn't think of an even worse joke with which to annoy him, so I shut up and scoffed a large amount of chocolate.

Having come as far as Oslo it seemed the only crazy option was to head even further into the wilderness. There was enough money left, mostly of Venetian origin, to keep us going through a few days without busking, so we bravely plunged into The Unknown.

The train whose twice daily destination was The Unknown, and a nice-sounding place called Flam in particular, had large red seats that swivelled around. We claimed a corner of the otherwise open-plan carriage as our own, and relaxed and let the beauty and ruggedness of the remoter parts of Norway pass us by like objects on Bruce's conveyor belt.

It was the first day of August and there wasn't much snow around. In fact I didn't see any. Some of the landscapes we passed through contained very little vegetation other than a few pine trees on the rocky slopes. For a few miles the railway followed the course of a river along the base of a valley, rather like the mountain railway from Nice to Annot, except, unlike France, the surrounding lands here looked as if they could support primitive life forms. My theory was confirmed when I spotted a hiker with an American flag on his rucksack.

To pass the time we sang songs, counted our money (which actually equated to less than we thought in Norwegian currency), and helped ourselves to water from the carafes kindly provided by Norwegian State Railways in each carriage. It took most of the carafes on the train to fill all of our water bottles, but we forgave NSB for that minor oversight.

The only major stop en route was a junction called Myrdal where the line split between Bergen and Flam, and we took the latter. The train finally stopped just in time to avoid dropping into the fjord, which presumably meant we had arrived at Flam. Looking out of the window I could see that Flam was actually a dead-end in the middle of nowhere. There wasn't even a station: everyone jumped off the train onto the ground. In front of us was a timber-framed hotel/restaurant/ souvenir shop/ticket office, into which most of our rather thirsty fellow travellers seemed to be headed. But it was early evening and we had to find somewhere to put up the tent.

The campsite was not exactly hard to find. The hotel/etc was on one side of the unfenced track, and a large field with a shed and a toilet block and some tents was on the other. We went in the opposite direction to our wealthier counterparts and spoke to the man in the shed. The bill for two nights in his field would have put us up comfortably in a French chateau for a week.

We picked one of the remoter corners of the field for our tent, well away from a party of French scouts who were no doubt wishing they had stayed in a chateau instead. With the tent almost complete a light drizzle began to set in, so we wrapped up in our warmer togs and set off in search of food and shelter.

The obvious 'choice' was the hotel, and I examined the menu while Alastair peered in through the misty window. The prices were staggering: three meals came to more than our original food budget for the entire trip. Alastair moaned with despair as a waitress walked past carrying a tray with the left-overs of a meal, the value of which would keep a Third World village in food for a week. Paul tried to restore his internal imbalance with a small lump of nasal residue, but still he was hungry.

'There's a couple more buildings along there,' he pointed. 'Maybe one of them sells food?'

The first building, again made of deeply varnished pine with a large overhang under which we sheltered briefly, was a bank, and was shut. It had no great culinary offerings.

Following the road by the waterside a little further past two houses and a tree, we found a pub with a balcony over the water and an adjacent jetty. It looked beautiful through the drizzle, its wooden protrusions reflecting vaguely on the water, and its menu board was only moderately expensive rather than exorbitant.

We gave our orders to the barman.

'I am sorry but it is not awailable tonight.'

'What isn't?' asked Paul.

'Ewerything,' he said.

'Is this a cheese shop?' mumbled Paul, obscurely. Alastair ordered a beer in compromise, so did Paul, and I asked for a coke.

'I am sorry, we are waiting for deliwery tomorrow.'

'For what?' I asked.

'Deliwery.'

'Well what have you got then?' asked Paul, exasperated.

The barman reached below the counter and produced three dusty bottles of a fruit juice that we had never heard of.

'It's on special offer,' he said.

We bought them, together with the last packet of peanuts on the shelf, and sat outside on the large wooden balcony. I could see the water gently rippling against the pillars below us through the gaps in the boards, but was in no way tempted to drop any precious peanuts through them. We were rather despondent with hunger and disappointed that our Italian riches were worth nothing in this country. The only conversation was about the notice fixed to the handrail that said in English, 'Boats for Hire'. This sounded fun, and the prices listed below came to much less than a meal for one, which we were not going to have anyway. Paul went in to ask the barman, but his expression on his return was no more cheerful than it had been before.

'The willagers have broken them all,' he said, sitting down and helping himself to the last peanut.

'The what?' we asked.

'The willagers.'

'Oh,' we said.

a mug full of dollars

Stewart

Waking up in Flam the next morning was one of the hungriest moments of the summer. It was as if we were at the remotest possible point from a McDonald's, and no pizza delivery service on Earth was going to send out a moped. The mist was heavy on the hillsides, but you couldn't eat it. The grass was lush and green around the tent, but you couldn't eat it. Even the hairy bar of soap in the shower block took on the appearance of a piece of cake, but we had to resist.

The morning train bringing the next load of tourists was due to arrive soon, and we prepared to greet it in our own special way.

'Well she was just seventeen, you know what I mean!' we yelled, jangling the guitars and generally jigging around in such a way as to make it clear that we were hungry and would accept a meal in the hotel instead of cash. We were standing adjacent to the train, between the two doors through which most of the people were exiting, as if we were an official welcoming band. But something must have gone wrong because we didn't earn anything at all.

That settled it. We were going by train on a day trip in search of food. There was a junction back at Myrdal — the line to Bergen had to be more promising. The train we were on went all the way back to Oslo, so we had to change at Myrdal. Unfortunately, the new train had come from Oslo and was completely full. We struggled through two or three carriages with our guitars before concluding that this journey would have to be made sitting on the floor, something which we hadn't expected to do in the civilised north.

The carriage had pairs of seats all facing forward to where we were sitting in the corner, below the shelf with the carafe of water. It wouldn't have taken an expert sociologist to ascertain the origin of our new companions. The preponderance of golfing trousers, chequered hats and enormous cameras nestling on blubbery stomachs gave the game away somewhat.

There is something uniquely fascinating about middle-aged Americans when they retire and travel the world. The uniform they are required to wear when abroad (so that, like schoolchildren, they will never get lost), is one of the most obscene apparel concoctions to be seen outside of Italy. For the men, regulation golfing trouser length is to a couple of inches above the ankle, in order to display the pink socks to their full effect. Their baseball caps must be worn backwards, and their cameras must be mounted at all times around the neck. For the women, the most fashionable green cotton trousers from 1974 must be worn, to remind them of when they had good taste. Make-up must be applied with a cement trowel in such a way that it will clash with the silver NASA anorak. Permitted phrases in general conversation include, 'Gee honey', 'Say that's real neat' and 'Can you get a hamburger here?'.

Other than these attributes, it was also obvious that they had rather a lot of money. But how best to make them want to give it to us? I knew that if the party of middle-aged tourists had been British they would steadfastly refuse to acknowledge our scruffy presence in their sanitised world, but that being American they would feel less inhibited if we started singing.

'If we start playing down here they'll ask us to stand up and sing, then we can pass round the hat and take all of their money,' I proposed, in hushed tones.

We quietly strummed a few chords, teasingly avoiding the winked eyes and hand gestures indicating that they wanted us to stand up and sing. Finally they could resist no longer and their tour guide came over and asked us to sing to them. Fully taken by surprise, of course, we agreed. After all, I thought, why bother to look out of the window at some of the world's most beautiful terrain when you could watch scruffy, hungry Inter-Railers thrashing their instruments at the front of the carriage?

The songs were extremely well-received, even though we tended to lose our rhythm when the train threw us off-balance around the corners. Then one of the old men stood up and took a paper cup from the dispenser next to the carafe of water, which he passed around the carriage collecting money for us. This was too easy! After only three songs the cup was returned to us brimming with dollar bills, about forty in all.

'Say, that's real neat,' said the old man, demonstrating to the others how to clap before returning to his seat.

We gave them a free song for their generosity.

'Gee honey,' said the man's wife, and then stopped because she couldn't think of anything else to say. 'Can you get a hamburger here?'

The train entered a long tunnel through the mountainside as we settled down once again, feeling rich. Once back in the daylight we were almost upon Bergen, where we said goodbye to our grateful benefactors.

Bergen was wet, rainy, damp, and cold, and a bit drizzly. And did I mention the interminable precipitation? Lucky I was wearing a hat, really, as I didn't have a coat.

'Nice day,' said Alastair.

'Shut up. Where's the bloody food?' snapped Paul.

It was lunchtime, late lunchtime, and we went first to a bar that looked as if it served food. We didn't even think about the money when ordering drinks, but when they came to more than ten quid for three we thought twice about eating there as well. There were some market stalls down by the harbour and some ordinary shops, so we strolled down the cobbled road, gazed shiveringly and unappreciatively at the boats from the quayside for a moment, then bought a mountain of junkfood from a supermarket. Picnics in the rain had never tasted so good, and there was still enough Norwegian money left to buy a postcard.

I imagined Viking warriors setting forth from the harbour at Bergen all those years ago. They would need to plunder and pillage all the villages in a county to be able to buy a round of drinks when they got back to their town, where they would be once more walled in on three sides by mountains and virtually cut-off from the world in cold isolation. No wonder they wanted to get away.

Back at Flam that night we were relieved to find our rucksacks where we left them, undisturbed in the tent. With a population of about two, the crime rate in Flam was obviously low, which was lucky considering the nearest police station was hours away, and we settled down to sleep with full stomachs and full pockets.

money runs out

Stewart

Our final morning in Flam was a warm, dry one. It was going to be a nice day, but we were due to spend the next thirty hours or so on trains from where we could not appreciate the weather. We had been isolated from the world for too long, and it was a long journey back to central Europe. There was just time for a quick game of strip-frisbee using a plastic plate and getting as far as boxer shorts before feeling rather stupid and deciding to get on with packing up the tent and walking over to the railway line.

Flam had been like a holiday within a holiday, a quiet, restful couple of days away from crowded stations and busy cities, and we were sufficiently recharged to tackle more of the continent. There is only so much natural beauty and poetry a mind can take, and so it became necessary to free ourselves from paradise and to slum it once more on dirty pavements. These offered no aesthetic appeal but were less taxing on the mind. In the cities you didn't need to keep saying to yourself 'fuck me what a lovely fjord/glacier/penguin'. You could be consistently critical of everything in sight and not have to feel bad about it.

Flam had been truly inspirational, but soon something anti-inspirational is needed to restore a mental balance that will enable one to continue to appreciate beauty. Beauty is nothing in the absence of ugliness, and we had to leave the countryside for that reason.

In other words we couldn't handle another day without a burger. Thousands of other Inter-Railers were still crawling all over Europe from burger bar to burger bar and we were beginning to feel a little left behind, missing out on the fun.

The only thing different about the journey back to Copenhagen was that it was a different journey, as it was not necessary to travel via Stockholm this time. This saved us half a day and meant that we were on the night train to Copenhagen that evening, travelling via Gothenburg.

Alastair spent rather a more pleasant night than did Paul and I on our patch of corridor floor. There were two utterly scrumptious Norwegian girls in one of the compartments, and Alastair somehow managed to worm his way in with them, from whence he mysteriously did not reappear until the morning, much to our chagrin. The only pleasure Paul and I had that evening was in managing to scrounge some cream-crackers from an Australian teacher who wasn't called Bruce. He was 'doing' Europe on his own with a packet of crackers. We were starving, of course, and in return for us promising not to sing to him he fed our hungry stomachs.

'Thanks Bruce,' said Paul.

Copenhagen and the welcome relief of the Inter-Rail Centre was upon us by lunchtime the next day. There were considerable crowds leaving the platform as we hopped from the train, and the escalator going up to the central concourse was full. However, the down escalator was empty. Alastair declared never-ending madness, took a deep breath, and ran up the down escalator complete with rucksack, hat and guitar, soon to be followed by Paul. I watched, more shocked than amused, as I waited my turn in the crowd. It looked as if they weren't going to make it when a face appeared at the top, but fortunately whoever it was did not mind being late for his train and was content to wait for the struggling Inter-Railers to complete their astounding feat. In the end I was only a few seconds behind the others, but they hadn't waited.

I found them sorting out their wash gear down in the Inter-Rail Centre, preparing to shower. I couldn't be bothered so I strolled into the other washing area to fill up my water bottle. This was my favourite room in the centre because it was usually full of semi-clad females. It was more or less the female toilets and washrooms, but the Danes are very liberal about such matters and don't go as far as to mention the fact on the always-open door.

Refreshed and unusually un-smelly we headed once more into the centre of Copenhagen for a bit of busking. This session, however, was not at all lucrative. The streets were busier than they had been before, and it was hard finding a place to play that didn't obstruct a shop. We counted our earnings and added both coins to what was left in the main kitty. It came to the grand total of not a lot. The cost of camping, eating and drinking in Norway for three days had used up nearly all our cash, and some burgers were needed fast if we were to think of a solution.

'We're broke guys,' said Paul, simply.

'Ob,' I said, because I had discovered it was Danish for tampon.

Only with the aid of the Burger King could we make plans that would radically re-structure the entire trip, according to the ideas that were brewing in our minds, so off we went.

Paul

As we sat on the plastic bench seats for the umpteenth time, again staring at the lonely-looking dills, we felt as if the whole restaurant was moving. It was truly weird that we should all be experiencing the same phenomenon simultaneously, but the thousands of miles of rail travel had begun to take their toll on us. When it was apparent that the problem had nothing to do with either the restaurant or the stability of the Earth, it occurred to me that this swaying feeling could be a symptom of permanent psychological damage, but thankfully my fears proved to be wrong, wibble wibble.

We had to face the fact that our time in Scandinavia had left us almost penniless: the Venetian bounty had run out, leaving us far below a desirable level of affluence. As we sat gazing at the middle of the table, wondering why the Danes were so frugal with their Krone this time, Stew and Al decided between themselves that we should return to lucrative Venice and earn some more cash to enable us to continue travelling in the manner to which we had become accustomed.

I, on the other hand, had completely taken leave of my senses. I had decided to return to Vienna to find Liesbeth.

'I'm going to Vienna!' I announced, in a way that momentarily silenced them both.

'Does the body rule the mind or does the mind rule the body?' asked Stew rhetorically. 'This surely proves conclusively that the John Thomas rules everything in Paul's case.'

Alastair was quick to agree with him,

'Don't be stupid, Paul. Vienna is a capital city, you don't know where Liesbeth is staying, you don't know where to find her and you don't even know if they are still in Vienna. They might have gone home.'

Something in Alastair's voice, however, lacked the conviction of Stewart's condemnation. This was almost certainly because Alastair was prone to falling in love and doing things of an equally foolish magnitude. But the boys could not change my mind. I was not fully aware of the chances of finding one Dutch tourist in a city of a few million people, but even the thought of having to sleep down-and-out alone in a Vienna station was not enough to deter me.

That evening we took a night train to Hamburg, but our paths diverged in the early hours of the morning and we arranged to meet up again at midday at Innsbruck station two days later. If for any reason this didn't happen we were to make our way home to England separately.

I watched the others disappear into the tangle of rails that passed as a rail junction without a care in the world. It was as if I had been sedated heavily enough to remove all fear of going into the unknown — a bit like all those spaced-out American servicemen in Vietnam. I was disappointed to note, however, that my train would not leave for another couple of hours. I nestled down among all my belongings on the station floor and tried to get some rest, but the subconscious fear of being knifed, robbed, or simply missing my train prevented me from falling fully asleep.

When the train finally came I was overjoyed to find that I seemed to be sharing it with only about ten other people. This struck me as a bit odd because Vienna was such a nice place. There is no logic in the world: I mean, why did so many people want to go to Venice when it is so expensive, restrictive and crap and only a handful want to go to Vienna? I was grateful, nonetheless, that I could spread out and relax for a change.

During the journey I woke occasionally to see the names of stations flashing by outside. Wurzburg, Wels . . . I didn't recognise any of them, but I was too knackered to care. In fact someone could have told me I was going to Brussels again and I wouldn't have bothered to get off until I had fully rested.

split up

Stewart

Getting back down to Venice was tricky after Munich. Having woken up on the floor of a carriage surrounded by stern-faced commuters trying to sit around us we got off the train only to find there were no scheduled trains to Venice. The only solution was to bodge it.

Inter-Rail Rule 10: Bodging. If the timetable at the station doesn't go where you want to go, just take any trains that seem to head vaguely in the right direction until you discover that you are further from your destination than you were before you started.

Bodging was a skill at which we became highly unproficient: we could probably get lost on a ghost train at a fun-fair if we tried. Getting to Venice on this occasion involved various little zig-zags through Austria and Italy. From Munich we headed to Innsbruck, from where there were still no suitable trains for the rest of that decade. So next we took one going to Bolzano, since it sounded quite Italian and was probably in the right direction.

The problem was that after several long delays on remote sections of mountain track we were told to get off on a station not far from Bolzano. The train driver had decided to stop there for the day as he had had enough, even though it was a couple of hours before the Verona connection. It was now late afternoon and the air was thick and sweaty and left mysterious sticky, damp residues on our shoulders and thighs.

The station was not large. It had two tracks, one ticket office, half a toilet, a Nestlé chocolate dispenser, and four armed guards. Just like any other rural Italian station. Some flies that had been happily buzzing around a pile of human excrement and tissues in the centre of the track suddenly rose up and flew, in a complex formation that would have inspired the Red Arrows to even greater acts of lunacy, to the more tempting odours on our bodies. My flailing arms whipped the rancid air like a berserk windmill, but the flies flew such an irregular course as to be unswattable.

I pulled a bar of chocolate from my rucksack, but it flopped limply under its own weight and began to ooze out of the corners of the wrapper. I put it back for future consumption in a colder climate.

Alastair and I trotted up and down the platform, sheltering among the various inadequate patches of shade, and checking the timetable to see if there was an earlier train out of there. There was none, of course, and we were having second thoughts about the wisdom of the entire capitalistic venture.

At 18:02 hours precisely the Verona train pulled in. There were no completely empty compartments, so we picked at random one which contained two very old men. They greeted us in their native tongue, but we, wishing to avoid any kind of rapport with the stale-smelling gentlemen, simply grunted that we were English, which shut them up for a little bit.

Suddenly they spoke to each other disturbingly fast in Italian, then stopped. The train was still motionless, to allow the driver time to finish his cigarette. One of the old men slowly turned his wrinkled neck, as if being careful not to crack it under the strain, to look out of the window. Upon spying one of the policemen standing menacingly in front of the chocolate dispenser as if daring someone to make his day, the old man nudged his friend, spoke with great volume and rapidity, and the two of them broke into a strain of deep, haughty laughter. We could not help looking bemused, so one of them tried to explain using the English he had picked up when he changed sides in the war.

'That policeman,' he said, 'I can remember yes my father. He beat very hard for, I zink, take off his clothes. After church. He was no then policeman.'

After that fascinating revelation I took out my water bottle for a drink, but then thought I ought to offer it around now that the ice had been broken. To my considerable disappointment the old men gladly accepted it, took their fill, and passed the bottle back lightly dribbled with sticky saliva. Despite my own thirst I put it away without taking a drop.

We waited for them to say something more about the policeman, but they seemed to have switched off their brains and were sat smiling in silent contemplation of their earlier amusement, as if it were entirely sufficient for a day's excitement. Some commands were barked on the platform, salutes given, whistles blown, and the train began to carry us and the grinning zombies on to Verona, from where there had to be a Venice train.

We spent another couple of hours on the Verona platform. There was a concrete overhang above the ticket office, with a small ledge.

'That's Juliet's balcony,' I told Alastair.

'Oh,' he said. 'Who's Juliet?'

We toyed with the idea of trekking briefly into town and catching a glimpse of the Roman amphitheatre and the real balcony, but as I had already seen them on a previous trip, Alastair was content to let me describe them to him, which involved much less effort.

'The Roman amphi-theatre is bloody big, and it's pretty old too,' I said.

'Oh,' he said, satisfied.

We were eventually able to depart from this cultural stopover and head to Venice.

Paul

I was woken by the friendly shout of,

'*Ausweis bitte!*'

Oh shit, I remember thinking, I'm still in Germany. But then my brain woke up to join the rest of my body and reminded me that they also speak German in Austria. I fumbled about and eventually found my passport and handed it to him. As usual he didn't actually want to see it to check that it was mine: simply holding up a piece of black card is enough for most border guards.

'*Wann kommen wir in Wien Bahnhof an?*' I asked him, knowing that my grammar was wrong but confident that he would understand.

'*Drei stunden.*' This was good news, almost too good. I gathered my things together and looked out of the window to see if I recognised any of the surrounding countryside. Needless to say I didn't, but I was full of enthusiasm at the prospect of finding Liesbeth again. It was only later that I realised that I had asked a border guard something that I should have asked a ticket inspector, and was relieved therefore to discover that the phrase 'Not my job, mate' has no foreign equivalent.

I strode purposefully out of Westbahnhof as if I had lived in Vienna for all my life and started to find my way towards the tram stop. Suddenly I was aware that someone was following me and trying to catch up. I stopped dead and spun around to face my pursuer, expecting to see a six foot meat-head. The only person within ten feet of me, though, was a small, frail-looking man in his mid-thirties.

'Do you speak English?' asked the man in an undisguisable west coast American accent.

'Yeah, pretty fluently,' I replied, foolishly, as I didn't really want to talk to him at all.

'Oh great! You are English. This is just fantastic. What's your name?'

I looked him up and down with an air of contempt that I hoped would be obvious enough for him to realise that I didn't want anything to do with him. Unfortunately this didn't work and after an embarrassing silence I had to answer him.

'Paul,' I replied, keeping things as curt as possible to enhance my chances of being rid of him. He proffered me his hand.

'I'm Gary.' His hand felt like a wet dishcloth, and he was dressed in a two piece hessian outfit with open-toe sandals. 'Do you know the city at all?'

'No. Never been here in my life,' I lied, hoping that at any time I would say the right thing and he would wander off somewhere else.

'We can explore Vienna together then. I'm going to Stefansplatz. Do you want to come with me?'

Of course I didn't, but Stefansplatz was exactly where I wanted to go so I decided to let him tag along. Being a typical example of his genre he was constantly talking and taking no notice of anything that wasn't directly to do with him. From his monologue I managed to glean that he lived in San Francisco (which was enough to confirm my suspicions that his name did not really contain the letter 'R' at all) and that he didn't have a house — he lived in a van on the edge of a park, did yoga in the morning and didn't have a job as such. He just 'bought and sold shares, man', didn't eat meat and lived mainly on yoghurt. What a wanker.

Suddenly I had a brainstorm of such staggering brilliance that I had to check I had not plagiarised it from Stew or Alastair.

'I think that's the tram we want,' I said, pointing to the tram that orbits the city day and night. We boarded it and started our circumnavigation of Vienna. We must have circled the city twice without Gary noticing that anything was amiss. Then my plan started to work: he fell asleep, his head resting on the window, completely oblivious to anything around him (nothing new there). I saw this as my opportunity to escape. At the next stop I jumped off, leaving my new found 'friend' asleep on the tram. It was not long before I found an entrance to the Vienna underground and caught a train to Stefansplatz.

I surfaced from the underground full of confidence that I would soon find someone who would know where I could find Liesbeth. I looked around for Daniel, supposing that as he was a professional busker he would be out on the streets earning money, but to my dismay I could not find any trace of him. Stranger still, there was no sign of Vienna's resident professional madman, Waluliso.

I began to worry. Well, there was still Robert Krisch to try so I made my way to a phone box where I was surprised to note that I still had enough change left over from my last Austrian visit to make a phone call. I called AEG and asked to speak to him, but the receptionist informed me that there was no one called Robert Krisch working for them nor had there ever been.

I gave up worrying and began to panic.

Stewart

By the time we arrived in Venice we had been travelling for twenty-four hours since Copenhagen. It was late evening, and the only tourists around were those who had finished eating and were taking a stroll around the streets looking for buskers. We were only too happy to oblige.

We played a few of our quieter songs — *Yesterday, Here There and Everywhere*, and *El Condor Pasa* in a fairly large square where people were milling around the central fountain. Midnight was approaching so we didn't want to wake any of the neighbours by doing our usual rocky stuff, but equally it was hard to get much attention without making any noise. A few Lire notes fluttered their way into the hat, but the sound of chinking coins certainly wouldn't have disturbed anyone.

'Issa good,' said a voice. I looked to my right to see a man leaning against the fountain. 'You must, eh, sing, *She Love You*, you know?'

He was a small man, oddly dressed in a light-coloured suit and carrying a white boater and a small daysack. He reminded me of Ford Prefect, only a little more strange. And he was so drunk he could barely stand.

'It's too late,' I objected. 'People are sleeping.'

But he could not understand much and remained insistent, and we remained reluctant. Finally he produced some money, stressing that it was just for one song. What the hell, I thought, we can always get out of here afterwards.

So we sang *She Loves You*, leaving out the latter half of the song, confident that he was too drunk to notice. He gave us the money and started demanding more music.

'Play, play, everyone wanta you play,' he sang.

We put our guitars away, and he changed his tune.

'You like cheese?' he asked, delving into his bag and producing some small pieces of soft cheese.

'Thank you,' we said.

'You want drink something?' he asked, ushering us drunkenly out of the square.

We did need a drink, and decided to let him buy us one before we made our great escape. He took us to a fast food place, one that we had inadvertently missed on our previous visit. Two cokes later on our part, and several beers from his daysack later on his part, we tried to say goodbye. It was not at all apparent why he wanted to keep giving us things, or what his motive might be. He didn't appear to be interested in the contents of our trousers — though things may well have been different had Paul been with us — and he didn't want our money, so what could it be? Could it be that he was just drunk enough genuinely to want to hear us sing and to reward us? I had never met anyone that drunk before.

By this point he was too far gone to be able to remember any more English words. Every sentence now took about five minutes to form, and seemed to contain more Italian than anything else. We thanked him sincerely, sat him on the steps of a bridge to stop him falling over, and finally made our escape. It was now one in the morning, and we had forgotten that it would be necessary to find somewhere to spend the night.

I had an idea. I remembered that on a remote corner of Venice there was a park. There were certainly no campsites, except on the Lido which was a little too far to swim with so much luggage. So the park it had to be, and we walked from St Mark's Square past the Bridge of Sighs and along the coastal edge until we were further and further away from the populated streets and pavements.

Leaning on the handrail of a bridge close to the park was a girl, looking rather lonely. She was a blonde eighteen year old from Sweden. Her name was Hannah, and she had been left on her own by her friends who had gone off to spend the night with American soldiers. Being gentlemen, we were too considerate to leave her to her fate in the dark, so we let her sleep with us.

The park consisted of a couple of acres of grass interspersed with a few trees here and there. The trees threw dark shadows over most of the land, and it was not the sort of place through which you would normally send anyone after dark without the protection of a Sherman Tank or two. But as it was illegal to lie down in any part of Venice except a hotel bed, and as the legal problems were only relevant where there were police to enforce them, the only possible place for people like us to sleep was the park.

Hannah pointed at a dark bulk that looked like a small hillock next to a tree and told us it was her friend lying with the soldier.

'He was so drunk he couldn't walk,' she said. 'We had to carry him there.'

'Where's your other friend?' I asked.

'They went to sleep at the station. It is safer there she says.'

'You'll be alright here with us,' said Alastair.

'Yeah, it's miles back to the station and they'll only arrest you for being homo sapien or something anyway,' I said.

We picked a patch of ground at the base of a tree some yards from her friend and the soldier, tied our rucksacks to each other and to the tree, then crawled into our sleeping bags and lay with Hannah between us. Other than the odd shadow of a person moving through the park things were fairly quiet and we went to sleep, unaware that some of the dark shadows were moving rather close to us.

Paul

I had at least expected to be able to find someone in Vienna that I knew, but this total absence of any friendly Austrians had taken me completely by surprise and for the first time I began to realise the extent of my folly. I desperately wracked my brains to think of an alternative plan as I couldn't even remember Daniel's address. After all, capital cities tend to look the same after you've visited so many.

The only possible alternative occurred to me: I'd have to go and see Reinhard. How would he take it? I'd only known him for a couple of hours and really I was only a friend of a friend. Well, I'd just have to risk it. I had no alternative. I found 'Klepp' where he worked and gingerly made my way to the basement where the sports department was. The moment he saw me he recognised me and I could tell by the look on his face that he wasn't displeased to see me.

'You have come to look for Liesbeth, yes?'

I was surprised by his perception and wondered why, if his brain worked so well, he was selling tennis rackets and skateboards.

'That's right,' I replied, seeing no reason to lie to him.

'Where have you come from?' he asked.

'Scandinavia.'

'Where are you staying tonight?'

For some reason I felt at ease with Reinhard, and although I accepted that I had a tendency to attract homosexuals when I was abroad, Reinhard was not one of them.

'Well, to tell the truth I hadn't really thought about it. I'm kind of in love, you know.'

'My girlfriend's in Oberosterreich so you can stay at my place if you want.'

What an angel, I thought.

'I'd love to. Are you sure that's alright?'

'*Aber naturlich*.'

I loitered in the shop, zooming around the sports department on little BMX-type scooters and prodding mannequins with a baseball bat, until he finished work. We then both caught the train back to Floridsdorf, the suburb where he lived. Reinhard turned out to be the perfect host. He let me have a shower, then decided my clothes were too disgusting to wear out for a night on the town and lent me some of his.

'How much money have you got?' he asked me.

'About a hundred and fifty Schillings,' I replied, firmly believing that this would be enough for a couple of beers.

'We will go to a restaurant tonight,' he declared, 'and I will pay.' He was adamant about this and I was definitely not going to argue with him. We ended up going to a pasta restaurant in the city centre where we sat at a table on the pavement taking in the warm evening air.

'So what are you going to do about Liesbeth? This is a big city.' He wasn't wrong there. It was then that I realised what a fool I'd been trying to find a foreign tourist in Vienna.

'I don't really think I've got any chance of finding her,' I replied, honestly.

'You need some sleep, my friend.' Again he was completely correct. 'I have to go to work tomorrow but you can sleep as long as you want and then drop the keys off to me at Klepp when you wake up.' I was astounded by his trust.

After the restaurant Reinhard took me to one of his favourite haunts, a bar that sold three hundred and sixty five different brands of beer.

'Cor, one for every day of the year,' I commented, before realising that everyone probably said that. To my retrospective embarrassment, I plebbishly ordered a bottle of Guinness before moving on to more traditional Austrian brews as recommended by Reinhard.

'We can stay here all night if you want,' said Reinhard.

It was a tempting offer and I felt I should take it up as one can't do that sort of thing back in England, but I was just too tired.

On the way home we saw Gary sitting on a bench in the city centre, eating a suspicious-looking sausage.

'You found somewhere to stay, then?' he asked, somewhat rhetorically.

'Yes thanks. What's that?' I asked, pointing to the steaming chunk of wurst in his hands. 'I thought you were a vegetarian.'

'It was the only thing I could afford. I'm sleeping in the station tonight. It will be cold I'm sure.'

'Yeah, it probably will,' I replied, forgetting to mention that the station was shut between three and six in the morning. 'Never mind, eh? Catch you later.' I walked away from the pathetic-looking man shivering on the bench and, by so doing, introduced myself to a genuinely new experience: feeling sorry for an American. Still, it was every man for himself as far as I was concerned, and for once in my life I had come out on top.

I eventually settled down on Reinhard's floor, for once confident and reassured by the fact that I would not be woken by a border guard, ticket inspector or anyone else for that matter. Bliss, I thought, as I drifted off into some well-earned sleep.

under arrest

Stewart

A gentle nudging woke me at about four in the morning. It was still dark and I took some moments to appreciate that I was in a public park in Venice. I looked up and saw Hannah trying to wake Alastair as well. Some figures were walking away from us.

'What's going on?' I asked her.

'My friend has been robbed. Someone slashed her sleeping bag with a knife while she slept and they took her money and passport.'

'What about the soldier? Surely no one would come up to her with him there?'

'He was so drunk he slept through it,' she said.

'Shit, that's really heavy,' I observed.

She had given up trying to wake Alastair by now, and was carefully hiding her valuables around her person.

'Where are they going?' I asked.

'To the station. It will be safer there. There are more police.'

'Do I detect a contradiction there?' I asked, sarcastically. To my surprise she laughed and said that I was probably right. I was beginning to feel that everyone from northern Europe spoke fluent English these days, and felt extremely ignorant of foreign languages myself.

The problem now lay in deciding whether to stay in what was obviously a dangerous place or to walk the couple of miles back to the station. Since the latter would inevitably mean carrying the dormant Alastair all the way only to get arrested for wearing odd socks or something when we got there we decided we might as well stay put. It was a pity that I felt it necessary to lie awake until daylight, peering into the shadows with my pocket knife in my hand, and making noises to deter anyone who came close by from thinking we were asleep and therefore easy targets. But the Venetian police were obviously more concerned with making sure people kept their shoes on in public than with protecting people at night.

Thankfully I didn't need to use the knife, except to cut the string that bound our rucksacks together. Never had I been so relieved to see the dawn (not that I had seen many), for with light came safety as the frightening shadows melted into harmless branches and bushes.

Alastair found it hard to believe what had gone on when he finally opened his eyes and wondered why I was so tired when he had slept so well. Hannah thanked us for looking after her but said she ought to get to her friends at the station now, so after the obligatory address-swapping we parted company and went back into central Venice in search of a fortune.

We spent most of what we had earned the previous night on a modest breakfast of yukky rolls and orange juice, then found a narrow street with an alcove into which we fitted quite nicely. A couple of shops opposite were opening up for the morning, selling crafts and bracelets and loads of other shit. The owners seemed quite intrigued by us, but there was no sense of any animosity so we felt perfectly safe.

Almost three songs and a measly few thousand Lire later two policewomen arrived. I smiled at them in my usual tactful way, and even when they demanded 'Passports!' I thought they were just checking routinely. But they didn't offer them back to us. Odd, I thought.

'Follow please,' said one of them, sternly, while the other helped herself to the hat and all its money.

Normally Alastair would have been only too happy to follow young women at their request, but their manners sent him into an explosive mode.

'What the bloody hell kind of country is this?' he exploded, explosively. I ducked the fall-out, then tried to defuse the situation. Aggravating the fascists was not going to help matters, and I told him to shut up and calm down. Putting on my diplomat's smile again I said we would follow them and was there any problem? Yes, we were the problem, it seemed.

Alastair calmed down when I explained that all that had happened was that we had come from Denmark to Venice to earn a fortune, nearly got mugged in the night, hardly earned a thing, been arrested, and what money we had was confiscated. That was all. Nothing to get uptight about, of course. I didn't mention my worry that we were headed towards the dungeon in the Doge's Palace, off St Mark's Square. This fear was unfounded anyway, since it was a different police dungeon that just happened to be next door to the medieval one.

Shortly before we arrived, however, one of the women began to realise from our whimperings that we were basically harmless tourists, albeit disguised as penniless tramps, and that perhaps we had a little more right to our money than she did. With this she handed back two-thirds of the money in the hat, indicating that she had to show something to her boss because rules were rules, especially in Venice.

Inside the police station was the classic police chief, a fat greasy Mussolini slouched behind a big old desk that was covered with urgent papers which he was busy ignoring. After a brief introduction from one of the women, he stood up and ranted at us for a couple of minutes. The sweat from his brow dripped distractingly onto the papers on his desk as his tirade reached its climax. His panting breath could have earned him a fortune had he chosen a career in telephone sex services, rather than harassing innocent visitors to his odd city.

His speech was translated roughly by the three of them as,

'You cannot play in Venice without a licence.'

'Can we have a licence, then, please?' we asked.

'No,' they said, continuing with, 'we can fine you eight hundred thousand Lire for playing without a licence.'

We put on sheepish looks and told them that we needed what little money we had to get back to England and that we would be leaving Italy immediately. By now the policewomen realised that there were much more deserving cases of their intimidation than us and started to plead with the old bastard on our behalves. He finally wrote down our passport details.

Oh good, we thought, we're being deported from Italy. Cool!

However, that was not to be, and he gave back the few Lire that were left in the hat and sent us on our humbled way.

'Where shall we busk now?' asked Alastair as we stepped out into the make-believe world of a tourist-friendly Venice.

'What? You can't be serious?'

'We'll be alright on the other side of Venice. We've come all this way, we might as well get a bit of cash before we go.'

'No way,' I objected. 'They'll crucify us if they catch us again. It's not worth the risk. How could we pay a four hundred quid fine?'

'By busking.'

'I think not,' I said.

We settled on a pizza in commiseration, then headed back to the station for the depressing retreat in the face of defeat at the hands of the Italian authorities.

Paul

I woke up to find myself staring up at a high ceiling and not a baggage rack for once, and then remembered that the reason for this was that Reinhard's house was not a train. I looked around and saw that I was alone. Reinhard really must have trusted me. What was the time? It was only 10:15, and this surprised me considerably as the night before I had felt so knackered that I thought I would sleep for a week.

I collected my things, had a cursory wash (not wanting to get used to a level of hygiene that I would not be able to enjoy on a regular basis once I was back 'on the open rail' as they don't say in Inter-Railing circles), let myself out of the flat and caught the train back into Vienna city centre.

Well, I thought, at least it could never be said that I didn't try to find Liesbeth. I pondered what I would do for the next twenty-two hours until I had to meet the boys in Innsbruck. Nothing sprang to mind. I walked along Karntnerstrasse as slowly as I could to maximise the amount of time that I was spending doing something useful as I knew that it would only be a matter of minutes before I would find myself alone and bored in a railway station, pathetically trying to hurry the hour hand around the clock face using the power of my mind. Then, in the distance, I managed to pick out among the throng of tourists two blonde girls walking the same way as me. Engine room, ahead full!

The chances of the two girls being Liesbeth and Ans were astronomically low, but I had to be sure. After all, I had come through several countries to look for them. As I drew closer my heart started to pound fiercely within me, accompanied by some activity in the bowel department, to the extent that I thought it must be audible to the other shoppers. I feared my heart might muscle-up to my rib-cage and try to break its way out, but no one took any notice of me. (The anonymity of bassism — Stew.)

I caught up with the girls, double-checked just to make absolutely sure that I wasn't hallucinating, took off my hat and plonked it firmly onto Liesbeth's head. She panicked for a minute, thinking that she was being assaulted by some kind of dirty old man, which wasn't the effect I had in mind, but upon seeing that it was just me she relaxed and smiled at me with a perfect row of teeth as if she was auditioning for a toothpaste advertisement. She didn't seem as surprised to see me as I was to see her, but the reason for this became apparent later on.

We proceeded as a trio to Klepp where we met Reinhard. He was finishing work early that day, and so we all went to a café off Stefansplatz and had a drink together.

It transpired that as soon as I had fallen asleep the previous night, Reinhard had got on the phone and called all his friends until he had ascertained where Liesbeth and Ans were staying and had arranged for them to meet me at midday at Klepp. Unfortunately I had woken up a bit earlier than anyone had anticipated, and had therefore spoilt the surprise to a certain degree, but no one seemed to mind — least of all me. I've no idea how much of a phone bill Reinhard ran up that evening or how much sleep he deprived himself of, but I know I owe him a gigantic favour and if I ever meet him again I fully intend to repay him.

That evening Reinhard and I caught another train to the village where the girls were staying — a small place called Gumpoldskirchen (obviously named by someone with a sense of humour). Reinhard took me to a wine bar and again insisted on paying for everything. Despite the fact that I am an uncultured pleb and hence do not drink wine, a thoroughly enjoyable evening was had by all as I sat gazing wide-eyed at Liesbeth across the table.

Some kind of itinerant photographer visited all the tables in the bar taking photographs of each of us. He later reappeared with the pictures set in tacky keyrings. Reinhard had evidently decided that he had no further use for money and that he should get rid of it all as soon as possible and thus bought all four of them, donating the two of Liesbeth and Ans to me.

At the end of the evening we said our fond farewells (sob, sob!), promising to keep in touch as I prepared to find my way back to Innsbruck. Needless to say, Reinhard wouldn't hear of it and insisted that I spent another night at his flat to continue the rest and recuperation programme that I was enjoying at his expense. I didn't refuse, ob.

As I drifted off to sleep again I thought that Reinhard deserved a medal from the Austrian government for hospitality above and beyond the call of duty. Reinhard Weber: Austrian Ambassador of the year.

Stewart

We tactfully avoided being water-cannoned this time by taking the first train out of Venice, which seemed the most sensible way of evading incarceration. We were fortunate in that it was going to Mestre, which was directly north, but unfortunate in that it was full of Inter-Railers except for, mysteriously, one carriage.

'Bugger this,' I said, unwittingly climbing into the first class carriage, and helping myself to an empty compartment.

'Why is no one else here?' asked Alastair.

'They'll be along soon,' I replied, as the train began to move.

The guard didn't arrive until we had passed the enormity of Venice station, crossed the railway bridge, and we were drawing level with the grotty industrial area on the mainland. The moment he saw us he knew we were not first class material, our having been to a state school marking us forever with an air of normality. Sort of.

He glanced at our second class tickets and pointed at the silver figure '1' painted back to front on the window. So what? I thought, looking at the compartment. It only differed from second class in that it had little white tea-towels hung over the head-rests to cover the dandruff, and the reading lights weren't broken. The rest of the train was full, there were no first class passengers, and these seats were empty. The logical conclusion of which was that we had to go and sit on the floor outside a toilet in the next carriage, getting dripped on by people as they came out of it. This pissed me off enough to make me scribble 'Out of Order' on a piece of paper and affix it to the door. Problem solved. So remember,

Inter-Rail Rule 11: Always carry a black pen, paper, and some gaffa tape. If you are forced to sit or sleep by the toilet door in a train carriage, write 'Out of Order', '*En Panne*' or whatever on the paper and stick it to the door. This is guaranteed to stop people treading on you or asking you to move out of the way, but it might not prevent them urinating on you.

There was another day before we had to meet Paul, assuming, by some miracle, that the rendezvous would actually take place as planned, but we weren't going to bother travelling to Rome and back to fill out the time. It was imperative to get out of Italy before we were summoned before Il Duce and ordered to grow a moustache, and if avoiding that meant waiting in Innsbruck for a day then that was what we would do.

The train carried on from Mestre in roughly the right direction, then, bodging the route slightly, we crossed the border at last into a civilised domain. I sighed deeply and felt the tenseness seep from my body, enjoying the relief afforded by German language advertisements by the trackside and the sight of cars that were being driven by people who had passed some kind of driving test. There had been some lengthy delays on this journey, the resultant boredom of which drove us to sleep.

Hours later, a guard gently woke us to inspect our tickets. We handed them over, little realising where we were. He stared at the name 'Innsbruck' and thought for a moment.

'This train to Innsbruck goes not,' he explained. The day had swept by, and so had Innsbruck. 'You can turn back at Worgl,' he added.

We wrote the name 'Worgl' into our Inter-Rail tickets and waited. The station popped up twenty minutes further up the line, and off we jumped. It was getting on for early evening and there was some urgency in getting back to Innsbruck before nightfall in order to find a suitable field or wood in which to camp.

'There's the platform,' I said, spotting a train opposite that seemed to be pointing back to Innsbruck. There were two other tracks as well, but they were unpopulated. I dragged Alastair down through the subway and up onto the platform with the waiting train.

'Shouldn't we check the timetable first?' he asked, sensibly.

'No, there's no time. It's obviously the right one and they're about to leave,' I replied, stupidly. No sooner were we aboard when the train pulled away.

'But how do you know it's going to Innsbruck?' he repeated.

'It's going back down the line we've just come from. It's bloody obvious. Trust me.' Those last words were for my own benefit, as it began to dawn on me that I might have been a little hasty. There was no one in the compartment to ask, so we sat back and waited.

My gut reaction that this wasn't the right train swelled a little as the train began to veer round a bend that hadn't been there on the way up, and developed into a fully blown treacle tart when I saw the points some distance behind us.

'Phew!' said Alastair, opening the window a little further. 'You don't half express your guilt in funny ways.'

'Alright, so the train driver knows a short-cut to Innsbruck. What's the problem?'

'We'd better ask the guard,' said Alastair.

Again the guard was friendly and sympathetic to our navigational inadequacies. Having established that this was by no means the way to Innsbruck he wrote down the name of the next stop, a mere forty-five minutes away. Looking through that Inter-Rail ticket now, his entry is still illegible: it starts with 'Sch', followed by a long squiggle. This jolly, though practically illiterate guard, also wrote in the return journey from Sch-something to Innsbruck, so I have no record of the place in my own handwriting. I have also failed to trace the place on my European map, which isn't surprising as it would have made Flam look like a sprawling metropolis. As soon as we got off the train I went to check the timetable for the next train out of there. No one else had left the train with us, and no one boarded it. And looking at the timetable I could see why.

'I'm really sorry,' I said. 'It's all my fault.'

'Yes it is,' said Alastair, double-checking what I had already double-checked.

'Where are we going to sleep?' I wondered.

We walked out of the station and wandered a little way along the lane in search of somewhere suitable. I had an idea that a corner of a field would provide adequate shelter, but all the fields here sloped upwards to the farms and there were no hedges. We didn't fancy the idea of waking up at the wrong end of a farmer's shotgun. With no other shelter within easy hiking distance, we elected to return to the quietness of the station and sit in a corner behind the lockers.

There was just enough room here to lie out, so, tied to our rucksacks for security, we prepared to spend the night.

reunion

Paul

Reinhard woke me up with a cup of steaming coffee.

Clearing the crud from my eyes I asked him what the time was.

'We must leave in fifteen minutes if you are to get to Westbahnhof on time.' This was not what I wanted to hear and had I known him a bit better I would probably have ignored him and got up in my own time, but sadly today that course of inaction was not an option. I drank the coffee, not having the heart to say that I would have liked a couple of pounds of sugar in it too. Reinhard helped me to collect my things and showed me to the door.

'See you then,' I croaked. 'Thanks for everything, man. I'll write.'

'Hey, I'm coming with you to the station. You are my guest. We look after our guests in Austria.'

I wished the same thing could be said of England. The difference lay in that Reinhard wanted to escort me there and that he wasn't just saying it because he felt obliged. Then again he wasn't English.

The train we took from Floridsdorf to Westbahnhof shook, rattled, and vibrated in a very British sort of way. Every passing of a set of points was accompanied by a painful jarring of the spine. Though the side-effects of Inter-Railing had caught up with me again I tried not to let my discomfort show as I knew that Reinhard would probably start needlessly apologising for the uneven ride quality of Austrian trains.

When we arrived at Westbahnhof, it became apparent that Reinhard had again been hard at work with his phone the night before by the fact that Liesbeth and Ans turned up to see me off as well. And at 06:45 too. How sweet, I thought.

With characteristic Teutonic efficiency the Innsbruck train pulled out of Westbahnhof exactly on time with Reinhard and the two girls jogging alongside it and me hanging out of a window shouting last minute farewells. Eventually they could no longer keep up and with a final wave I slumped back into my seat. Within a few seconds of losing sight of them, the full extent of Reinhard's generosity became apparent to me and I had to try hard to choke back a tear. Inter-Railers are big and clever, however, and they definitely don't cry.

It's a good job that today is Saturday, I thought — no rush hour. Be that as it may, I was prepared to take all precautions to ensure that I had as much space as possible. I spread my crap about the compartment to cover as much potential seating area as possible before getting out the photo-keyring of Liesbeth and gazing at it dementedly until I fell asleep.

The jolt of coming to a standstill at another anonymous station woke me just in time to make myself look as uncouth and diseased as possible for when the passengers would come filtering through the train looking for a place to sit. There were a few 'near misses' as people almost designated my compartment as the one for them. I knew I would have to look even worse next time to achieve the same result.

As I pondered on how to effect such a deterioration in my demeanour someone passed by outside wearing a personal stereo. As all rail travellers will know, personal stereos are a source of acute annoyance to anyone not wearing one themselves. I, however, could do better than the humble Walkman. I dug into the depths of my rucksack and pulled out the small but nonetheless quite-loud-enough-thank-you tape player which my ever-adoring little sister had loaned us for the duration of our holiday — thanks, Spam. I delved into the rucksack again and pulled out a handful of cassettes, selecting the one I deemed to be the most anti-social.

'Uriah Heep it is then,' I said to the empty compartment.

The plan of playing this appalling mid-seventies rock worked for another couple of stations until the train became so full that people were left with no option but to sit with me. As they began to fill the compartment, politely asking me to remove my crap from the seats, it occurred to me that the Austrians don't deserve this type of treatment: they seem to be such tolerant people and I wondered why on Earth they ever signed up for Anschluss with Germany back in 1938 or whenever it was. Anyway, it was 10:30 and the train was due at Innsbruck in half an hour, so it was hardly a major sacrifice to make.

Stewart

To the farmers who arrived at Sch-something station first thing in the morning, presumably to commute between fields, the sight of two lost Inter-Railers asleep on their floor must have brightened up their rural lives no end. There was a bin close to us, which, the night before, I had noticed contained a discarded rug. I had considered taking it for myself, but the sleeping bag was warm enough.

The first thing I saw on waking up, however, was a toothless farmer dropping the rug over us, and tip-toeing back to his amused friends. I suddenly felt ridiculous, lying in bed in public, stared at by the fascinated coterie of the rug-dropper. I nodded to show my appreciation of the mangy, flea-bitten textile that they had placed on me, then folded it onto Alastair so that the smell would wake him.

The novelty of our vulnerable presence soon wore off, and the farmers trickled onto the platform. We weren't far behind, eager to catch the only train out of there that morning.

The only train was late, and when it arrived I could see why. There must have been about a thousand Yugoslavian peasants on it, few of whom apparently had any previous experience of using doors. All the big, pull-down windows were open, and through them poured all the peasants in the space of about five minutes. They each passed their old, brown suitcases full of turnips and their string bags of carrots out to the peasant in front before jumping through themselves. The men were unshaven, the women were unkempt and unshaven, and the turnips were brown and muddy.

'They must be off to a peasants' convention,' concluded Alastair. He was probably right, because the Austrian farmers who had woken us seemed to have formed some kind of welcoming party.

'Yeah,' I said, kicking the squashed remains of one of the more unfortunate vegetables under the train.

The window was still open in our chosen compartment, though we had been brought up to use the door. It was just as well that it was open because Yugoslavian peasants in those days were about as familiar with bodily hygiene as Paul's feet, and breathing on the train was like putting one of Paul's shoes up to your face in mistake for a gas mask.

Paul

I would be lying if I said that I wasn't just a little worried that I wouldn't meet up with the boys and thus have to make my way back to England on my own, but God must have been smiling on me in a big way that day — probably because I hadn't got too carnal with Liesbeth in Austria — and I found

Stewart and Alastair sitting on the stone steps outside the station exactly where we had arranged back in Copenhagen. Quite an astonishing achievement, I think you'll agree.

They weren't happy. Instead of greeting me and telling me what a fab time they had had in Venice and the pots of money that they had earned there they began to relate a tale of woe involving Yugoslavian peasants, Italian policewomen and the inside of a Venetian police station. Ha, ha, I thought. That only served to reinforce the belief that I had made the right decision in going to Austria.

'Off to McDonald's, ob,' said Poo. 'A few cheeseburgers will see me well on the road to recovery.'

Stewart

With only a week's worth of Inter-Railing left on our tickets we felt it wise to head north once more, so as not to be too far from home in case of any delays. In other words, I wanted to see Anja, and Alastair wanted to see Maaike. Before leaving Innsbruck we made a couple of phonecalls: Anja was free any time, but Maaike could only see Alastair on Monday when she was able to get down to Amsterdam from Hoorn. Paul conceded that it was only fair for us to visit the Dutchies, since he had gone back to Liesbeth.

Frankfurt was the furthest north we could get direct from Innsbruck, and from there I was to head off by myself and meet up at Amsterdam the following afternoon. What they got up to was their business.

Paul

'Ooer! Frankfurt looks a bit dodgy,' remarked Poo as he alighted the train. 'Look at all those prozzies.'

'It's nothing we haven't seen before,' I replied, testing fate to the limit. 'Let's go and find a timetable so we can see what's happening.'

Poo's train was due in a matter of a few minutes. Alastair and I walked him to his platform wishing him luck with his mission to deflower Anja and telling him that we hoped we'd never see him again.

'Yeah, and don't be late for Amsterdam, wanker,' Alastair reminded him, contradicting himself somewhat in the process. Poo returned the compliment and after taking a quick snapshot of me and Alastair for the Mad Brothers photo album which was to be collated upon our return, he boarded his train. Presently he appeared in the window where he remained, shouting insults at us until he was out of earshot.

'Best we get some cheeseburgers down us then,' I suggested. 'After we've checked out the timetable, ob.'

I inspected the timetable thoroughly before shouting 'Bollocks' at the top of my voice.

'What's the matter, mate?' enquired Alastair.

'The next bloody train to Hamburg is leaving in a mere nine and a half hours. Well that's just great, isn't it?'

'Why don't we go somewhere else then?' he asked, being annoyingly sensible for the second time in one whole holiday.

'Suggest somewhere,' I challenged. He couldn't, so we agreed to go and calm down over a pile of burgers.

Frankfurt station had its own little branch of Wendy's, which was pretty fortunate as neither of us particularly fancied venturing outside the relative safety of the station to find anything to eat.

'At least there's a waiting room,' commented Alastair with his mouth full of cheeseburger, 'but I think you need a ticket to get in and I wouldn't be surprised if Inter-Rail tickets don't count.'

'Well, we'll find out shortly I dare say. Do you think we should sleep in it if we can?' I asked.

'Unless you've got any other ideas we'll have to. Look at all those dodgy-looking bastards out there. We wouldn't last a night among that lot.'

I looked through the glass partition to see what he was talking about: three tramps were busy beating the shit out of each other over a bottle of wine.

'Yeah, OK. Waiting room it is then.'

We staggered out of Wendy's, our bellies filled to capacity as usual, and made our way over to the waiting room.

'Shit!' said Alastair upon examining the notice next to the door. 'Does that German writing by any chance mean it's not open until one in the morning and closed from five onwards?'

I studied the notice carefully before giving my verdict,

'Yes, I'm afraid so. That's a bit of a crap arrangement. What are we supposed to do for the next three hours? There's all sorts of weird-looking people out there.'

Alastair suggested that we just find a place to sit down and rest until the room was open. We found a bookshop in the station that was fronted by an invitingly clean patch of ground and decided that we would wait there until we could move to more suitable surroundings.

After about half an hour we were approached by a middle-aged man in an expensive-looking suit. Having ascertained that we were English he started to chat to us in our own language,

'What are you doing here in Frankfurt?' he asked.

'Oh, we're just passing through: 'in transit' as they say.'

The man looked a little confused before continuing,

'You must not sleep here tonight. It is too dangerous. You can stay at my place if you want.'

Alastair looked to me worriedly before leaning over to me and whispering,

'I'm going to kill you when we get out of this. You attract them wherever you go, you bastard. Get rid of him will you? I'm not feeling too well again.'

'We are only going to be here for another hour,' I said, lying through my teeth, 'so I don't think we'll need to. Thanks anyway.'

'If you have any problems, come and see me,' he said before stalking off.

'Not fucking likely,' I muttered under my breath, although I'm sure it was loud enough for him to have heard me.

We sat in front of the shop for a little while, observing the comings and goings and the wheelings and dealings of the Frankfurt pavement businesspeople. We saw dozens of prostitutes soliciting and then being picked up, young lads being led off by rich-looking middle-aged men, coppers having words with all of the above and drug dealers pushing their merchandise openly. One dealer caught sight of us and made his way over.

'You want?' he said, opening up his clenched fist to reveal a polythene bag full of white powder.

'No, not really, sorry,' I said, as apologetically as possible.

'What is it?' whispered Alastair.

'Sulphates . . . I think,' I replied, trying to sound as if I knew what I was talking about.

'You WANT!' he practically ordered, thrusting the white package towards us.

'No . . . we . . . don't,' Alastair spelled it out for him. 'Fuck off!'

I prepared to be knifed, but to my considerable surprise and to my lasting relief the dealer just turned round and walked away. There would almost certainly be someone in the station who wanted some speed.

Shortly after our encounter with the drug man a group of six policemen, wearing body armour and carrying Heckler and Koch submachine guns, tore past us shouting to one another and generally instilling a sense of panic and confusion in all who saw them. We never did find out who they were chasing but as there were no gunshots I guess whoever it was got away.

After this incident I suppose we must have had a fairly reasonable amount of time undisturbed as we managed to fall asleep on each other. I wouldn't like to think what it must have looked like to anyone passing by. Inevitably we were woken from our shallow sleep, this time by the sound of *Silent Night* being sung badly and excessively loudly in very close proximity to us. Alastair and I looked at each other in dismay.

'What do you want, you pissed old fart?' I asked, annoyed at being so needlessly woken.

'*Bitte?*' he replied. I told him again, only this time in German. He wanted some money as he was singing carols and it is customary to give such singers money in Germany, he told me.

'It's August now so fuck off for another four months,' I jeered before slumping back onto my rucksack. He didn't move. 'Go on. *Verpiss dich!*' I said, choosing the most effective from my mental list of foreign swearwords. Then I pretended to go back to sleep, keeping one eye slightly open to check that the irritating old bastard went away.

After two minutes he was still there. I stood up, stretching my spine to its fullest extent and puffing my chest out to look as fearsome as I could. 'Will you FUCK OFF!' I bellowed at the top of my voice. The man looked quite hurt but I couldn't be bothered to feel sorry for him: he had annoyed me far too much to stand any chance of a quick change of heart on my part.

Alastair and I stayed awake after this until the waiting room opened at the somewhat strange and unearthly hour of one in the morning. I was more than slightly interested to see that outside the waiting room was an armed guard. I was really worried that they would search us for drugs or something — not that I had any on me, I just didn't much fancy a body-cavity search. We filed in slowly behind loads of other people: women with babies, old men, businessmen, cooty-looking Inter-Railers and examples of all walks of life in between. The room was quite bare, comprising only a couple of benches and some officious-looking notices on the wall.

'Do you think we'll be safe sleeping here?' asked Alastair.

'Well, it depends what you mean by safe. Safe from all the lowlife outside — yes. Safe from those psychotic-looking guards — I can't be too sure.'

We lay down our sleeping bags regardless and soon fell asleep, only to be woken what seemed like a matter of a couple of minutes later by the armed guard shaking us by the shoulders. But it was five in the morning and the waiting room was now officially shut.

Stewart

At Mainz there was a three hour wait until the connecting train to Zwolle, which departed at two in the morning. It was a cold night, and I put my denim jacket on over my jumper and buttoned it up fully. It was too late and too dark to go anywhere, and I was too tired to read a book under the flickering fluorescent lights.

There was a large digital clock on the platform, slowly flicking away the minutes. I made the foolish mistake of looking at it frequently, which slowed its progress down almost to a standstill. 23:14. I was terrified of falling asleep and waking up at about five or six the next morning, and yet my body craved sleep almost as much as it craved Anja. 23:16. The platform was a couple of hundred yards from end to end. To walk up and down it would use up a few minutes, so I loaded up and started marching, occasionally breaking into an on-the-spot jog when I was sure no one was watching. 23:29. The rucksack was getting heavy so I went back to my bench. Still 23:29.

For a few moments I was fine, studying the particles in the concrete with decreasing interest, until my eyes began to falter. This time I gave in to them, confident that something would wake me during the next couple of hours.

23:37, said the clock as I jumped awake. It seemed as if I had slept for hours: the number of dreams that had swept in and out of my brain were enough to fill an entire night. I got up and walked another circuit, passing for the umpteenth time the chocolate vending machine and wishing beyond hope that I had some Deutschmarks left. 23:41. The old shilling coins refused to work, of course. I sat down again. 23:42. I resolved not to look at the clock for at least an hour, and started jogging on the spot to stay warm and awake, though I soon decided I preferred being cold and seated.

An hour later it was almost midnight. Shit. That was never an hour. A drunk staggered onto the platform and sat next to me. Shit. Why couldn't I just be with Anja now? I hoped she would appreciate what I was going through to be with her.

'You Australian?' he asked, looking at my rucksack.

'Yes,' I lied.

'Do you have a cigarette?' he added, slipping slightly on the bench and adjusting his greasy jeans.

'No,' I grunted, shuffling away in the traditional British manner.

'Hey, you wanna buy some?'

'No thank you.'

'I don't mean cigarettes,' he grinned, slipping again. 'It is good. You want some?'

I didn't. The only benefit his presence gave me was that it kept me awake, which I would rather have tried to do alone. After some further minutes of drunken harassment that involved progressively less English and more German, a policeman walked onto the platform, covering his nightly beat. A subtle shift of my eyes was enough to explain the situation to him, and to my great relief he asked to see the drunk's identity papers, called someone on the radio, and then dragged him away. He didn't bother to look at my credentials, which was just as well in view of the cold night.

00:40. Here we go again, I thought, though the agonisingly slow night passed without incident until the prompt arrival of the train to take me to Anja.

sex world

Inter-Rail Rule 12: (Men) Don't wear short trousers if you want to visit the Reperbahn.

Paul

The guard at the waiting room was becoming increasingly agitated at the time it was taking us to pack our sleeping bags and generally get our act together. He started shouting foreign babble at us but it was too early even to think about trying to translate what he was saying.

'I want to go back to sleep,' moaned Alastair as soon as we were out of the way of the guard. 'I think maybe we should find a train that's going a long way and stay on it so that we can catch up on lost kip.'

'When have we got to meet up with Poo then?' I asked.

'Um, let me see. Twenty-four, plus six and a half: thirty hours and thirty minutes,' concluded Alastair.

'Shit, that's ages away.' I studied the timetable hoping for some divine inspiration. 'This one to Hamburg looks good. It's a slow one too: it won't arrive until two-thirty this afternoon. The only downer is that it doesn't get here for another forty-five minutes. How's that?'

'It'll do,' replied Alastair.

The station was unpleasantly cold at six in the morning and my discomfort was exacerbated by the aches I had acquired by lying on the waiting room floor the night before. The lack of sleep and the fact that the station nutters were still about and giving people a hard time made me restless, and I stamped my feet in irritation at the lack of train. Alastair, on the other hand, was incapable of this level of activity and was ungracefully slumped in a heap on a station bench. The one consolatory

230

factor in this wait was that, unlike home, I was convinced that the train would arrive on time. And arrive on time it did.

It became apparent as we came to board the train that our plan to spend the journey asleep would not be realised. In the five minutes prior to the train's arrival, from nowhere, hundreds of conservatively dressed young men and women carrying suitcases had arrived on the platform and were obviously intent on boarding the same train as us. This alarmed me a little and I woke Alastair to warn him.

'Oh, that'll be the Born-Again Christians, I guess,' he said, rubbing his bloodshot eyes to get a better look.

'You what?' I gasped in disbelief.

'Yeah, that's them,' he confirmed. 'I forgot to tell you. Last night in Wendy's I overheard some Americans talking about it. The International Nutters of God Federation or something have just had their annual conference here and now they're going home.' He looked at me, savouring the look of horror on my face. 'I knew you'd be pleased,' he added.

Against all odds we managed to get ourselves a compartment and it wasn't until the train grumbled into motion once more that one of the aforementioned disciples put his head around the door.

'Is anyone sitting here?' he asked in an ever-so-nice home-counties accent. Sadly, Alastair and I were too tired to think up any convincing bullshit at that time in the morning, the result of which was that we had to share the compartment with two Happy Clappies all the way to Bonn.

I'll be fair, the two guys were unbearably nice and were the first example of this particular breed of religious variant that I had met who refrained from trying to ram religion down our throats. This is not to say they did not extend an invitation to us to join their 'club' and, to be honest, they put up a good case for themselves. But we considered that having to lead such a virtuous life at such an early age would rule out an indulgence in many of the sins of which we were so fond. Also, unbeknown to us at the time, had we taken up their offer, there would have been a serious conflict of interests later that day.

After Bonn we had the compartment to ourselves and the undulating motion of the train sent us into a deep sleep from which we did not wake until we reached Hamburg.

My first impression of Hamburg station, or at least the one we alighted at, was that it was fucking enormous. A huge vaulted ceiling hung miles above us, and about half a mile below that was a mezzanine floor on which hordes of people were milling about in front of a parade of shops. On further exploration of the station, we found it to be luxuriously appointed with restaurants, newsagents, drunkards and a bureau de change (or as the Germans romantically refer to them: Geldwechseln).

The only real discovery of value that our exploration brought to light was that we were both hungry. As the station looked even dodgier than Frankfurt we thought that it would be prudent to make our exit as soon as possible. We changed two hundred Francs worth of traveller's cheques for Deutschmarks, put all our unnecessary crap in an oversized locker and headed out of the station into another unfamiliar city.

The sky had an ominous look about it and the temperature was markedly lower than anywhere else we had been in Europe, Scandinavia included. I began to question the wisdom of wearing shorts in such conditions but returning to the station to retrieve my jeans would have necessitated reopening the locker and we weren't prepared to do that. We might have done, of course, if the bloody things would accept an old shilling instead of a Deutschmark, like they were supposed to.

McDonald's was typically easy to find, its garish exterior not even trying to blend in with the delightful façade of hideous concrete shop-fronts. As we were short on ideas of what to do at this point, we sat in McD's for a couple of hours, sipping on our drinks and tentatively chewing our burgers. This time-wasting tactic was not appreciated by the manager who stood, propping himself up on a handy column, glaring at us until we felt sufficiently intimidated to leave. About two minutes.

Slightly annoyed but more at a loss of what to do we shuffled out of the restaurant and into the street.

'Shall we explore a bit?' suggested Alastair.

It seemed a reasonable proposition at the time so I followed him to some nearby traffic lights and then right down another road.

'Umm, where are we going?' it occurred to me to ask after a couple of minutes.

'Dunno really. Just around. We've not got anything else to now so we may as well just meander about until we catch the train to Amsterdam.'

We continued wandering in roughly the same direction for another twenty minutes before an unexpected burst of rain forced a quick run for cover under the awning of a nearby hotel. We sat silently on the low wall staring into the middle distance until the rain stopped.

'We could have a look for the Reperbahn,' I suggested. 'It's the only famous thing I can think of in Hamburg.'

We agreed that a trip to this wholesome tourist attraction would kill some more time and may just prove to be more fun than sitting on a low wall as the circulation to our buttocks gradually deteriorated due to the cold.

We set off again and immediately realised the inherent flaw in this plan was that neither of us had the faintest idea where the Reperbahn was. Though I felt I was linguistically able to, I was loath actually to ask a local to direct us as I did not want to appear to be another British pervert.

As we paused on a street corner to rest we were approached by an emaciated-looking man dressed in a long coat and a scarf. It was strange apparel for August but it has to be said that his clothes were probably better suited to the current weather conditions than were ours.

'If he's a nancy-boy you're dead,' threatened Alastair.

'I am from Poland,' the man announced.

'Fascinating — and are you gay?' asked Alastair facetiously.

'No,' he replied, seemingly unoffended by Alastair's last remark, 'I am poor.' He reached into the depths of his knackered raincoat and withdrew some kind of gyroscope. 'I have been attempting to sell this instrument to buy food for my family but no-one will buy it. Would you like to buy it?'

'Of course we want it!' retorted Alastair. 'Why, I was just remarking to my colleague here how useful an old gyroscope would be to a couple of tourists in Hamburg and cursing myself for not packing one before we left. How much do you want for it?'

'It is worth twenty Marks but I will accept five for it.'

I was suddenly attacked by a wave of sympathy that took me completely by surprise. The old man looked so pathetic I really felt that he was telling the truth, and even though, contrary to Alastair's earlier comment, we had no use whatsoever for an old gyroscope, I withdrew a five Mark coin from my pocket and handed it to the man.

'Thank you, thank you,' he said as he thrust the useless junk into my hands. I didn't want it so I returned it to him and told him he should sell it to someone else. The man thanked me again and ran off grinning.

A few minutes later we rounded a corner and across a small traffic island was a silver-fronted building sporting a large blue neon sign that read: 'Sex World'. Naturally, as two young, red-blooded males, we were a mite curious. We approached the building that was curiously devoid of any windows. Outside a couple of glass-fronted cabinets displayed a variety of Polaroid shots of the inside of the club. The revelation of these photographs 'intrigued' us further as we excitedly discussed whether or not we should investigate this establishment. Our voices must have been audible inside the club for just at the moment that we decided to carry on until we found the Reperbahn, a small hatch opened up next to the recessed door of the club and a head popped out.

'You wanna come in?' it inquired. Alastair and I looked at each other, each hoping that the other would take charge of the situation. The head, sensing our hesitation, added; 'Seven Deutschmarks. Two free drinks, five cinemas, one live act. Stay as long as you want.' As if we needed any further convincing we informed the head that we would have to return when we had got some money. This, the head informed us, was fine.

Stewart

One thing I did not expect from a train that arrived at two in the morning was that it would be full. I managed to squeeze inside and walked over the sleeping bodies on the floor until I found a corner of floorspace for myself. In settling down — which involved propping up the guitar, rucksack and hat and getting out the dormant sleeping bag — I disturbed the Inter-Railer next to me.

'Weren't you busking in Zurich a couple of weeks ago?' he asked me.

'Er, yeah,' I said, half asleep.

'You were great,' he said.

'Thanks,' I replied, thinking he must have mistaken me for someone else. 'Wake me up at Zwolle, will you?'

'No problem.'

From Zwolle it took just an hour and a bit on the bright yellow Dutch trains to get to Assen, from where I rang Anja to ask her to pick me up. Alastair, in his wisdom, had advised me to kiss her very firmly as soon as we met, so as not to delay in any way the development of the relationship. But this proved to be impossible as her mother was driving the family Volkswagen and I couldn't bring myself to assault her daughter in front of her.

She lived in a nearby village called Rolde, an attractive place in which all the roads were made of bright red brick and everything was unspeakably clean, even more so than Austria. Her house was small, but it was part of a modern terrace that had been designed to incorporate lots of clever angles so that it was hard to see where one house began and another ended. The front door was set behind the subtle integral garage that protruded onto the front garden, which was, of course, littered with bicycles. I had never been inside a foreign house before, and I was surprised to note that it seemed quite habitable.

'Did you have a good journey?' Anja asked me.

'Yes,' I lied. 'No trouble at all.'

Now that I was there, all the hassles of the tedious journey were gone from my mind. I was in my Elysium. Anja and her mother, however, were not. Something was said in Dutch, then Anja translated,

'My mother will fill the bath for you.'

It suddenly dawned on me why she had not sat next to me on the sofa: I had not had a shower since Norway, since when I had slept rough in Venice and Austria and on various train floors in between, all in the same clothes.

'She will wash your clothes also,' she added.

'Thank you very much,' I replied, guiltily self-conscious.

Bathed, shaved, and in clean clothes, I went to find Anja in her room. She was sitting on the bed, listening to a crappy foreign record that I pretended to like, and I sat beside her.

'Well,' I said, 'turned out nice again, hasn't it?' My longing to hold her grew unbearably intense, but I had to resist while she showed me her interesting collection of photographs of feet, and then took a picture of mine for the album. Very nice, I thought. How Dutch.

'What do you want to do?' she asked me.

What did I want to do? Wasn't it obvious? I didn't shave for pleasure, I felt like telling her. I tried looking her in the eye, but I found it awkward.

'I've travelled four thousand miles to see you,' I said.

'Castellane is only sixteen hundred kilometres from here,' she observed.

'I got lost.'

As she smiled I took her hand, expecting her to wrench it from my grasp with a shriek and hide it deep within her black dungarees. But no such humiliation occurred, and her smile broadened. There was no need to hold back now, and I kissed her.

Paul

We set off back towards the station, occasionally breaking into a half-jog such was our 'enthusiasm' to return. We opened the locker, collected some more money, slammed another two Mark piece into the slot and tore back to the club. If my brain rather than a certain other part of my body had been running things at the time I would almost certainly have changed my shorts for a pair of jeans. Sadly, however, the nether-regions were in full control that evening and the thought did not even enter my head.

Once inside the club, we accepted the gracious offer of a free beer and stood with our backs to the bar, sizing the place up. It was cleaner than I had anticipated with the bar running along the longest wall. The stage (which had no doubt witnessed some Thespian triumphs in its time) was at the back of the club with a straight staircase running up to the first floor. The cinemas referred to in the sales pitch were distributed over the two floors.

After viewing our fellow perverts suspiciously for a quarter of an hour we decided to take in a film. The screens were showing the sort of pornography that you only really find on the continent and it kept us entertained for some time as we wandered between screens sampling the various fetishes that were being catered for. The live act started after about an hour and we hurriedly made our way downstairs for the highlight of the evening. We slipped innocuously into a shady corner and watched the proceedings. To start with the entertainment consisted mainly of women dancing around provocatively dressed only in their underwear which was gradually shed over the course of about five minutes. This, we decided, was pretty bloody tedious and the sort of thing that we could probably have seen at home had we been in

Soho. We need not have worried as things quickly took a turn for the better. Or worse, depending on one's point of view regarding such matters. Presumably, these first displays of choreography had been the support act for what was to follow. The next performers seemed to be more confident than their predecessors and set about removing their garments in a far more flamboyant manner which occasionally required some audience participation. This made us thankful that we had chosen to lurk in such a remote part of the club. The act continued becoming more lewd by the minute and culminated in an interesting union between one of the women and a recently opened bottle of Champagne. Or, more probably, Asti Spumante.

When it became evident that we had seen all that we were going to with respect to live performance, we traipsed back upstairs to enjoy some more foreign cinema. It interested us that some of the performers were now mingling with us perverts. Surreptitious conversations were conducted and men were led off through mysterious doors marked 'Privat'. We were asked if we might like some personal service but we managed to stop ourselves short of accepting. Slightly later, a man approached us and started babbling on in German. Though I was a little the worse for wear on account of the beer I decided to try to understand what he was saying rather than the easier option of ignoring him. The man had to repeat himself a couple of times before the horror of what he was asking me sank in. He had asked me if I had ever had sex with another man. Though I had been 'educated' in an all-boys' school, I had to disappoint him by saying 'No'. I looked down at my shorts and silently cursed them for bringing this predicament upon me. He then went on to ask if I would like to have sex with a man, presumably him. I panicked. I looked at Alastair for back-up but he could not help as he had not understood our conversation. I shouted out for help and, in true *Mr Ben* style, as if by magic a club owner arrived. The owner immediately expelled the pillow-biting pervert and tried to console us by offering us further free drinks. We declined his kind offer and decided that we should probably leave at this point for fear of attracting further unwanted attention.

The station looked positively homely after Sex World. We removed our crap from the locker and found a clear piece of floor on the mezzanine and laid out our beach mats. We spent a pleasant hour or so eating cherries and spitting the pips over the edge onto the platform below, but fatigue caught up with me again and I had to get some sleep. I got into my sleeping bag and fell asleep instantly.

Three hours later I was woken by the obnoxious sound of unruly singing piercing the relative calm of the station air.

'What's going on, man?' I asked my fully-conscious companion.

'That train has been over there for about half an hour and it appears to be full of drunk, English soccer fans,' he replied.

'Bastard English. Can't escape them,' I muttered.

Our train finally arrived on time from Copenhagen, and, to my enormous relief, it was practically empty. The train was the most comfortable thing in the world to me at the time and we were both asleep within minutes of our departure.

Stewart

After a lunch of traditional fruit pizza, Anja took me to a lake on the back of her bike. I had never ridden a giant Dutch bike before, but found myself a passenger on the luggage rack of something that was not dissimilar to a Penny Farthing and which had no apparent brakes. Anja energetically pedalled me along the red brick roads and out onto the cycle lanes that ran parallel to the country roads. Then to get to the lake we had to ride through a gate marked Private Property.

'It doesn't matter,' she said, charging through the entrance and along the footpaths until we came, finally, to a halt on the grassy bank by the lake.

It was a warm day, though a little cloudy, and Anja assured me it was normally much hotter. The lake was bordered on all sides by trees, and the place seemed deserted.

'Let's swim,' she said, taking off her dungarees. This took me by surprise, but then I noticed she was already wearing her swimsuit.

'I bet it's cold,' I moaned.

'No,' she said, 'this isn't England.'

I walked over to the water in just my boxer shorts, and dipped my hand in to feel its icy temperature. Looking up again I saw Anja standing knee-deep in the water, her swimsuit rolled down to her waist, the sight of which nearly knocked me backwards into the water.

It was too cold to swim, however, and the rest of the day was spent lying half-dressed and half-asleep on the grass, learning how to count to one hundred in Dutch, and wishing I'd been more forward with Anja in Castellane. (We only got to number five there.)

Back at the house I was introduced to her rabbit, Steunzool, which means 'Arch Support'. Rather a strange name, I thought, though it probably lost a lot in translation. He looked quite cute, so I picked up the little white shitting machine and it shat all over me. Great. Restraining the temptation to throw Arch Support onto the carpet I maintained self-control and gave him carefully back to Anja, before running outside and jumping around maniacally.

With my shirt washed a second time, I was ready to accompany Anja on a small tour of her friends' houses, and thus gained a taste of many Dutch interiors, finding them all to be as annoyingly tasteful as her own. One of her friends smoked a brand of tobacco called Shag. I pointed at the packet and told her I found it amusing.

'There is a lot of it in Holland,' she said.

'I know,' I replied, although no one else understood the joke.

Meeting the rest of Anja's family that night was not too much of an ordeal, as only she and her brother spoke English. We watched a sub-titled Monty Python episode in the evening, the humour of which Anja appreciated even more than I did, probably because she liked to laugh at the British.

Knowing that I had to get to Amsterdam the next morning I didn't want to stay up too late, and declined the chance of discussing feet in more depth in favour of sleep. To my surprise and disappointment I was given my own bedroom for the night, which was definitely not what happened when English boys stayed with foreign girls on television shows, but if they did it wouldn't be worth watching I suppose.

dutch culture

Paul

The clean, beige fabric interior of the DSB train provided a level of comfort hitherto unknown to us within the realms of Inter-Rail. I could quite happily have remained, recumbent upon my row of three luxuriously appointed seats, had it not been for Alastair waking up with the excitement of knowing that he would be seeing Maaike again in the very near future. Much to my disdain, I was forced to join him in the world of the conscious. Amsterdam Centraal was only a matter of a few minutes away and Alastair was already preparing himself for his impending date.

'It's only nine-thirty,' I observed, to his obvious satisfaction.

'Yeah, I know,' he replied nonchalantly. 'Good isn't it.'

I couldn't find it in myself to argue with him as it would have been unfair to bring him down off his heightened emotional pedestal.

'When are we meeting Poo again?' I asked, very much in need of having my memory refreshed.

'Midday,' came the reply. 'And he'd better not be bloody late.'

Our disembarkation coincided with the usual offers of drugs, sex and accommodation, all of which we declined on the pretext of having no money — this, I decided was the logical way to deal with people who are trying to sell you something that you don't want rather than just telling them straight that you are not interested. The only potential loop-hole in this concept is if the dealers offer credit, but I am led to believe that this is not common.

With these disagreeable purveyors of accoutrements for immoral living out of the way and well off the scent of our somewhat meagre wallets, we made our way to the main hall of the station. It was typically clean, and, having claimed a corner by the front doors, we slumped against the wall to await the arrival of Poo who would swell the ranks of the Mad Brothers to their more usual number of three.

It came as no surprise that twelve o'clock passed with no sign of Stewart. Alastair was beginning to express his annoyance that his potential time with Maaike was being depleted by Stewart's unpunctuality when the familiar form of Poo came shambling up to us wearing a triumphant grin. We greeted him with a typical display of tolerance and sympathy,

'You're late, Poo,' reprimanded Alastair.

'Only ten minutes,' said Stewart, taken aback.

'That's six hundred seconds,' I added, entering the persecution game.

'So?' replied Stewart, still unable to see what all the fuss was about, which was hardly surprising as there was no reason for it at all. 'I've had to come a hundred miles this morning. Shall we eat then or what?'

'We've come a lot further than that — from Hamburg, and we still managed to be on time,' continued Alastair, not interested in higher pursuits such as filling one's face at McDonald's. He then announced that he was off to phone Maaike.

I stayed with Poo, reassuring him that we weren't really angry with him. Alastair soon returned, informing us that his ladyfriend would be with us within the hour. We elected to keep him company until she arrived, despite the indubitable disadvantages of being exceptionally hungry and there being little to do at the station unless one was a junkie or wanted to contract an interesting social disease.

Stewart

The pain of leaving Anja that morning with little more than happy memories and a picture of her feet was dissipated somewhat by our agreement to meet up the next summer, but even so I felt sick for the first few miles of the journey to Amsterdam. However, I had prudently skipped Anja's typically Dutch breakfast of dry toast covered with hundreds and thousands, and eventually managed to replace the butterflies in my stomach with the more familiar feeling of hunger.

While we were waiting for Maaike's arrival at Amsterdam I suggested we find out what time the next train for Paris left, so Paul went over with me to the information counter. There was a small queue in front of us so, to relieve his boredom, he started singing *New York, New York* to himself, and strutting about a little.

'That's very good,' I said.

His confidence boosted, he started singing more loudly and dancing as if he had a cane in his hand, tipping his hat up at passers-by and generally looking utterly ridiculous. When it was our turn to be served I expected him to stop and actually ask the woman at the desk for a timetable. All he did instead was to dance from side to side and sing a special performance for the hard-working woman who obviously needed a little insane entertainment.

'When is the last train to Paris?' I asked, brushing Frank Sinatra aside for a moment.

'Oi, watch it,' said Old Blue Eyes.

'Quarter past ten,' said the woman, calmly, no doubt used to having mad people sing at her as she was working in a city that had cannabis coming out of its ears.

'*Dank u wel*,' I said.

'You're welcome.'

When Maaike turned up, Paul and I left her and Alastair to get on with their cultural afternoon. We, meanwhile, went in search of our own kind of culture — the kind that begins with Mc and ends in a visit to the john. We had changed some money at the station bureau de change and went off to feed upon the ninety Guilders, keen on this penultimate day of the holiday to spend as much as possible.

Blissfully unaware of the canals, the coffee houses, the brothels, and all the other tourist attractions, we crossed the bridge in front of the station and followed the sign for McDonald's into a side alley and onto a main traffic-free street. It was bustling with Hare Krishna disciples on a march, a few buskers in doorways, and thousands of shoppers buying imitation brand goods to bring back home for people they didn't like very much. And there, amongst all this confusion and noise, stood a towering, three-storey McDonald's.

We set upon the menu with our fistfuls of cash, ordering a bit of everything plus a bit more, then took it upstairs to the top floor where we could watch the goings-on in the street from a safe position.

Paul set up his milkshakes on the table: strawberry, vanilla, and chocolate next to each other, and a straw in each one so that they converged at his mouth.

'Here goes,' he said, and switched on the suction to full power. Three colours of drink slowly made their way up the straws and into his gullet, a feat which failed to impress all who watched. Then he took a bite into the first of the three Big Macs on his tray, followed by a bagful of French Fries and a bite of apple pie. My efforts were less impressive, but even so our initial meal lasted well over half an hour, which is probably a record for McDonald's.

We allowed ten minutes to let the feast settle inside us before I ventured downstairs again for round two. I wondered how Alastair was getting on at this point? He was probably eating something really grotty like a posh meal that he had to pay a fortune for, and would be forced to go on a canal tour or something. Pretty daft I thought, considering we had a canal at home. I ordered a couple more Big Macs and all accessories for Paul, and took another giant coke and some cheeseburgers for myself.

'Oi mate,' mumbled Paul, the quality of his speech very much impeded by the gobfull of burger, elements of which were trying to get back out of his mouth and away to freedom, 'I've been thinking.'

I listened intently as I didn't want him to have to repeat anything.

'Yes — go on,' I encouraged him.

'As you were late today, everything I do from now on will be six hundred seconds later than I should have done it.'

'Eh?'

'You've shunted my life out of synch by ten minutes, and now I'll be late for everything else I ever do.'

'Shut up and eat,' I said.

Even after this there was still more money left than we actually wanted, so yet another feeding foray was planned for a little later. This was to be an entire afternoon spent in McDonald's, which, had we been working there, would have represented enough service experience to get us pushed one step up the McPromotion Ladder.

Paul
By the end of the final glut-out I was physically incapable of moving and was therefore forced to remain in the restaurant

until I had downloaded some of what I had eaten into the Amsterdam sewage system. Finally, both of us still unsteady and thoroughly bloated, we clumped back to the station to meet up with Alastair as we thought that we had a moral obligation to take him home with us.

He and Maaike were waiting for us, seated on some stone steps at the side of the station; Alastair was looking dirty and cooty like Poo and me, but Maaike was clinically clean by comparison and immaculately dressed. Alastair tried to assure us that he had not done anything of which he should be ashamed while Maaike stood by in silence, no doubt able to understand every taunt and innuendo which we threw at him.

I left the lovebirds to get on with their melancholy farewells in private while I checked that the noises coming from around the corner were not really audible evidence of Stewart being violently ill. Thankfully it was someone else being ill and, judging by their overall demeanour, from an overindulgence in something other than hamburgers.

Alastair finally rejoined us, as hyperactive as he normally was when he had good reason to be happy. We had a quick discussion and decided that as the train we were supposed to be catching was not due for another four hours we should try to bodge our way to Le Havre. The only train that we could take that held any promise of bodging success was one bound for Brussels. After much procrastination and to our extreme reluctance, we agreed to catch this train to Belgium, home of the Belgians.

The journey was not a quick one and the doubts which we had initially held about going to Belgium were consolidated when we realised that we weren't even going to pass through the country at any great speed. One positive thing came from the journey, however. Between us we managed to write one song, which pleased us no end as songwriting was the original reason for taking the guitars abroad.

Later that evening we found ourselves, as a result of our bodging, marooned in Brussels Central station and unable to continue until three-thirty in the morning when our train would arrive and spirit us away to the slightly more civilised surroundings of Paris. In the event, we were lucky to get out of Belgium at all that night.

In one of the wide corridors that ran through the station was a large television screen, hanging from the ceiling. We settled down to watch it with a group of other Inter-Railers, not that any of us could speak Flemish of course, but it was something to do to pass the time.

I don't remember falling asleep in the middle of the corridor propped up on a pile of rucksacks but I certainly remember waking up there. The TV had gone to bed for the night and there was no sign of any life except us. Well, there was one exception — the cleaning man, hosepipe in hand, who was steadily advancing on us and showing no sign of stopping for a tea-break, as would have been the case in England. I hastily woke the others and we just managed to get out of his way before he arrived at where we had been sleeping, blasting the dirt off the floor with a jet of water that was a bit too similar to the one we had seen in Venice for my liking.

By some miracle we had not missed our train, so we ran to our platform just in time to see the big Inter-City pull in. Once we were aboard, sleep was the only option. By early morning we were in Paris, Gare Du Nord, and shortly afterwards found ourselves at St Lazare, though how we got there is still a bit of a mystery to me. I was so tired, possibly even asleep on my feet, that I remember nothing of the connecting journey in the Metro.

three smugglers

Paul

The train to Le Havre left at eight that morning. Home felt very close now and for the first time since I had boarded the initial train of the holiday, I was looking forward to being in my home town again or, more specifically, in my own bed again.

The thought of our impending homecoming was enough to keep me awake for the duration of the journey to the grim port from where our ferry would sail. At this point, we studied the leaflet provided by HM Customs that informed us that customs men collected foreign pornographic magazines and would welcome any contributions. They also made you pay a lot of money for giving up your literature to the national collection, which made us wonder what to do with the prurient art mags which had been bought during the first few days as a kind of symbol to represent our emancipation from our mothers' apron strings. The conclusion of this discussion was that we would take them back to England with us as trophies: after all, we had taken them across a couple of dozen borders without incident.

Our ferry finally left Le Havre on time at three o'clock that afternoon, to our considerable relief. No matter how many ferry crossings one makes, they are never interesting unless one has the vast sums of money necessary to purchase such luxuries as a cup of coffee or a pint of beer. We, however, hardly had a bean, having eaten almost thirty pounds worth of McDonald's foodstuffs the day before. We knew that we would have to spend the rest of the journey doing nothing. This was probably the best course of action as we were all so tired that sleep was the only thing that was within our capabilities at the time.

I remember sitting on a stairwell next to Alastair and then waking up, slumped against him with an unsightly trail of dribble hanging out of my mouth and leading down to my T-shirt. I had begun to lose control of my bodily functions and wished that the ferry would hurry up so that I could get home before I really embarrassed myself.

A while later, Stewart came bounding down the steps to tell us that he could see the all too familiar lights of Southsea funfair. As soon as I saw those I wished that I was on my way back to mainland Europe.

As my mind filled with the mundane images of England, it occurred to me that if we were searched in customs we would be unable to use the communication barrier and feigned ignorance of the law as a form of defence. I started to worry, and thought that maybe we should re-consider our decision.

'Don't worry, they never stop you in the Green Channel,' lied Stewart, reassuringly. 'And if they do I'll just say it was your idea.'

'Thanks mate,' I said.

To be on the safe side we each hid one of the three pieces of contraband deep inside our rucksacks. If anything happened we were all in it together; not that anything could go wrong.

'Nothing to declare boys?' asked the Customs Fascist as we walked through the Green Channel.

My first instinct was to run for it, but I managed to hold myself back and croak,

'No.'

'Been on holiday have you?' he continued, noticing our short trousers and shaking knees.

'Yes.'

'Where have you been to?'

'Everywhere,' I said, relaxing a little and thinking this was a doddle.

'Everywhere, eh? Such as?'

I couldn't help showing off and started reciting our entire route, tactfully leaving out Amsterdam for obvious reasons.

'Quite a trip,' he observed. 'Was that all?'

'Don't forget Amsterdam,' blurted Poo, helpfully.

Shit, I thought. Goodbye free world.

'Would you open your bags please?'

'Er,' I said, feeling faint. Alastair and Stewart slowly lowered the rucksacks off their backs, eyeing each other worriedly. There was no hope now. Our dubious imports were going to land us in court.

'We'll take this one first,' said the fascist, helping me lift my rucksack onto the inspection table. He released the toggle at the top and opened up the flaps, then put in his hands and began to rummage. My heart sank as he probed deeper, at any moment likely to fish out the evidence.

Then the smell hit us all at once. He frantically pulled out his hands to waft the unholy stench from his face, and covered up the decomposing shoes whose plastic wrapping he had so unfortunately disturbed. The source of the radiation temporarily checked, he pulled the toggle tight and practically threw the rucksack into my arms. Nothing on Earth could have persuaded him to explore the interior of our rucksacks after that.

'Off you go,' he spluttered, between coughs.

Outside, I didn't wish to dwell on my heroism and asked how we were getting back.

'It would have been in a police car if it wasn't for your personal hygiene standards,' said Stewart, barely able to comprehend that the feet he had been cursing for the last few days had now saved him from an embarrassing fate.

'Yeah, thanks mate,' agreed Alastair.

'Come on, we were lucky. Go and ring your parents, Al,' I said.

An hour later, the familiar shape of Alastair's family Citroen hove into view with its headlights flashing in recognition and greeting. Stewart's parents turned up too to take him home so I was left with a choice of carriage. I decided on the Citroen and with many parting salutations we pulled away and continued down the final stretch of the motorway towards home.

I was a little puzzled when no one answered the door to my house when I knocked upon it and was even more surprised to find a big pile of mail on the doormat. Then I remembered that everyone else was on holiday too. I sank to my knees and then lay out on the floor, face down, thinking, I'll just stay here for a couple of minutes.

I awoke an hour later, finding respiration rather harder than usual. Oh, yes, that's it, I thought, I've still got my rucksack on.

Never again.

Index of Profane Words
Liable to Induce Childish Amusement
in Mentally Weak Persons

Anal 164

Arse 178

Belgium 12, 166-7, 248

Bollocks 16, 64, 97, 101, 141, 181, 223

Bottom 38, 50, 53, 55, 58, 62, 80, 103, 156-7, 170

Brussels 166-7, 194, 248

Bullshit 17, 42, 83, 89, 104, 164, 231

Fart 10, 25, 40, 84, 151, 226, 240

Fuck 47, 55-6, 64, 71, 80-1, 87, 114, 123,
 134, 167, 190, 225-7, 232

Nob 41, 44

Piss 16, 28, 52, 70, 73, 98, 107, 160, 165, 173,
 214, 226

Shit 16, 20, 27-8, 40-2, 45, 48, 50, 52, 56,
 59-60, 69, 72, 84, 89, 94, 97, 104, 111, 114,
 128, 131, 142, 153, 164, 167, 172, 181, 198,
 207-8, 224, 228, 230, 241, 252

Toss 160

Tossed 128

Tosser 40

Wank 52

Wanker 28, 31, 46, 64, 81, 129, 160, 163, 200, 223

Wanky 79

OTHER TRAVEL BOOKS
FROM SUMMERSDALE

Don't Mention The War
A Shameful European Adventure
Stewart Ferris & Paul Bassett

The Gringo Trail
Mark Mann

The Trail to Titicaca
Rupert Attlee

Running A Hotel on the Roof of the World
Five Years in Tibet
Alec le Sueur

Year of the Roasted Ear
Travels, Trials and Tribulations in South-east Asia
Donna Carrère

Zen Explorations in Remotest New Guinea
Adventures in the Jungles and Mountains of Irian Jaya
Neville Shulman
Foreword by Rebecca Stephens

Two Feet, Four Paws (New Edition)
The Girl Who Walked Her Dog 4500 Miles
Spud Talbot-Ponsonby
Foreword by Ffyona Campbell

Small Steps with Heavy Hooves
A Mother's Walk Back To Health in the Highlands
Spud Talbot-Ponsonby

The Sea On Our Left
A couple's ten month walk around Britain's coastline
Shally Hunt

And Mother Came Too
Joy Viney

FOR A CATALOGUE, PLEASE WRITE TO:

SUMMERSDALE PUBLISHERS LTD
46 WEST STREET
CHICHESTER
PO19 1RP
UK

www.summersdale.com